BY THE SAME AUTHOR

Fiction

THE GIRL WITH THE GLORIOUS GENES
(A. B. Carbury, *pseud*.)

Biography

JUGGERNAUT: The Path of Dictatorship

MEN OF POWER

NAPOLEON SPEAKS

THE WORLD AND WILLIAM WALKER

History

THE COMING OF WAR

A MATTER OF LIFE AND DEATH

AMERICA'S LAST CHANCE

TRUMAN, STALIN AND PEACE

Business

JOHN D. ROCKEFELLER'S SECRET WEAPON

HOW TO ATTRACT GOOD LUCK

BUSINESS AS A GAME

A. H. Z. CARR

Finding Maubee

G. P. PUTNAM'S SONS
NEW YORK

FINDING MAUBEE

1

AS everyone who has been to the island of St. Caro knows, it has the highest rate of illegitimacy and the lowest rate of crime in the Caribbean. Police headquartered in the sleepy little capital of Gracedieu (pronounced Grassdew) spend much of their time rounding up fathers of newly born babies on the say-so of young mothers. Hauled into court, the abashed young buck confronts the well-curved girl in the case, the plump baby in her arms, and a wise and experienced judge of his own race. The "trial" is often over within a minute.

Judge: "John Fredericks, this girl Dolores says you are the father of her child."

John (with an unhappy grin): "I guess if Dolores say me the father it must be so."

Dolores (with a tender smile): "You are good boy, John."

Judge: "Very well. The court orders you to pay the mother five dollars a week for the care of the child until further notice. Next case."

The girl would, of course, usually prefer to be the mother of an "inbaby"—born in wedlock—but there is no disgrace in giving birth to an "outbaby," acknowledged and supported by the father. It is only in connection with "bushbabies," whose paternity is cloudy, that problems arise. When the young man feels that the court is being imposed on by a girl known to be "easy"—that is, to have a multiplicity of lovers—he is likely to say, "No, I tell you, mon—I mean Your Honor—me not the father, and I can prove it." ("Me" and "I" are often used interchangeably on St. Caro, where elementary schooling has only begun to make inroads on the traditional dialect.)

"How can you prove it?"

"Well, if me the father I have to be with her nine months

before baby is born, right? Middle of last May. All right, I got my little black book, Judge. It show where I been every night all year. Me no with her 'til August. See for yourself, Your Honor, here the little black book."

The judge, appraising the girl, the genuineness of the man's indignation, and the authenticity of the little black book, may agree. "Paternity not proved. Next case."

Modern methods of birth control have not yet penetrated very far in St. Caro, and most of the island's lively blades have learned to keep their little black books with as much care as a businessman preparing accounts for the scrutiny of Internal Revenue—and with much the same purpose, for too many proved paternities can mean financial ruin. Calypso singers in Gracedieu's nightclubs sympathize with the local "repeating papas."

> "Henry Brown, we are sorry for thee,
> Cause you have thrice achieved paternitee.
> It would be wiser, mon, it would be best-a,
> If you stay away from girls during siesta."

More than one repeating papa, finding that almost all of his wages were garnisheed for the care of his outbabies, has taken ship for foreign parts. Others have gone to some remote corner of the forty-mile-long island and found work under assumed names. But every now and then one of the unfortunate fathers becomes embittered, heads for the hill country of the interior, and takes up the life of a professional outlaw, mixing petty theft with persistent adultery.

The most notorious of these freebooters, David Maubee, turned to crime only after he had fathered two inbabies, six outbabies, and an undetermined number of bushbabies. A calypso which became a favorite of St. Caro's steel bands went as follows:

> "Let us tell you the story of David Maubee,
> Who sought for a life of tranquilitee.
> He had to pay money to eight different women,
> So now he rob tourists while they are swimmin'.

He have found the way of life which is safest and surest—
Like all of us here he live on the tourist."

David Maubee's favorite method of operation was to enter
the cottages and rooms rented by American visitors on the
beaches of St. Caro and pick up exposed watches, cameras,
jewelry, or cash. Periodically, outraged tourists and anxious
resort owners reported his depredations to St. Caro's chief of
police, tall, black Xavier Brooke, who made sporadic efforts
to find the outlaw. But Maubee had too many friends among
the girls of the towns and the sugarcane cutters of the
plantations and he knew too many hideaways to be found
easily. Occasionally, according to reports, he would even
drop into a friendly bar for a convivial drink or two, but the
twenty constables scattered through the island never saw a
trace of him, or at least never said so if they did; he was a big,
strong, fast man whom no one wanted to tackle. In any
event, the losses suffered by his victims were not serious. His
story had become part of St. Caro's collection of spicy
legends, and his name appeared in more than one Caribbean
guidebook.

Even the women who had borne his children harbored no
grudge against him. On the contrary, they were proud to
name their boys David and their girls Maubeela. There were
rumors of mysterious gifts made to one or another of these
progeny from time to time, after Maubee had done particularly well for himself at some tourist's expense. Some called
him the Robin Hood of St. Caro, and the prevailing conviction was that it would be a shame to hunt him down.
Although Xavier Brooke was too good a policeman to share
this view, he did not feel more than mildly frustrated by his
failure to clap Maubee in jail; and the island as a whole
grinned and shrugged when the subject was mentioned.

Another popular calypso said:

"Police don' wan' get Dave Maubee sore
Cause provocation is against the law."

One morning the weary smile with which Xavier usually

heard Maubee's name turned to a scowl. He had picked up the telephone in his little office to hear the voice of Horace Chalk, the acting governor of the island. "Brooke? I've just had a call from Mango Beach. Maubee has done it this time. Walter Searle says he's murdered one of the guests at the inn. Man named Lattner. Killed him with a machete."

Xavier's first reaction was one of astonishment. Assault, robbery, and rape were frequent enough, even in easygoing St. Caro, but murder was a rarity; and he could not imagine David Maubee doing anything so foolish as to kill a tourist. It would mean the end of the government's forbearance.

Into the phone, however, all that Xavier said was, "That's bad, Governor." Experience had taught him the inadvisability of asking Chalk questions. The answers were likely to flop around and to have a sting in the tail, like a whip-ray.

Sitting at the other side of Xavier's battered desk at the time was a friend of his, Ted Motley. He was the publisher, editor, business manager, and chief reporter of the St. Caro *Sentinel,* the island's only newspaper—an anemic tabloid which managed to survive on the advertising of Gracedieu's shops and bars and the government's official notices. It was published weekly during the tourist season, and at other times whenever the fit came on Motley.

He was a thin, sandy-haired, bespectacled young man, whose long nose, receding chin, and open expression made him look a little like an amiable fish. The red Bermuda shorts and yellow cotton shirt that he habitually wore added to an effect of mild idiocy that deceived the unwary. Cool distrust of all human motives, including his own, was the essence of his outlook. He hailed from Vermont and was accustomed to say that his chief reasons for living on St. Caro were scotch at half the U.S. price, accessible girls, a hatred of snow, and laziness, in that order.

Xavier was one of the few men on the island with whom Motley felt a sense of genuine fellowship. They were about the same age, the early thirties, but different in every other respect. Xavier made a figure of considerable dignity. He stood over six feet and had a warrior's body—slender and muscular, with a long arm reach. His close-cropped black, wiry hair made a curious contrast with his lean, angular face, the features of which, apart from their color, were more European than African. This was natural enough. Among the Spanish, French, Dutch, and British soldiers who at one time or another had come to St. Caro as conquerors before the island was bought by the United States, a number must have found their way into Xavier's ancestry. His surname came from a British plantation owner who had owned his great-grandfather as a slave.

As an exceptionally promising boy in Gracedieu's schools (which ran through the sixth grade) he had been selected to go to the mainland for high school, three years at a Florida college, and a year at the federal police school in Washington, D.C. One of the results was that he no longer talked like a Carovian. The lilting cadence and broad "a" had almost dropped out of his speech. He was careful, however, not to indulge in refinements of diction or displays of vocabulary which would have separated him even more sharply from most of St. Caro's black community, and in the line of duty he could match the local patois in any part of the island.

As soon as Motley realized that Chalk was at the other end of the telephone, he leaned across the desk toward the receiver to listen, but Xavier held up a prohibitive palm. Chalk was saying, "Now hear this, Brooke." Many years before, in World War II, the acting governor had been a lieutenant in the United States Navy, and he liked to think of himself as an old sea dog. It was his habit to greet visitors to the island with a bluff, "Glad to have you aboard." A booming voice went with the nautical style.

He went on, "I want you to take charge of this case personally, Brooke. Drop everything else. Your job is to bring in Maubee. Bring him in alive if you can, but dead if you have to. Stay with it until you've got him. Report to me directly. Time we had some law and order on this island." It was Chalk's illusion that he contributed to order when he gave orders. "Do I make myself clear?"

Xavier covered the transmitter with his hand and swore softly in the old Carovian manner: "Shit of a dead rat." Into the phone he said coldly, "I understand." Motley winked at

him. Suddenly Xavier's somber look changed to a broad
smile. Chalk had said, "Another thing. I want you to locate
Ted Motley and tell him to get over to my office right away.
Send a couple of your men to comb the bars or wherever else
he might be at this hour."

"Yes, Governor," said Xavier. "I will find Mr. Motley. Of
course he may be drunk, but I will sober him up and get him
to your office." He grinned as Ted thumbed his nose.

"You do that," said Chalk. "How long do you think it will
take you to track down Maubee?"

"Can't tell yet, Governor. Could be a day. Could be a
week." Xavier stopped himself from adding, "Could be
never."

"Well, while you're away leave Marco Ferrer in charge of
your office. He is perfectly capable of handling the routine."
Xavier gritted his teeth. Ferrer, one of his two deputies, had
been promoted from sergeant a year earlier at Chalk's
insistence, and his designs on Xavier's job were only too
apparent. As if reading his thoughts, Chalk went on, "Keep in
touch with him and I'll call him from time to time to check."
He hung up, and Xavier said, "Crap of a sick chicken."

Ted said, "What's it about, Xave?" He pronounced the
name "Zave"—in St. Caro Xavier rhymes with "savior."

"Been a murder at Mango Beach."

Ted's face lighted up. "Who got killed?"

"Man named Lattner, I think Chalk said. Cut with a
machete."

Pursing his lips in a soundless whistle, Ted repeated,
"Lattner. Carl Lattner. I saw his name on the Mango Beach
guest list. He's the head of a big company in Cleveland or
some place. This will raise a stink. Who did it, do they
know?"

"Chalk says David Maubee. Wants me to find him and bring
him in, quick."

"Hey!" Enthusiasm shone in Ted's face. He had an old-
fashioned habit of snapping his fingers when struck by an
idea, and he did so now. "It's a story! Bet I can get
Associated Press to take a thousand words." As St. Caro's
correspondent for American wire services, he picked up an

occasional fee. "No wonder Chalk wants to see me." He snapped his fingers again. "I feel the power of the press stirring in my veins."

"Better restrain that feeling," said Xavier.

Ted laughed. "All I have to do is report a crime wave. People getting sliced by machetes. St. Caro's inns riddled with thievery. Mainland newspapers carry the story. Read by millions. Think of the effect on the winter vacationers just at the height of the season. Scared silly. Reservations get canceled. Planes come in here half empty. Hotels lose money. Shops go broke. People can't get jobs. Hunger and pestilence stalk the island. Riots outside Government House. And all at my whim."

"Not so funny," Xavier said. "You just write even a little bit like that and I will personally tie you to a manchineel tree in a heavy rain and stuff the apples down your throat."

"I live here too, so I will spare you. Only question is, how do we handle the thing?" Ted's face became serious. "A lot might depend on how fast you find Maubee."

"A lot might depend on whether he did it."

"What do they have on him, did Chalk say?"

"No. Just said Walter Searle phoned him from Mango Beach and for me to get Maubee. Peculiar, Searle going to Chalk instead of calling me. He's always been friendly."

"Oh, he's got the inn to protect. Could be his wife told him to call Chalk. It's her money in the place, after all."

"I don't like it." Xavier's solid jaw tightened. "I'm going to call Searle right now."

Ted, who had been about to rise, sprawled back in his chair. "Good idea. See if you can get some facts. More I know when I see Chalk, better I'll be able to handle him."

Xavier picked up the telephone and signaled the operator. Automation and the dial system had not yet arrived on St. Caro. Telephones were few and service was erratic, but lines had been strung to the coastal towns and to most of the hotels and inns. A minute later he heard Walter Searle's voice.

"This is Xavier Brooke, Mr. Searle. Governor Chalk tells me you have trouble out there. I thought perhaps you tried to notify me and couldn't get through."

Searle hesitated, apparently trying to decide whether to take advantage of the excuse that was being offered to him. Finally he said, "Chief, I should have called you. Sorry about that. But things are pretty confused here, and this was something I knew the governor would want to hear about right away."

Frankness and courtesy in whites always touched a responsive chord in Xavier, and his tone softened. He said, "That's all right. I'm calling mainly to find out whether I should get Dr. Evans from the hospital to come out with me. Establish the cause of death on the spot."

"No need for that," said Searle. "One of our guests is a doctor—Dr. Richardson. From Los Angeles. Noted heart specialist. He examined the corpse. No doubt how it was done. Got him in the back of the neck with a machete. The weapon is right there."

"All right. You realize, of course, that nothing should be touched until I get there. One other thing. The governor mentioned David Maubee. Got some reason to suspect him?"

"Not just suspicion, Chief. A practical certainty. He dropped his little black book. We found it right next to the body."

Xavier was almost as surprised as if Searle had reported finding Maubee's right eye. He said, "I'll be out there just as soon as I can," and hung up.

Ted was watching him closely. "What does he have on Maubee?"

"Says he lost his little black book at the scene of the crime."

A grin split Ted's bony face. "Now that's a touch the great American public would go for."

"Take it easy, Ted, till I see for myself."

"Umm. You've got a soft place for Maubee, haven't you?"

Xavier shrugged. "He's a criminal, I'm a policeman."

"Sure. Naturally. Fact that you knew him as a kid and went to school with him makes no difference. You're a tough cop. We all know that." Ted stood up. "I'd better get over to Government House and see what the great man has on his mind. Later I'll run down to Mango Beach and you can fill me in." As he was about to open the door that led to the outer office, he stopped and came back. "Xave, here's a suggestion. How about sending Marco Ferrer out to get Maubee? Let him take the rap if he can't be found."

"Can't do that. Chalk says I should do it personally and leave Marco in charge while I'm away."

Ted strummed an invisible guitar and sang throatily, with the Carovian inflection, "I smell a goose is bein' cook', and the goose belong to Xavier Brooke."

"Very funny."

"Don't let them get you down. Remember, the mighty St. Caro *Sentinel* is on your side." He waved and went out.

Rising from the creaky wooden swivel chair behind his desk, Xavier checked the pockets of his immaculate tan trousers and shirt to make sure that he had his wallet, notebook, ball-point pen, badge, and sunglasses. The badge, bearing the title "Chief of Police," was gold-plated—a gift from a grateful tourist whom Xavier had befriended. The only other outward sign of his rank was the gold ribbon at the base of his white sun helmet. From a drawer he took a gun holster, which he clipped to his wide brown belt. The old Smith and Wesson .38 revolver had never been fired in the line of duty, and he carried it primarily for appearances' sake.

Unlocking a drawer in an ancient cabinet, he thumbed through file folders until he found one labeled "Maubee, David." Its thickness testified to the amount of pilferage of which the outlaw had been accused over the years. In the depths of the folder was a small card containing a set of Maubee's fingerprints, made in the year before he turned to crime, when he was a clerk in Gracedieu's post office. This Xavier extracted and carefully tucked into his wallet.

In the outer office his two deputies were at their desks, and a young trainee was monitoring the two-way radio. Marco Ferrer had an air of youthful animation and a swarthy, strikingly handsome and self-assured face. George Michelle, the other deputy, was older, a big black man with an earnest expression.

"Been a murder at Mango Beach," Xavier said.

Their responses were characteristic. George repeated, "Murder!" Marco said, "Hey, that's great. Who got killed?"

One of the things that Xavier disliked about Marco was that he never seemed to be at a loss for a flip remark. But his glibness, if an irritant in the office, had helped to make him a popular figure in Gracedieu's Puerto Rican neighborhood, where he was much in demand as a speaker at weddings, funerals, and celebrations. On the whole, Xavier got on well with Puerto Ricans—for one thing, he had learned to speak fluent Spanish—but between Marco and himself there was an instinctive antagonism. After outlining the facts of the murder, he added, "I'm going out there. George, you come with me. Marco, you remain in the office and handle things from this end until I get back." He turned to the trainee at the radio, Peter Obee, a slim nineteen-year-old. "Peter, you will stay with the radio and assist Marco. I'll keep in touch with you."

"Yes, sir. Roger, Wilco." Peter took great pride in the technical jargon of the air waves.

Marco, his bright, shrewd eyes crinkling, said, "Suppose Maubee tries to get away by boat? How about setting up a watch at the harbors and checkpoints on the roads?"

The question irritated Xavier even more than Marco intended. Long experience had taught him that no constable stationed on the roads was going to catch Maubee, or even a glimpse of him. He would not be so foolish as to steal a car. He would either walk or pick up a bicycle and move at night along the old plantation footpaths that crisscrossed the island. If he chose to enter a town it would be in the dark by back lanes no one would be watching, even if there were enough constables for the task, and there were not.

A harbor watch would similarly be a waste of manpower and time. Motorized fishing boats and pleasure craft, with their ignition locks, complicated controls, and dependence on uncertain gasoline supplies, offered little hope to a Carovian on the run. As for small sailboats, there were so many coves on the island where Maubee might steal one that no watch was likely to stop him. If that was his intention, he would certainly not have waited; he would already be at sea.

But it was altogether unlikely that he would try to leave St. Caro unless he were sure of sanctuary somewhere. No matter on what island he landed, sooner or later he would be picked up. In the Virgins, in Puerto Rico, in any of the Leewards to the south or the Bahamas to the north, a stranger without visible means of support would be suspect; and there was a continuous exchange of radio information about island-hopping criminals among the police departments of the Caribbean. In Haiti, the Dominican Republic, or Cuba, if he could not prove himself politically acceptable in French or Spanish he would find himself in a convict gang at forced labor. Nowhere else could he hope to hide so successfully as on St. Caro, which he knew as he knew his own hand.

But Marco's suggestion had implications that did not escape Xavier. Resist it, and if Maubee thereafter was not quickly found, Chalk would certainly raise the charge of negligence. Fall in with it, and Marco would be able to tell the governor that no steps had been taken in the search for Maubee until he had suggested them. The life of a public official, Xavier had come to know, was full of such little traps. He said briskly, "You got to remember, Marco, soon as we begin to search that way, the whole island will be talking. And the governor isn't going to want a lot of talk. That's why we should keep things quiet until I see the situation at Mango Beach. After that I'll decide what to do."

He was glad to see Marco's face lose something of its satisfied expression. With a nod, Xavier put on his sunglasses and went into the bright street, followed by the silent George.

2

ON the other side of the street and a hundred yards away was Government House, an imposing white three-story mansion built by the British a century earlier, its dignity accented by a high white iron fence. There was enough of a fresh morning breeze to flutter the American flag on its tall white pole. St. Caro was famous for its balmy climate, never really torrid, seldom really cool. A reckless writer for a prominent travel magazine once compared the island's soft, perfumed air to "the skin at the base of the throat of a beautiful woman in a moment of ecstasy." That year the tourist influx almost doubled.

In front of the wide-open gate of Government House stood a United States Marine sergeant, a husky black, who gave a friendly salute as Xavier and George walked toward him. Gracedieu's only police car stood next to the governor's limousine in the driveway, for the street was too narrow to permit parking.

"Calling on His Excellency?" said the sergeant and winked, with the eye only half shut and the corners of the mouth drawn down. An American sociologist once wrote a paper suggesting that this particular variety of wink had originated among the blacks of the old slave plantations as a silent form of comment on their masters. Times had changed but the memory remained. Xavier winked back, and he and the sergeant smiled, with the knowledge that they had put Acting Governor Chalk in his place.

"Just getting the car," Xavier told him. "Going out to Mango Beach."

The sergeant nodded. "I hear Dave Maubee murdered a tourist."

"The grapevine is sure working," Xavier grunted.

The side of the shining black police car announced **POLICE** in white paint. It was an old gear-shift Ford sedan—automatic transmissions did not hold up well on St. Caro's roads. As they drove down the twisting, paved street toward the shopping district, small black children waved and the faces of the people ambling along the sidewalk turned toward them curiously. Many of the women tourists wore tight shorts and soft, clinging shirts, and the prettier ones were appreciatively noted by Xavier out of the corner of his eye as he drove. The colorful displays in the shop windows, the blue sky reflected in the glass, and the dazzling brightness of the sidewalks made a picture that never failed to give him a feeling of pleasure and pride in his town. He had lived in Jacksonville and Washington, he had visited San Juan, Port-au-Prince, Santo Domingo, and Kingston, but he considered Gracedieu, with its white, pink, and yellow houses, its clean streets, and its comparative freedom from motorcars, to be infinitely preferable to those grander cities.

In a minute he stopped the car. He had maneuvered George into coming with him mainly so as not to humiliate the older deputy by putting him under Marco's authority. George was a good, responsible man who would carry out orders to the letter, but who worked best when given exact instructions. Xavier said, "Maubee's got a sister in Bamboula—Alice. Married to a man, I forget his name, but Sergeant Ackee in Bamboula will know. I don't think Maubee would do anything that could make trouble for them, but we ought to make sure. George, I want you to get your motorcycle and ride over to Bamboula. Get hold of Ackee, and the two of you check the house. If he's there, be careful. If he isn't, tell Ackee to assign a constable to watch the house for the next few nights. Then come back here. I'll have another job for you."

"I'll do that, Chief," George said, and got out of the car. Before turning away he punctiliously saluted. He had great respect for Xavier.

With George gone, Xavier reflected for a moment, and then turned the car toward the outlying district of the town where he lived. The streets there were unpaved and dusty, and the houses small, but they were not ramshackle. His own, a little larger than most and freshly painted in cream color, with a neat little yard around it, stood out among them with a certain authority. He was especially proud of the interior, furnished with solid pieces made from native woods—some by his own hands.

His wife, Toinette, came out of the kitchen, surprised to see him at that hour. "What you doing home?" she demanded. "Hungry already? Or maybe you don't trust me." She was a café-au-lait beauty who had been a nightclub singer before she married Xavier and became the mother of his two children. Her smile was as warm as Caribbean sunlight.

He kissed her. She looked delectable in her short housedress and little apron. Her eyes were very large and faintly Oriental in cast, with long lashes, and her silken skin glowed in the luminous shadows of the room. She had been born in St. Caro's small French colony, established by privateers of an earlier century, and there was something remotely Gallic in her features and in the cluster of soft black curls that she wore close to her head. The children were at school and he was strongly tempted to make love to her, but his sense of duty restrained him. "Got to go to Mango Beach," he said. "Murder out there. Can't tell when I'll be back."

"Murder! Now you be careful," she said. "Don't you go fighting no murderers." Her grammar, to which they had given considerable effort, tended to deteriorate in moments of emotion.

"I'm always careful."

"Taking somebody with you?"

"No."

"You ought to have a man to help if there is fighting. Why not take Marco? He look—he looks like a pretty tough fellow."

"He would probably stab me in the back."

She frowned at him. "That's a bad thing to say."

"I told you before, he is after my job."

"You worry too much. Not even Chalk is so foolish as to make a Ricano chief of police in Gracedieu."

"You are wrong. Ricanos are now forty percent of our population, and more coming all the time. Chalk thinks he could make himself popular with them if he puts Marco in my place."

"But Marco is not an educated man like you." Toinette had never ceased to be impressed by the fact of Xavier's mainland education.

"He is a politician. That is more important."

She shook her head dubiously. "I better make some sandwiches for you to take along."

"Maybe that isn't such a bad idea."

As she began to busy herself with bread and cold chicken, he could not resist putting his arms around her from behind and running his hands slowly down the racing curves of her body. "You stop that," she said mildly. "You want me cut myself with this knife?" He let her go reluctantly, upon which she turned and kissed him with such intensity that his high-minded resolve evaporated. Their capacity for rapture had survived all the years of their marriage. The way she was made, with eager breasts and rounded thighs, like a young girl, had never ceased to fascinate him. For a few seconds they stood pressed together, eyes closed, his face buried in the soft hollow at the side of her throat, while their questing hands evoked the humidities of love. When he heard her gasp, he whispered "I love you," picked her up lightly, and carried her into their bedroom.

Half an hour later, as they lay warmly in each other's arms, he remembered Mango Beach, sprang out of bed, and reached for his clothes. "I ought to be kicked!" he exclaimed. "Some policeman!"

She laughed. "Some man!" She sat up in the bed and sang a snatch of a popular St. Caro song: "Me don' wan' be your washwoman. Me don' wan' be your cook. Me jus' wan' be on every page of yo' little black book."

He looked at her in surprise. "What made you think of that?"

"I'm glad you don't have a little black book no more," she

said fondly. On their wedding night, they had made a solemn ceremony of burning it. Watching his long, muscular legs slip into his trousers, her mood changed. She said thoughtfully, "Xave. Why does Chalk think Marco is so much?"

"Politics."

"What you mean?"

As he buttoned his shirt, he said, "Chalk is only acting governor. Governor Roberts is in Washington. People say the President is going to make him a big judge on the mainland. Well, when that happens, Chalk wants to become governor. Lots of other people on the mainland would like the job, but the acting governor is bound to have a pretty good chance."

"So?"

"So the best way for Chalk to get the job is if the Legislative Council says he is the man." He referred to St. Caro's only elective body which had responsibility for proposing laws and advising the governor. "If the Councillors say they want Chalk, he has practically got it. Nowadays Washington likes to oblige us natives when it comes to governors."

Toinette shook her head fretfully. "How does that help Marco? I don't get it."

"Simple," he said, putting on his socks and shoes. "Nearly half the Council is Puerto Rican nowadays. And Marco is a big man among the Ricanos. The Councillors will listen to him. He can help them get elected. So if he says he wants Chalk, they want Chalk."

"What about *our* Councillors? Why you no go—why don't you go talk to them?"

"You got to be a politician for that."

"Well, be a politician."

"Not me. It's not my line. A man has got to follow his own nature. Anyway, you see how the deal works. If Chalk promises Marco my job, Marco helps Chalk with the Councillors."

Toinette stamped her bare foot on the wooden floor. "They can't do that. You the best police chief St. Caro ever had. Everybody say that."

"Everybody *says* that," Xavier corrected. "Well, maybe so,

but all I have to do is make one mistake." Such as, he added to himself, not bringing in Maubee.

"Then don't you make no—make any mistakes." She clapped a hand to her forehead. "Oh, my. The sandwiches. Wait!"

"Never mind the sandwiches. I got to go." He thought of telephoning Mango Beach to say he was on his way—one of his perquisites as chief was a telephone, seldom used, in his home—but he decided that it would not hurt Searle to fret a little.

"Don't stay up for me. I may not get home at all tonight. Can't tell how things will go."

"Just so long as you don't stay with no woman."

"Not likely now," he grinned.

He kissed her hastily and, grabbing his sun helmet, rushed out to the car. As he drove away, he saw Toinette's bare arm and a bare leg waving at him through the partly opened door, and he chuckled delightedly. An old Carovian fisherman's proverb came into his mind: "Kiss right in the mornin', fish bite in the afternoon." It was true that he always felt luckier and stronger after being with Toinette. No real Carovian could ever feel very guilty about taking time from work to make love. First things came first. Lattner was merely a corpse and a problem. Toinette was alive, and they needed each other. In his view, if a man had a beautiful wife and did not make love to her when she wanted to, something had to be wrong with him.

3

AS he drove, he sang softly, "Me jus' wan' be on every page of yo' little black book." One tune or another was always going through his head. Carovians were a singing people. But not the smiling people they once had been. The habit of showing happy smiles in the presence of whites had slowly fallen away after the abolition of slavery and had nearly vanished with rumors of the Black Power movement on the mainland. The native face had become serious, as the sense of freedom and the problems of freedom grew.

Skirting Gracedieu's harbor, where white and pink sails dotted blue Caribbean water, he took the Coast Road for Mango Beach, eleven miles away. Outside the town the asphalt surface stopped abruptly, and the road became a rutted irritation, holding his speed down to a bare twenty miles an hour. Much of it ran between stubbly fields of cut sugarcane, but here and there a distant herd of small cattle, or a tamarind tree jutting up like a hand against the sky, or a banana grove, or a sudden clump of coconut palms caught the eye.

Once he had to pull far to the right to let an oncoming yellow bus, decrepit with age, rattle by him on the narrow road. Black faces within grinned at him, the driver saluted, women waved. At another point, as he passed a heavy thicket of mixed growth, he thought he saw the shiny dark leaves of a manchineel tree, and he made a mental note of its location, for the government was trying to get rid of the poisonous manchineels. A funny old song that he had heard when he was a small boy tugging at his grandmother's skirts in the family kitchen came to him:

"Hippomanee Manzanilla, that the fancy name—
Us call it manchineel, but it all the same.
Cook a little manchee juice in your husban's stew
An' that the las' time he ever nag at you.
Obeah man, obeah man, me tired of my ol' lover.
Obeah man, obeah man, bring me anuvver."

Musing, Xavier shook his head ruefully. Obeah was banned by St. Caro law, but in practice the government policy was simply to leave the obeah men alone so long as they did not provoke trouble, in the belief that the old magical practices would eventually die out. Among the sophisticated whites of Gracedieu there was a fashion to defend obeah. They said the obeah men and a few witches who were lesser practitioners of the cult were really the psychiatrists, marriage counselors, and birth-control specialists of St. Caro. Where else could an unhappy Carovian woman go for advice or, if her pregnancy was unwelcome, for the secret drugs that could produce an abortion? Xavier did not regard this kind of talk as funny. To him it suggested the willingness of whites to perpetuate ignorance and superstition among the blacks for their entertainment and advantage.

His thoughts took a different turn as he passed the remains of an old wagon that had been pulled off the road and abandoned. In it he caught a glimpse of a pair of young lovers lying on the floor of the wagon and peering at him through the broken slats as he passed. They could not have been more than fifteen, if so old. It was a common enough spectacle. In St. Caro everyone took it for granted that sex experience began with puberty. Continence among the young was regarded as a joke and fidelity as a temporary aberration. Some said that back in the old days the owners had deliberately encouraged early intercourse among their slaves, with a frequent change of partners, in the mistaken belief that more and healthier children would be born; and the custom had survived.

Xavier's stay in Florida had made him more conscious than most Carovians of the ways in which the psychology of slavery tended to perpetuate itself on both sides of the color

line. In the eyes of some white men, Horace Chalk among
them, he could detect a glint which sneered, as clearly as
words, "Educated nigger." The right reply, he had long since
determined, was a cool and unwinking stare, compelling the
offender to look away.

The current fashion among black extremists of calling white
Americans "pigs" struck him as weak and beside the point.
Much of the human race, including blacks, if given a chance
to indulge their greed behaved like pigs. Nevertheless, when
he thought of the Horace Chalks of the world the phrase
sometimes came to him: "pigs without pigment."

He had no doubt about the island's future if Chalk became
governor. Education, housing, food prices—the things that
really counted—didn't interest Chalk. More than once he had
said in Xavier's hearing that the governor's main responsibility was to attract more tourists and light industries that would
operate with cheap native labor. Innkeepers and store owners
would doubtless be enthusiastic about their profits, but
Xavier could not for the life of him see how Chalk's program
would improve the life of ordinary Carovians.

The sea was now at his right, and there was a row of
graceful little white clouds on the horizon, evenly spaced,
like ballet dancers. To the left in the distance were the St.
Caro hills. If that was where David Maubee had gone, finding
him would be like playing blindfold tag. In Xavier's nine
years on the police force, there had not been a real manhunt
on the island.

Ahead of him, on a low rise that commanded the beach
below, was the inn. Among visitors to St. Caro, a Mango
Beach luggage label was a mark of status, for the place was
designed for upper-bracket American business and professional men ("Stock Exchange reports received daily by radio and
a telephone in every guesthouse") and their families ("Our
own beauty salon and boutique featuring latest continental
styles"). The inn boasted a nine-hole golf course with a view
of the sea, tennis courts, fishing boats, and a wide beach on a
cove where wire nets assured protection from wandering
sharks, barracuda, and men-of-war. Forty or more separate
guesthouses were spread over a dozen green acres, with broad

curving belts of trees and floral shrubbery to provide privacy.

To see the place from a distance was like looking at a paint catalogue. All the houses were built of stained redwood in the contemporary Swedish style, with terraces, roofs, and trim in red, azure, pale yellow, or green. As if to achieve an effect of instant gaiety, the same colors were used on the bodies of the little sports cars that dotted the grounds. ("With every guesthouse, Mango Beach is ready to provide a sports convertible for your private use.") A sprawling central structure, painted blue and white, with much plate glass, sheltered the offices, public rooms, and restaurant. ("The most sophisticated bar this side of Paris, and superb food in our famed Marine Room or, if the guest prefers, in the privacy of his own cottage.") Xavier recognized that Americans knew better than anybody else how to get people to pay out money. Their trouble was that they thought too much about what would sell and not enough about whether it ought to be sold.

Driving slowly along the inn's winding asphalt road, Xavier passed a broad café terrace, with green tables beneath red and white umbrellas, facing a large blue swimming pool exotically curved; and just beyond was a green and white pavilion with a tiled dance floor, where a row of steel drums glinted in the shadows. ("The ten-piece Mango Steel Band, famed throughout the islands, plays nightly for your pleasure.") As the car pulled up in front of the office, Walter Searle came out, together with a small, slender woman wearing a short white beach robe and sandals and a black boy whose pink shirt bore the monogram of the inn. "Now, Andrea, be reasonable," Searle was saying. "I'm sorry as I can be about the dog, but what can I do about it? He may just have wandered off—"

"He never would!" she cried. "Someone may have stolen him. The least you can do is have a search made—"

"Percy has been searching."

The boy nodded. "Yes, ma'am, searched all over the place."

"He may have wandered over to the servants' quarters and somebody—"

"We've been through all that." Searle flung out an exasperated hand. "Well, I'll see what I can do. Be a good girl,

Andrea, have your swim, and we'll talk about it later. Right now I've got other things on my mind."

"Oh, I know." Her burnished dark hair swirled indignantly around her shoulders. "But Carl is dead, you can't help him, and my poor Pepe may be lying in pain somewhere. You're heartless, Walter." There were tears in her eyes as she turned away.

Searle turned back to the car shaking his head, with a slightly glazed look in his eye. "What a woman! Damned little Mexican hairless, you'd think it was a child the fuss she makes over it. Who knows who got it? A mongoose, or maybe some kid picked it up. I ought to have refused to let her bring it, but she's been coming here for years, so—" He shook his head again, collected himself, and offered Xavier a hand. "I've been waiting for you."

He was a tall, vigorous man of about forty, with a handsome face and abundant brown hair. Ten years earlier he had come to St. Caro as a tourist, perceived the possibilities of a luxury inn at Mango Beach, and bought the land for it; but St. Caro gossip said that only his subsequent marriage had enabled him to find the money for the lavish development of the place. In white shorts, a white sport shirt, and tennis shoes, he might have conveyed an impression of health and holiday if he had not sounded weary. He turned to say a word to the page, and the boy hurried away. "I've sent for Dr. Richardson. He's playing golf, but he said if I'd let him know when you arrived he'd join us at Lattner's cottage. Why don't we drive over in your car? It's all the way across the compound." He pointed to a distant yellow roof.

A number of tanned men and women watched them curiously from guesthouse terraces. "This is a bad business," said Searle. "Could raise hell with us. Two couples have left already. I certainly hope you can catch Maubee and get the thing settled fast." When Xavier did not reply, Searle went on, talking with a kind of galloping garrulity, almost a compulsion. "Lattner is, I mean he was, important in Ohio. His family and his company are going to be on my neck. I've notified them through the governor's office, and Chalk's secretary just phoned to say they've had a cable. The family wants the body flown back to Cleveland right away for the funeral. I'd like to get it into the hands of the mortician this afternoon and fly it out tomorrow morning. That all right with you?"

"Could be," Xavier said. "Depends."

They were approaching an isolated cottage with a wide terrace on one side facing the dark blue sea and on the other a cluster of mango trees. A small yellow sports car stood in the shade of the trees. Searle continued to pour out his troubles. "Rotten situation from every standpoint. He was one of our stockholders."

"Has he been coming here long?"

"No, last year was his first season with us. He liked it so much, he bought in. Stockholders are allowed to reserve the cottage of their choice. This was Lattner's. His family probably won't want to keep it." It occurred to Xavier that every remark Searle had made so far concerned only the business problems arising from Lattner's death, not the man who had died.

With the motor shut off, the only sounds were bird cries and the distant slosh of the Caribbean surf. Searle took a key from his pocket and unlocked the yellow door of the cottage. It was Xavier's first inspection of the interior of a Mango Beach guesthouse, and he was surprised by its simplicity. The furniture was ordinary, the maroon-tiled floor rugless. The only authentic touch of the affluent society was provided by a small built-in refrigerator and a bar, on top of which was a half-empty bottle of rum and a few glasses. A large glass jalousied window with a panoramic view of the sea was the chief attraction of the living room. Yellow drapes, capable of providing privacy when drawn, hung alongside.

Through the open bedroom door Xavier could see the body, lying prone on the floor, the head turned to one side, revealing the gape of a deep cut in the back of the neck. A machete, its long cutlass blade darkly stained, lay close by. The blow had sliced through Lattner's spinal cord, and blood had spread a heavy brown stain over his blue linen jacket and the collar of his white sport shirt. Xavier took off his sunglasses and, out of respect for the dead, his helmet.

Violent death could stir more emotion in him than was advisable in a policeman. He had been ten years old when his father was knifed and killed in a fight in a Honduras lumber camp and not long after his mother had died during an operation.

He stood on the threshold of the bedroom for several seconds. The room was deeply shadowed, for slatted wooden jalousies had been turned to cover the windows; but a glowing table lamp revealed some detail. The machete, he noted, was one of the expensive sort that Carovians call "show-shows," with a heavy decorated blade nearly two feet long and a ceremonial handle of polished dark wood. For the most part they were sold only to tourists; the machete used in cane cutting had a shorter blade and a plain handle.

"Nothing has been touched." Even a short silence seemed to make Searle nervous. "I left the lamp on, too, just as it was." He gave the impression of wanting approval. Xavier crossed to a window and adjusted the jalousies to flood the room with daylight. All of the windows were unscreened. The insect life of St. Caro was notably unassertive—a thousand varieties of birds saw to that.

To judge from dark hair and firm features, Lattner had been in the mid-forties—a stocky, muscular man. The body lay at the foot of a large bed, on which the yellow bedspread had been neatly folded, exposing fresh and unwrinkled sheets and pillowcases. "I suppose the maid turned down the bed?" Xavier asked.

"Yes, we do that for every cottage, every evening, while most of the guests are in the restaurant."

When at the scene of a crime, record all available data bearing on the character and habits of the principals involved. The axiom had been impressed on Xavier at police school. He circled the room slowly. The yellow-tiled bathroom was impeccable. One closet was full of Lattner's expensive clothes, neatly hung; in the other were his golf clubs, tennis rackets, and fishing rods.

"Maubee must have taken the camera and binoculars," Searle volunteered. "Lattner was proud of that camera. His watch is gone, too." A band of pale skin on a tanned wrist showed where the dead man had worn it. When Xavier examined a miscellany of toilet articles on top of the dresser, including a man's cologne, the manager added, "He paid a lot of attention to his grooming," and after another moment, "Looking for anything in particular?"

"Just getting an impression." Books and a magazine on a bedside stand had caught Xavier's eye—two paperbacks with lurid covers and a copy of *Playboy*. "What kind of man was Lattner? Aggressive?"

"You got it in one. Interesting but tough. A little crude, in fact. The business buccaneer, if you know what I mean."

"A woman chaser?"

"Well—yes, you could say that. He had a forceful way that appeals to a lot of women."

"Did he have many opportunities around here?"

After a moment, Searle nodded abruptly. "You know how it is in a place like this. Always a few bored women on their own looking for adventure. A widower like Lattner—a successful man in the prime of life—well, you can imagine. Fast talker, too—had a lot of stories, a distinctive line. Not my business to know which guest goes into which cottage, but for Lattner I'd say it could have been one or another woman almost every night. Not last night, though."

"How do you know that?"

"Why, Chief, it stands to reason. Look at the bed. Look at the bar. No sign of a woman. Anyway, why waste time? We know who did it." He reached into a pocket and brought out a small, worn diary with a black, smooth imitation leather cover. "Dr. Richardson saw this under the dresser when he examined the body. Probably fell out of Maubee's pocket and got kicked aside in the struggle."

Xavier opened the diary to the first page, where an ill-formed but bold scrawl read, "Property of David Maubee." He said, "I thought nothing had been touched."

"Nothing was, except that. What difference does it make?"

"Might want to test it for prints."

"Fingerprints? You mean you go in for that kind of thing?"

"Yes, even in St. Caro we know about fingerprints. I guess yours will be all over this book."

Searle gestured irritably. "I took it for protection. Figured that when Maubee realized he'd lost it he might spread the word for one of the help to get it back to him. You know how it is, he's a kind of hero to a lot of the boys."

"I'll look at it later." Xavier put the diary in his pocket, bent over the body, gripped a rock-hard shoulder of the heavy corpse, and rolled it over on its back. It moved like a statue. Only the whites of the wide-open eyes showed, like washed stones, and the lips were retracted in a death grimace that could be read as either sardonic or anguished. Searle made a sound as if he were about to be sick. "Good God!" he muttered. "Close his eyes, can't you?"

With a contraction of his own stomach muscles, Xavier tried to pull down the eyelids, but they resisted. *"Rigor mortis* well advanced," he said. It occurred to him that he had not used the phrase since leaving the police academy. The dead face, with its surface tan, looked as if it had been carved in some repellent clay by a sculptor full of hate for humanity but, even so, the broad forehead, strong cheek bones, and pugnacious jaw suggested a considerable force of personality in the living Lattner. An old Carovian saying crossed Xavier's mind: "Death and Mr. Whip have cold faces." Mr. Whip was the old slave term for the plantation overseer.

He knelt and tried to open the pale lips, but the clenched teeth would have required a chisel to pry them apart. With distaste he brought his nose close to the corpse's mouth. "Faint smell of rum," he said after a moment.

"That isn't surprising."

"Heavy drinker?"

"Heavy enough. He liked rum."

Rising, Xavier looked around him. "Maybe the glass is in the other room." When a glance and sniff at the tumblers on the bar showed them to be spotless and odorless, he opened the cabinet below and found it empty. So too was the refrigerator.

"I don't see any mixer. Did he drink his rum straight?"

"Might have. Usually, though, he liked it with green coconut water." The thin juice of the unripened coconut was

a favorite mixer for the island's knowledgeable rum drinkers.
The label on the opened bottle was that of St. Caro's most
expensive brand, almost as dark as Haitian rum. Holding the
neck of the bottle carefully in a handkerchief, Xavier un-
capped it, smelled it, poured a few drops into his palm,
cautiously tasted them, and nodded approvingly.

Searle looked surprised. "What did you expect? Think
somebody tampered with it?"

"Just checking. There ought to be a glass around somewhere." Crossing to the bathroom, Xavier found the tumblers
there similarly unused. "Would you say that Lattner was the
kind of man who would swig rum out of a bottle?"

"I wouldn't know. He might have. Maybe he didn't take a
drink here at all." Searle made no attempt to conceal his
irritation. "How about some action before Maubee gets
away?"

Xavier suppressed a smile. "Action" was a tourist's word,
which usually meant sight-seeing, exercise, gambling, or sex.
American impatience with the leisurely pace of native life
struck him as naïve. Over the centuries the islands had
learned that life rewards action only slowly and grudgingly.
Carovians when they saw a hurrying man said, "Crazy to
fight the sun." He bent over the body again. A pair of dark
spectacles in a leather case protruded from the breast pocket
of the blue jacket, and the other pockets yielded only a
pencil and, in the light gray trousers, a handkerchief.

"Do you know whether he was in the habit of carrying
money?"

"He usually had a wallet on him. Isn't it there? Maybe it's
in the dresser." When a search of the drawers revealed
nothing but clothing, Searle said, "Ought to be some travelers' checks around, too. And the key to the cottage. Maubee
must have taken them and the wallet. He would, naturally."

"Not naturally. Money, yes—but the wallet, the key, the
checks—he wouldn't want all that incriminating stuff."

"He might have picked them up to go through later. He
could always throw them away."

Xavier stared at the grinning dead face speculatively. "Who
found the body?"

"My wife and the maid. Our housekeeper left last month, went back to the States, and Mrs. Searle has been supervising the maids until we can find a replacement. Gives her something to do." He seemed slightly defensive. "She had just assigned a new maid to this cottage, and they came over here around ten this morning. Lattner was usually on the golf course by then. My wife knocked, didn't get an answer, tried the door. It wasn't locked. When they saw the body, they ran out. The maid was screaming so loud I heard her all the way across the compound, so I got in a car and rushed over."

They heard footsteps and turned to see Dr. Richardson and the boy who had been sent for him. The doctor had a craggy face, a brusque manner to go with it, and the build of a football tackle run slightly to fat. A rough-grained briar pipe was between his teeth, suiting the solidity of his jaw and the rich russet brown of his complexion. "Caught me right in the middle of my best round yet," he growled at Searle. "Could have broken eighty for the eighteen. But all right, I'm here." He turned to Xavier. "You the policeman?"

"Yes. You the doctor?" Xavier's tone matched Richardson's.

Searle said hastily, "Dr. Richardson, Chief Brooke." The doctor's eyes met Xavier's for a challenging instant before he put out a hand to be shaken. Xavier recognized the type. The usual skin prejudice, plus considerable class prejudice, in a personality that could not be bothered to conceal them. He radiated authority. His thick hair was almost white, but it was the premature white of the very blond, blue-eyed Anglo-Saxon. It did not age him; he looked the vigorous fifty that he probably was.

A pink shirt in the doorway caught Searle's eye. "Who told you to come in, Percy? Wait outside." Disappointment dripped from the boy's "Yes, sir," as he went out. The doctor was talking to Xavier. "I examined the body over two hours ago. Rigor was noticeable then. Indication is he was killed early this morning—sometime between one and four. Hard to tell closer than that, in this climate."

"No doubt about the cause of death?"

"You kidding? With the neck sliced like that? Wound inflicted by a sharp instrument, heavy blade." He indicated the machete with the toe of his sport shoe. "Must have killed him instantly."

"That grin on him, doctor. The *rictus sardonicus*. Would you say that was normal?"

Richardson eyed Xavier quizzically, seemed about to comment on the medical term, changed his mind, took a reflective puff at his pipe, and said, "Normal enough. Retraction here is pretty extreme, yes. It happens like that sometimes. Not pretty."

"No, sir. Like a soul in hell. He'll have to be taken to the hospital at Gracedieu. Would you be willing to assist in the autopsy, doctor?"

"Autopsy?" The doctor looked as if he had not expected to find so sophisticated a procedure on St. Caro.

Searle said, "What do you need an autopsy for? We know what killed him. Let's get the body to Cleveland without delay. The Lattner family is waiting for it."

"It's the law, Mr. Searle. Murder case calls for an autopsy."

"Oh, come off it, Chief. You know you can skip the autopsy if you want to. The doctor here will certify the cause of death. Just say the body is being sent home. The Lattners aren't going to like it if the body has been cut up without their permission."

Dr. Richardson glanced understandingly at Searle and nodded. "The body is going to start to decompose pretty soon. Sooner it gets to the undertaker, the better. Anyway, I'm not anxious to go into Gracedieu and fool around with cadavers, not when I'm supposed to be on a holiday. If it comes to that, you've got your own medical examiner, I suppose, but he'll just tell you what we already know."

"If the murder had been committed on the mainland, doctor, you'd expect an autopsy, wouldn't you?" Xavier spoke softly.

The doctor shrugged. "That's different."

The difference was obvious to Xavier. In a tropical island, with the tourist trade to protect, why bother with

legal technicalities? "The law calls for an autopsy," he said.
"The hell with that!" Searle snapped. "Let the governor
decide. I'll call him."

"You do that," Xavier said. "Tell him you want me to
violate the law in a murder case for your convenience."

The doctor broke in. "Well, you fellows work it out. You
don't need me any more. If you want to send over a death
certificate, Brooke, I'll sign it. I'm off to lunch, now." He
turned and was out of the cottage before Searle could finish
saying, "Thank you, doctor."

4

"YOU going to call the governor?" Xavier asked.

Ignoring the question, Searle turned his back and stared out of the window. It was a reaction that Xavier had seen before in whites who, when challenged by black authority, felt affronted and confused. After a few seconds, he said, "Then I'll call the hospital." He lifted the telephone from the bedside table, got through to the hospital, and asked to have Lattner's body picked up as soon as possible. "You'll probably want to check with the doctor here at the inn who examined the body," he told the weary voice at the other end. "Yes, I know you're full up with live tourists. A dead one will be a little change for you. Don't blame me. Tourist gets himself murdered, it's tough for everybody."

Cradling the phone, he said, "Mr. Searle." Searle turned around, his face hostile. "You say Dr. Richardson found Maubee's black book. Where exactly?"

Searle pointed. "There."

"That the only reason for suspecting Maubee?"

"I'd say it was enough."

"Anybody see him around the place?"

"Not that I know of. If he sneaked in at one or two in the morning, nobody would be likely to see him. It was a dark night—no moon."

"Was Lattner in the habit of locking his door when he left the cottage?"

"I don't think so. The guests are encouraged to lock up when they go out, but most of them don't bother. The staff here is trustworthy—they know anybody suspected of stealing would never get another job on the island. And the guests don't take Maubee and such types seriously. Besides, that door"—he flicked a finger at the closet used by Lattner for his sports equipment—"has a Yale lock. Same key as the door to the cottage. For jewelry and cash the guests can use the hotel safe if they want to. Generally they leave the lights on if they go out at night." He looked at the lighted lamp. "Okay to turn it off now?"

"Go ahead. Had any other cases of theft?"

"Over the years, only a few. Petty stuff. Each time a door had been left unlocked in a dark cottage with valuables lying around. Whether Maubee was in on those I don't know. But I suppose he must have looked the inn over more than once."

"Any idea what Lattner was doing last night up to the time he was killed?"

"I know he played bridge with some other guests in the card room at the main house until after midnight. Then he must have driven over here. Like to hear what I think happened?"

"Yes, I would."

"The way I see it, Maubee must have been hiding in those trees over there, and he saw Lattner drive up after his bridge game. He always drove across the compound—said it was too far to walk after all the other exercise he got. But Maubee would never break in while he was here, so it stands to reason he went out again. Maybe to the pool pavilion—the band was playing and he liked to dance. Must have left his door unlocked, and Maubee simply walked in, figuring he had plenty of time. But for some reason Lattner came back again and surprised him. Lattner was strong—he would have tried to hold him. I don't suppose Maubee would have been carrying the machete, too awkward, so perhaps Lattner had this one lying around. A lot of visitors buy them to take home. Maubee probably grabbed it, Lattner tried to duck and got it in the back of the neck. Then I suppose Maubee emptied Lattner's pockets and took the watch. If that closet door was locked, he would have tried the key on it, helped himself to the camera and binoculars, and sneaked off."

"Do you know whether anyone saw Lattner at the dance pavilion?"

"I didn't ask."

"Then all we really know is, Lattner left the card room around midnight and got killed here between one and four. With Dave Maubee's little black book under the dresser. We need more evidence than that. If you don't mind waiting a minute, I've got to get something out of my car."

As Xavier opened the trunk of the car and lifted out a canvas valise, he was aware of the pink-shirted page, Percy, watching him with bursting curiosity. He was a small boy, with lively eyes, a knowing expression, and skin so shiny black as to seem almost blue in the sunlight. Xavier said, "Been working here long, Percy?"

"Yes sir, Chief. Three years now."

"Don't you go to school?"

"Finished school long ago."

"I may want to talk to you later. Stay around."

"Yes, sir!"

In the bedroom Xavier opened his bag and removed an old Graflex camera, a small insufflator with a soft rubber bulb, a jar of fine gray dusting powder, and a strong magnifying glass. Since learning print-developing technique in the States not many opportunities to apply it had come his way, and he welcomed this one. As he knelt before the machete and began to dust the polished handle and the sharp blade, he saw out of the corner of his eye that Percy had tiptoed into the cottage and was standing open-mouthed at the bedroom door. Searle saw him too and snapped, "Outside, Percy."

"Yes, sir." The boy took a reluctant step backward, and then stood motionless, as if trying to make himself invisible. When Searle glared at him, saying, "I told you"—Xavier interrupted. "Oh, let the kid stay. He isn't doing any harm and we may want him for something." He glanced up to note Percy's delighted smile and Searle's compressed lips before blowing gently to remove the excess powder from the machete and studying the result through the magnifying glass. Presently he shook his head. "Just a mess. Not a clear print in the lot. Let's try the other side."

This time a print on the handle of the machete riveted his attention. "Something there. Looks like the ball of a thumb." He scanned the faint tracery of lines again. "From the position it would be the left hand." Reaching into his wallet, he extracted the official card containing Maubee's prints. A minute passed while he compared the card with the evidence of the polished wood. "Not much doubt," he said slowly as he rose. "Same whorl, same scar, and Maubee's left-handed."

"Well, there you are! That's all you need. Now it's just a question of finding him."

"I'll have to take the machete into Gracedieu."

"Yes, of course. I suppose they'll need it for the trial."

Xavier doubted that there would be a trial. With a murder charge against him, rather than be taken into custody Maubee would probably fight and perhaps even kill, or be killed. But if by luck they got him into jail, he would not deny his guilt. Carovians under arrest almost always confessed when they were guilty; the legal technicalities on which Stateside criminals relied meant nothing to them. Everything would be settled at the preliminary hearing. Governor Chalk would pick a judge and appoint an attorney to represent Maubee, who would plead guilty. It would all be over in ten minutes. Chalk would no doubt manage to transfer the sentencing to Washington, in order to get the case off the island, and Maubee would wind up in a federal penitentiary.

The important thing now was to make sure that the fingerprints could be introduced as evidence. Xavier moved the machete carefully into a patch of sunlight, adjusted the Graflex for close-up work, and took two or three pictures of the print he had identified.

"Let's play it safe," he said. "In case these don't turn out and the prints get rubbed off, we better have some confirming witnesses. Mr. Searle, would you mind looking through the glass at this print on the card, and that one on the handle? Tell me if in your opinion they look alike."

Searle knelt, studied the prints, and said, "Identical."

"Come here, Percy." The boy came into the room, his eyes shining. "Want to help? Look at the card first, then at this print on the handle, and tell me what you see."

With an expression of sheer ecstasy, Percy peered through

the magnifying glass. "This black thumb—that gray one. They just the same. That Dave Maubee's thumb?"

"Seems so. Suppose a month from now somebody asks you what you saw just now. What would you say?"

The boy hesitated for a moment. Perhaps he felt some conflict of loyalties between Xavier and Maubee. Then he made up his mind. "Me say I saw both thumbs and they the same."

"All right. Don't forget that. If it's all right with you, Mr. Searle, I'll just borrow a pillowcase from the bed to wrap the machete and a sheet to cover Lattner's body."

"Go ahead. Percy, we won't need you any more. You can get back to work. All through now, Chief?"

"Not quite." Xavier eyed the bottle of rum on the bar. "Could be Maubee took a drink while he was here. Might have needed it." He dusted the bottle for prints and to his surprise found none that were more than smudges. "I don't get it," he said, thinking aloud. "Should be Lattner's prints on here anyway. Unless Maubee took a drink and then wiped the bottle. But if he thought about fingerprints why didn't he wipe off the machete handle too?"

Searle said, "Probably just forgot in the excitement."

Xavier nodded, but without conviction. "Have to take the bottle along." Using another pillowcase for protection, he stowed it in the canvas bag.

"Anything more for you to do here?" Searle asked.

"The mortuary wagon will be coming for the body."

"You don't have to hang around for that. If you say there has to be an autopsy, I'm not going to argue. When the wagon arrives, I'll show the driver which cottage."

"I'll probably still be here then."

"What on earth for? The longer you delay, the harder it will be to pick up Maubee's trail."

"I want to talk with Mrs. Searle and the maid who was with her when they found the body. Got to have their statements for the record."

"I don't see the point of it. She can't tell you anything I haven't told you."

"Part of my job, Mr. Searle. Would you like me to go to your office, or will you ask Mrs. Searle to come here?"

"A lot of officious nonsense." The manager was visibly fighting to keep his temper. Finally he said, "No, I don't want you to go back to the office. The guests are having lunch now and seeing you drive up would just start the gossip again. And I don't want my wife to come here with that"—he looked at the shrouded body—"still around."

"We can close the door and I'll talk to her in the living room. Want me to drive you back across the compound?"

"No, I'll take Lattner's car. All right, have it your way. I'll ask my wife to come here after lunch, if she feels up to it. You'll have to wait, though. We're lunching with friends."

"I'll wait. Speaking of lunch, maybe you'd ask Percy to bring me a couple of sandwiches. Didn't have a chance"—he grinned inwardly—"to take any along. I'll be glad to pay."

"No need for that. Ham all right? I'll send them over." Searle strode out of the cottage. It occurred to Xavier that for a big, successful man he seemed to have about as much character as a wet paper towel. Perhaps that was what came of being married to a rich woman who held the purse strings. A man had to be lucky to have a wife who knew how to make him feel strong—like Toinette.

5

XAVIER closed the door to the bedroom and sat down in front of the window facing the sea. A few swimmers were coming out of the blue water onto the black sand and, beyond, two sailboats had caught an offshore breeze and were racing toward the horizon. Sometimes Xavier wished he could get on a boat and sail down to all the islands he had never seen. Almost on the edge of the water, in front of a pink cabaña, waiters were setting up a luncheon table, while others were serving drinks on the terrace of a thatched hut surrounded by coconut palms. It was all a little too much; it did not seem real; it was not real; it was merely a momentary glitter on the surface of the real St. Caro. With a shrug, Xavier brought out Maubee's little black book and began to leaf through the pages.

"May 14. All afternoon. Louisa Ellis. She say she 15, but she married two years. Third house behind the shoe store on Hooper St. in Bamboula. B-2. Perfume."

It was traditional for young Carovian bucks to rate girls on a nine-point scale running from A-1 at the top to C-3, thus pithily describing their qualifications as bedmates. Some said that many years earlier a British engineer had introduced the system as a joke, but it had caught on and spread throughout the island. The girls themselves were aware that they were being rated by their lovers, and many of them, filled with competitive ardor, did their utmost to justify a higher classification. "Honey, didn't I give you a real A-1 time tonight?" "Ain't I your A-1 girl?" As for the cryptic word "perfume," that was merely Maubee's reminder to himself that he had promised the girl a present when he visited her again.

"June 2. Mary I don't know her last name on the worf [wharf] in Morganstown. She try make me rape her and when I won't she did it for me anyway. B-3."

"June 9. Spanishtown. Isabel Cannon. That the right name for her. She move to Port Cambo next week, sing at Mac's place. A-1. Some figure."

The name Isabel appeared frequently thereafter. "October 14. Isabel. Her place on Poco Street. Yes yes. Record player." "Yes yes" was another familiar form of testimonial. A rough calculation indicated that Maubee, within the past eight months, had spent no fewer than a hundred nights or afternoons with more than thirty different women, of whom only three were rated A-1. His standards were evidently high. The chronicle was not complete, for the last half dozen pages of the book, carrying the record of a few weeks' activities, had been torn out. To conceal something of which Maubee was ashamed? No way of telling. One thing was clear— Maubee was even more of a menace to the girls of St. Caro than to tourists. On that ground alone he ought to be taken out of circulation. Xavier chuckled. If he had not been married to Toinette, he might have felt a twinge of envy, but he had become a wife-loving man—a type sometimes ridiculed by Carovian youth. "Wife-lovin' man," Gracedieu nightclub entertainers sang, "you don' know what you're missin', when you let one gal monopolize your kissin'."

His reflections were interrupted by Percy, who trotted into the cottage with a small plastic bag containing a couple of ham sandwiches and a can of cool beer. "Mr. Searle say these for you."

"Thank you, Percy." Xavier reached hungrily into the bag. "Mr. Searle want you back at the office?"

"Yes, sir. He tol' me come right back."

"Well, sit down. A few minutes won't matter. If you have any trouble, tell him I made you stay."

"Yes, sir." They smiled at each other. "You bossed him real good, Chief."

"Never mind about that. Everybody got his job to do. How old are you?"

"Fourteen."

Which was to say that, being a Carovian, Percy was sexually aware. "You knew Mr. Lattner?"

"Yes, sir."

"I understand he drank a lot."

"Yes, sir!" These two syllables in Percy's mouth, pronounced without the "r" and with varying intonation and emphasis, could express agreement, doubt, anticipation, resignation, or delight.

"He drank rum?"

"He big on rum. Bartenders all laugh about it. Sometime he sit at the bar an' put away a bottle in an hour. But he held it good. Never showed it."

"He drank it straight?"

"No, sir. Me never see him do that. Always with green coconut water. Bartenders cut open two, three, four greenies just for him, every day. Every day me had to bring a bottle green water up here an' put it in his fridge. Lattner always say it better than any sleeping pill and full of vitamins—more rum he drank, healthier he got on account of the green water." Percy related the saying without a smile. St. Caro's native population regarded the juice of the coconut as a staple of life provided by a benevolent deity.

"Did you like him?"

The boy reflected and shook his head. "He stingy. Rich man, but he tip mean."

"They say he was a wolf with women."

"Everybody know that. The maids call him ol' ass-pincher." A big grin and sparkling eyes went with the remark.

"The maids? He fool around with the maids?"

"Yes, sir. But that was las' year. This year he go for the white meat. But he still like to get his hand on our girls when he catch 'em alone."

"You know who his white women were?"

Percy hesitated. "Mr. Searle fin' out I talk about the guests, he fire me. That a big rule with him."

"Don't worry. What you tell me, that's just between us. What about these women?"

The words came out in a laughing torrent. "First it was Mrs. Dillon in number 14. You saw her this mornin'. She the one lost the dog. They say she in the movies, but she a boozer. She and Lattner, they turn it on, until Miss Bruce, she a redhead, she come and Lattner he go for her. She use' to go down to the beach with him late at night and they swim naked, I see 'em. She really built, that one. She go back to the States couple of weeks ago. Another one, Mrs. Keys, live in number 30. Her husban' go away an' after that Lattner there all the time. They say she some kind of sci"—he struggled for the word—"scientis'—but she paint pictures."

"Anybody else?"

The merriment faded and the boy looked faintly uneasy. "Don' know for sure."

"Come on, Percy. Who?"

"Some of the waiters say, maybe Lattner try make the big time with the boss lady."

"Mrs. Searle? Why do they think that?"

"They say the way he looks at her, he hot for her. She no angel, either. She drive out a lot at night by herself. They say she pretend to be real cool, but underneath she like everybody else."

Scurrilous gossip about white employers was a favorite pastime among black Carovians. Xavier put on a skeptical expression. "They say that. Anybody see her going to Lattner's cottage?"

Doubt crinkled Percy's eyes. "Ain't heard nobody say that."

"Do you know where she goes?"

"No, sir."

"Anybody who might know?"

Percy reflected. "Maybe Mrs. Dillon. The maids say she a big snoop—know everybody's business."

"Mrs. Searle, does she have children?"

The idea seemed to amuse the boy. "They say ol' Searle don' give her babies 'cause he no good in bed. They say their sheets always too neat for her to be mama. They say she got to get it somewhere an' she don' get it from Searle."

Xavier wolfed down part of a sandwich to cover his chuckle. He could imagine the conversations of the inn's maids and waiters in their time off, with the pages hanging avidly around their circle. The eyes and ears of the staff were sure to be everywhere. If a white who was popular with the help was known to be playing around, the gossip about him or her might be friendly and even admiring, but if the transgressor was disliked for any reason, a crumb of fact could be quickly magnified into slanderous fiction. Percy could not be relied on for accuracy, but something useful might be learned from him. "What about Mr. Searle?" Xavier asked. "Has he got a woman?"

"Him? The maids say he no had a woman for a year. They say he take a yellow pill every night, make himself sleep."

Xavier sensed that he had exhausted this vein in Percy's gossip mine and decided to try another. "Who was the maid with Mrs. Searle when she came here this morning?"

"Jenny. Jenny Meggs."

"The maid before her, who looked after this cottage—what's her name?"

"Carolla." It was a common name on St. Caro.

"Her last name?"

The boy suddenly dropped his eyes and his voice altered into a higher register, signs that Xavier recognized as prelude to evasion. "Me don' rightly remember."

"Don't lie to me, Percy. How old is Carolla?"

"Don' know." The boy reconsidered. "Twenty, maybe more."

"Did she get fired?"

"Don' rightly know."

Xavier looked at the now serious face above the pink shirt with mingled annoyance and compassion. He had often seen similar reactions in Carovians under questioning. Percy was willing to gossip ruthlessly about white women, but not about a black girl whom he liked and who might be in trouble. What trouble? The boy might be frightened into telling, if he knew; but after that he would never help the police again. If it became necessary to find out about Carolla, there were other ways to get the information. Xavier said, "All right, Percy. You don't have to tell me. Better get back to your job."

"Yes, sir." Percy left the cottage looking subdued and relieved. Xavier followed him outside, deposited his canvas bag and the wrapped machete carefully in the trunk of his car and, climbing into the front seat, switched on the two-way radio. A few seconds later he heard Peter Obee's voice: "Police headquarters. Over."

"This is Chief Brooke, Peter. Put Marco on."

"Marco not here, Chief. He go out this morning, not back yet."

"Did he say where he was going?"

"No, sir. Just out on business."

Xavier scowled at the mouthpiece in his hand. "Any calls?"

"Yes, sir. Little while ago, had a call from Deputy Michelle. He check the house in Morganstown. Nothing there. He coming in. Mr. Motley telephone a little while ago. He say he driving to Mango Beach—please you wait for him, he got something to tell you."

"All right, Peter. Now listen carefully. I'm at the inn. I'll be here for a while longer. An ambulance is coming from Gracedieu Hospital to take Lattner's body. Dr. Evans will do an autopsy this afternoon. I'll call again later and you can tell me if his report has come in."

"Wilco. Roger."

"All right. Over and out."

As he hung up his transmitter, Xavier heard the sound of a car coming up the driveway from the main building and was relieved to see that it was the mortuary car—actually a converted station wagon—from Gracedieu. It would be easier to talk with Mrs. Searle if the dead man were out of the way.

He knew both of the men in the front seat and helped them bring the body out of the house and install it in the wagon. They seemed unusually businesslike—almost in a hurry, not availing themselves of the Carovian custom which called for a minute or two of idle chat under such circumstances. It occurred to Xavier that since Searle had undoubtedly told them in which cottage the body was to be found, he might have told them more. Turning to the man he knew best, the driver, he said amiably, "Better not do it, Charlie."

Charlie looked startled. He was a slim young man with a beard and an unsmiling face. "Do what?"

"What Mr. Searle told you to do."

Charlie and the other man exchanged a quick, anxious glance. "What you know 'bout what he tol' us?"

"I'll tell you what he told you. You pretend you take this body to hospital. But instead, you take it to the undertaker. He told you the governor says it's okay to do like he says. Right? How much did he pay you?"

The men stared silently at the ground. "All right, Charlie, and you too, Arthur, you listen. This is a murder case. For all I care you can keep Searle's money, but if you do what he says, I will personally stick you into jail and you will stay there for a year. And I will take away your drivers' licenses and you will lose your jobs. You understand what I'm saying?"

"We don' wan' do nothin' wrong," said the man called Arthur, unhappily.

"Then you better do just like I tell you, Arthur. Now Charlie, be smart, once in your life. Take this body to the hospital and don't lose time. I will take care of Mr. Searle. You got that?"

"Got it," muttered Charlie, climbing into the driver's seat. They drove off without looking back.

That was settled, Xavier knew. In an hour the body would be in the dissection room of the hospital. But if he had not intervened it would have gone to the mortician's for preservative treatment and crating for the air trip to Cleveland. It was all in character for Searle. For him the important thing was to appease Lattner's family; the law was incidental.

It did not seem likely that the women Percy had mentioned, Mrs. Dillon and Mrs. Keys, would have much to contribute, but the possibility that one or both of them had been among the last to see Lattner alive could not be ignored. To ask Searle to arrange the interviews would be a cause of

argument and a waste of time. Estimating that an hour or so
would elapse before Mrs. Searle appeared, he strolled through
the compound until he saw a pink-doored house bearing the
number 30. The drapes of the picture window, he noticed,
had not been drawn, and walking slowly past he was able to
glimpse the interior without actually stopping. He could see
no one, but Percy's account of Mrs. Keys' interests had been
close to the mark. A microscope was prominent on a table,
next to a jumble of books, a collection of artist's brushes,
and a dozen colorful little jars of paint. A small easel
supported a painting of a spray of leaves that stood in a vase
alongside.

When his knock at the door was unanswered, he continued
his walk until he came to cottage number 14, its roof and
door a muted blue. A small sports car, an MG of the same
shade, was parked a few feet away. The door of the cottage
opened before he could even knock, and the woman he had
seen talking to Searle said, "I saw you coming." A small, neat
snub nose and twinkling dark eyes gave her an impish quality.
"You're Chief Brooke, aren't you?" Her pale green shorts
and shirt with a wide white cummerbund were far too elegant
for sports, and she smiled like someone expecting to be
photographed. The youthful prettiness of her lightly tanned
heart-shaped face did not deceive Xavier, who had encountered cosmetic surgery in his time. From her hands he
estimated her age at forty.

She stood aside for him to enter, her long spill of black hair
gleaming in the sunlight. "I thought you'd get to me. I wish
you would help me find my dog, but I suppose you've got
other things to do. You want to ask me about Lattner. Ask
away. I'm just having a little after-lunch drink. Join me?"
The animation of her talk, the brightness of her eyes, and a
slightly slurred diction suggested that the little drink was
taking hold. There was a faint rumor of rum in the air.

A small table with two chairs, used plates, and an empty
wine bottle told of luncheon just finished. Alongside one
plate lay a pipe that looked familiar—a gnarly black briar. Her
eyes followed his. "Oh, my guest forgot his pipe. He'll be
wanting it."

"I met Dr. Richardson this morning." Xavier smiled.

"You don't miss any tricks, do you? Now about that drink. I'm having daiquiris. All right with you?" Ignoring his refusal, she went to the bar and manipulated bottles and glasses, talking continuously. "I will be glad to tell you about that bastard Lattner, and who is better qualified? Back in Hollywood—you know who I am, don't you? Down here I use my married name, Dillon, but I'm Andrea Morse." When he said nothing, she laughed at herself. "Such is fame. You couldn't care less, could you? Hell. What was I saying?"

"Mr. Lattner."

"Yes, Lattner. Back in Hollywood, I thought I'd met all the extant varieties of louses, or is it lice, but Lattner was a special species." The last two words gave her trouble, and she repeated them, with elaborate enunciation. When he took the drink she gave him and put it aside, she said, "Oh, you meant it. You won't mind watching me, will you? Have a chair." She sat down on the sofa, curled her slim legs under her, and sipped at her cocktail glass. She seemed entirely at ease. "What do you want me to tell you?"

"Had you known Mr. Lattner long?"

"Too long. Well, not really. I met him last year. I own this cottage, you know. At least, I have permanent rights in it, as one of Searle's stockholders. I come here every winter if I'm resting." She wrinkled her nose. "Recent years, I've been resting entirely too much. Would you believe it? The word has gone round the studios that I drink. Ridiculous!" She lifted her glass again. "You won't mind if I'm frank? I mean, my kind of frankness may shock you. But then, you don't look like a prissy person and what I don't tell you others will, so what the hell."

"That's a sensible attitude, Mrs. Dillon. You were speaking of last year."

"Yes, last year. Lattner and I didn't have much to say to each other then. I noticed him—he was a noticeable man. Not handsome, but terrific energy. You could feel it when he entered a room. Deep voice. Talked a lot, but knew what he was talking about. Played a fast game of tennis, socked a golf ball like crazy—you know? And it wasn't any secret he made

millions out of that company of his—Lattner Valve, or
whatever it is. Oh, yes, I noticed him."

Xavier decided to say nothing, and she waited only a
second before going on. "Then I found he was on a native
kick. I mean, you won't be offended, he went all out for
young black girls. Must have been something new for him,
pretty exciting, because he certainly didn't show much
interest in any white woman around. When he never even
made a polite pass at me I was—I admit it—a little piqued. If
you stayed up late enough and spied—I did once or twice
when I couldn't get to sleep—you could usually see some
dusky kid going into his cottage." She stared pensively at her
drink. "Made me wonder if I'd been too timid all my life.
Missing something on account of an ethnic hang-up. Believe it
or not, except for the way I talk, I'm a rather inhibited
woman. Ridiculous, too, because I'm really very fond of the
people of this island. I made a picture here years ago when I
was just a starlet—one of those horror things—*Secrets of
Voodoo*. Awful. You a movie fan?"

The best way to keep her talking freely, Xavier felt, was to
fall in with her wandering style. "Perhaps not a fan, but I
remember when that movie company was here." He refrained
from adding that he had been twelve years old at the time.
"But there is no voodoo on St. Caro, you know. Here we call
it obeah."

"Oh, I know that. I learned a lot about it when I made the
picture, but for box office it had to be voodoo. Most people
in the States never heard of obeah and, anyway, we pretend-
ed it was made in Haiti. I remember there was one handsome
black man—but never mind. What was I talking about?"

"You were saying that this year Mr. Lattner was more
attentive."

"Attentive! When I got here about six weeks ago, he came
at me like a football tackle. As if he had just seen me for the
first time. I think he hadn't realized before who I am.
Celebrity makes a lot of difference to some men, you know. I
made him pay for last year. I can be damned haughty if I
want to." She laughed. "I didn't fool him, though. He had a

bruising way about him—he played rough. If a woman needled him too hard he was likely to slap her fanny until she yelled. He did that to me, once, down on the beach. Held my wrists and walloped me. Can you imagine? I was ready to kill him, but it was exciting, I admit it. Then he brought me back here." She sighed, finished her drink, and got up to pour another.

"But you came to dislike him?"

"Dislike." She considered, tapping her lips with a knuckle. "No. I came to hate him. He humiliated me. In different ways. Does talk about sex make you nervous? No? Then I might as well tell you. I'm not ashamed of it—just angry at myself. For about two weeks he couldn't get enough of my company. Said he'd wanted me ever since he saw my first starring film, *The Girl With Everything.* Ever see it? Not bad, really." She studied Xavier's face, with her eyebrows slightly arched. "It's very easy to talk to you. You've got the same sort of face as my analyst back home, color excepted, of course. What was I saying?"

"That Mr. Lattner could not get enough of your company."

"Did I say that? An understatement, if anything. He made love like a wild man, hinted he wanted to marry me, got me into a regular state. I had stars in my eyes. I even swore off drinking at night for two weeks because he wanted me sober. Then all at once it was over. A redheaded bitch from New Orleans, she couldn't have been more than twenty-five, sails in on a yacht and takes a cottage."

"Was that Miss Bruce?"

"You've been asking questions. Yes, that's the one. A jet-set type looking for something offbeat. She found it, all right. Next thing I knew he was treating me like a sister—a sister he didn't have much use for. Polite nods. Smiles. Waves of the hand. 'How are you this beautiful morning, Andrea?' Every woman in the place was laughing at me. When I faced him and demanded to know what he meant by it, he just said these things all come to an end, and what was I complaining about? I'm glad somebody killed him. If they hadn't, I might have. Was it really David Maubee, as people are saying? If so,

he deserves a medal. Only thing that makes me feel better is
that he gave the redhead the same treatment he gave me.
Dropped her for another woman."

"Who was that? Mrs. Keys?"

"Oh, then you know. Yes. Barbara Keys. Been talking to
her?"

"No, not yet. If there is anything you can tell me about
her, I'd appreciate it."

She gazed pensively at the diminished liquid in her glass
before saying, with a shrug, "Why not? She's a Boston
Brahmin, but you'd never think it if you saw her in a bikini.
Came with her husband, an older man. They're both scien-
tists, botanists. He's a professor someplace. She's writing a
book on tropical plants and illustrating it herself. They
seemed like nice people. Third or fourth day they were here
they took some of us on a hike, showed us all kinds of rare
flowers and trees. It was really interesting. Then Professor
Keys had to fly to London, some conference or other, and he
left Barbara here alone. That was his mistake."

"Lattner seized his opportunity?"

"That's one way to put it. First time she came down to the
beach after her husband left, I was there when it happened,
he went up to talk to her. They took a swim together, and
something must have clicked, because a couple of days after
that, whenever you saw one of them you saw the other. She
was supposed to fly back last week and meet her husband in
New York, but she's still here. The redhead couldn't take it.
Cleared out. Not me. I was damned if I was going to be
driven out of my own cottage. I stayed on and I'm going to
stay until I choose to go."

She yawned a little. Her glass was empty and her speech
was thickening. The next drink—and she was rising to pour
it—might extinguish her spark. Xavier said, "Just one more
question. Did you happen to see Mr. Lattner last night?"

From the bar, with bottle in her hand, she replied, "No, I
had dinner sent in and didn't see anybody. I wasn't feeling
well. Why?"

"I'm trying to find out whether he went to the dance
pavilion after midnight. Up to then he was playing bridge."

"He might have. He liked dancing. That's what he usually did nights—I mean when he wasn't—" She stopped. Her eyes were taking on a hooded look, and she drank half her drink at a gulp. "Sure you won't have one of these?"

"No, thank you."

"Then get the hell out of here. I want to sleep." As he rose, she eased herself down on the sofa, stretched out with a cat's grace, and closed her eyes. Her legs were firm, smooth, and elegant.

"Good-bye," he said. "Thank you for your cooperation." When she did not reply, he went out, closing the blue door gently behind him. He had not asked her if she knew about Mrs. Searle's nocturnal expeditions, but it would have been an awkward subject to bring up, and it did not seem important.

6

BEFORE he became chief of police and married Toinette, Xavier had been the lover of several white women visitors to St. Caro. Each year scores of unaccompanied American girls seeking adventure and romance arrived in Gracedieu to stay for a week or two at the less expensive inns and guesthouses. Some of them were free of color prejudice and, if defeated in the competition for the available male tourists, could always find an excuse to begin a conversation with a stalwart, amiable, and well-spoken black policeman. One word easily led to another, until Xavier's off-duty hours came to provide him with profound insights into the ways of the American female on the loose in a tropical island.

He was aware that some blacks when making love to white women felt a sense of racial triumph—they were "getting something back." A few even tried to enslave the white girls who loved them by playing on their sexual needs. He himself had always felt that if a woman was good to look at, pleasant to be with, and ready for love, then black or white, the thing to do was to make her and himself glad to remember the event. As to whether a beautiful white girl or a beautiful black girl was the more desirable, he had never been able to decide. Whenever he saw Toinette as a woman, rather than as a wife, he felt that her silken in-between complexion could not be improved on.

Even after he had given up the black-and-white game, as Carovians called it, he could not help appraising attractive white women in terms of their accessibility. Mrs. Dillon he liked for her lively style, and in his earlier days he might have been tempted to help rid her of her "ethic hang-up," but he did not feel really drawn to her. It was otherwise with

Margaret Searle, whom he had often seen shopping in Gracedieu. The firm set of her full mouth over an arrogant chin, a high-bridged nose, and the authority in her deep blue eyes made it clear that she was nobody to fool around with. She would pick the lover she wanted when she wanted him. Anybody else would have to rape her, and many a man must have considered the idea. She was a tall woman in her early thirties, with an athletic build, marvelous legs, lightly tanned skin, and sun-bleached blond hair piled high on top of her head, as if to emphasize her queenly style. Her voice, deep and cultivated, went with the rest of her. Black opinion held that she was high class but too bossy. You only had to see her husband wait on her to know that.

She was wearing white shorts, a white shirt open at the throat, and tennis shoes. Her eyes looked tired, but her voice was crisp enough. As she stepped out of the small red convertible in which she and Searle had driven across the compound, she said, "I hope this won't take long, Mr. Brooke."

Searle said, "Yes, we're playing tennis in fifteen minutes. The body gone?"

Xavier nodded. "Shall we go inside?"

In the cottage she seemed entirely composed, glancing only once at the closed door to the bedroom. As she sat down, she gave Xavier her full attention, and the way she tapped a cigarette before lighting it let him know that she expected his.

"See if I have this right, Mrs. Searle," he said. "You came to this cottage about nine this morning? With a maid?"

"Yes, Jenny Meggs. I had to let her go home, she was so upset. She's very young."

"Did either of you go into the bedroom?"

"No. The bedroom door was open and I could see he was dead. Jenny screamed, and we got out as fast as we could. She kept on screaming and Walter heard her."

Searle, who was sitting next to her on the sofa, said, "That girl has powerful lungs. A scream like an air raid siren."

"She was terribly scared. I don't blame her—I was almost as upset as she was."

"You had just hired her, I believe."

"Yes, this was her first day. But I've known her for years. She lives right down the road, in Mangotown. She used to baby-sit if one of our guests had small children to look after. She's quite reliable. Her father is a minister."

"Did she replace another girl?"

"I suppose you could say that, but maids are always coming and leaving in a place like this."

"In the tourist season we take on extra help," Searle amplified.

"Did you let another girl go just before you took on Jenny?"

Searle grunted impatiently. "What's that got to do with Lattner's death?"

"Just a routine question. This girl you let go, Mrs. Searle. Was there a reason?"

"Of course. She wasn't doing her work properly, and when I told her so, she was impudent."

"Now look here, Chief," Searle said. He pointed a finger at Xavier. "I don't like this. You ought to be out after Maubee, instead of asking a lot of meaningless questions."

With no change of expression, Xavier continued to look at Mrs. Searle. "What's the girl's name? The one you fired?"

"Carolla Peters." Mrs. Searle looked faintly amused, possibly at the casual way in which he had disposed of her husband's protest.

"Would you mind telling me what Carolla said that made you fire her?"

"Why do you want to know that?"

"Let me get at it another way. Somebody turned down Mr. Lattner's bed last night. Was that Carolla?"

"I suppose so. I let her go in the afternoon, but she might have done that before she left."

"Wouldn't that be unusual? If you fired her, she would have been angry, wouldn't she? Not anxious to please anybody."

Mrs. Searle smiled. "I see why they made you chief of police. I hoped I wouldn't have to mention this, but Mr. Lattner had accused Carolla of stealing—taking money from a wallet he had left lying around. When I spoke to her about it, she said a lot of very rude things. That's why I had to fire her." Mrs. Searle extinguished her half-smoked cigarette with emphasis. "I think it's quite possible that she came back here when no one was around to see what else she could pick up, and turned down the bed to give herself an excuse in case Mr. Lattner came in. Does that answer your question?"

"It's a possible explanation."

"May I ask, Mr. Brooke, why you're so interested in Carolla?"

"Just trying to get the whole picture."

She looked at him with a skeptical smile. "You mean, because a man was killed in this cottage, and the maid who looked after the cottage was fired the same day, there must be a connection?"

"That's right, Mrs. Searle. Coincidences do happen, of course, but we like to get all the facts. When Mr. Lattner was here last year, did Carolla look after him?"

There was a momentary pause before she said, "Possibly. I don't recall, and we don't keep records of the maids' assignments. If you don't mind my saying so, Mr. Brooke, the idea of Carolla killing anybody with a machete seems far-fetched to me. But of course, she might have got Maubee to do it for her, if she knew him."

At a glance from her, Searle said, "If you haven't anything important to ask us, Brooke, let's cut this short. Nothing to keep you here any longer, is there? Come on, Marge."

She stood up gracefully. "Good-bye, Mr. Brooke. I hope you find Maubee."

Xavier watched them climb into the convertible, walking testimonials to the plushy life. Superficially they looked well suited to each other, but he wondered how long a handsome, educated, and childless woman could tolerate an existence at Mango Beach with a husband she didn't love and a house-keeper's chores to perform. He turned to stare out of the picture window. White-crested waves were rolling in, and a few surfboarders were displaying their skill for the brown sun-worshipers on the beach. How many of them were suffering from sunburn, indigestion, hangovers, and marital troubles? Very few things in life lived up to the advertisement.

But why guess about the Searles' private life? *Investigative officers should avoid guesswork and confine themselves to the accumulation and systematic interpretation of factual evidence,* said the leading textbook on police methods. Xavier was doubtful about this rule—his own experience made him feel that if a policeman didn't sometimes guess, he'd never get very far. But the moment would soon come, he reminded himself, when Governor Chalk would demand a full report from him. Things would go a lot smoother if he could open his notebook and describe his procedure, step by step. He sat down and was busily writing, when he heard a car with a complaining motor drive up to the cottage and Ted Motley's voice called, "Xave?"

"In here."

Ted was wearing a wide-brimmed planter's straw hat which, atop his skinniness, created the effect of a mobile mushroom. A big leather-cased camera hung from his neck, bobbing as he moved. "Ah, the scene of the crime. In there, I suppose." He opened the bedroom door. "Body gone. Damn. I was afraid of that. Chalk held me up. Where was the body?"

"At the foot of the bed."

"X marks the spot." Ted unlimbered his camera and snapped several flashlight shots of the cottage. "Where's the murder weapon?"

"In my car. I'll show it to you later. When I talked to the station a little while back they said you had something to tell me."

"Message for you from Toinette."

"How come?"

"I was in my office, about an hour ago, and she telephoned. She sounded a little upset, but all she said was for me to give you a message. She wants you to come home tonight."

"She didn't say why?"

"No. I said maybe she'd prefer to talk to you over the radio and I'd go to the station with her if she liked, but she said no, if I spoke to you, just to tell you that."

Xavier hoped that his uneasiness did not show in his face.

Toinette knew Ted well and liked him, but ordinarily she would not have asked him for a favor if there was a way around it. He tried to reassure himself. "If something happened to one of the kids, she'd have told you. Maybe something went wrong in the house. Stove, toilet." He felt sure it was none of these things. Why hadn't she phoned the station and asked Peter Obee to relay the message? "Thanks for telling me. I was thinking I'd stay overnight in Morganstown, but I'll go back home tonight." An urge to get away from his anxiety made him change the subject abruptly. "How'd you make out with Chalk?"

Ted grinned and coiled himself into a chair. "As you'd expect. He had a call from Searle, so he knows about Maubee's fingerprints on the machete, and he can't understand why you're not out on the trail. Also, he doesn't want me to send anything to the mainland. Thinks I ought to hold myself down to a couple of lines on the back page of the *Sentinel,* saying Lattner died as a result of a cut from a machete and you are investigating to find out how it happened. Nothing about murder. Nothing to attract attention. When you catch Maubee, I'm allowed to say, still on the back page, he'll be tried for murder. When he's convicted, two more lines."

"And you do like he says?"

"He put on a lot of heat. Hinted that if he turns thumbs down on me, the airlines, steamship companies, and stores will find other ways of advertising in Gracedieu. His idea is that anybody who makes his living here and reports news that discourages tourists is a traitor to St. Caro and an enemy of Governor Chalk."

"So go home and be a good boy."

"Like to know what I said?"

"You're going to tell me, so why should I ask?"

"I said freedom of the press was a constitutional right wherever the American flag flies, and that if he pulls anything like that on me my great-uncle, Senator Russell of Georgia, would be interested. That, I can tell you, gave him a shock."

"Is Senator Russell your great-uncle?"

"Hell, no, but psychological warfare or, in other words, lying, is used in all forms of political combat. Anyway, I made no promises, and if I can get a good story out of this I'll rub Chalk's nose in printer's ink."

"Better do what he says, for the time being."

"You surprise me, but all right, if you say so. Now about you? What have you got?"

"Not much. I'm a little confused. It's all too easy. Maubee's fingerprint. His black book. Worries me. Almost like he was saying, 'Sure, I did it. Now come and get me.' "

Ted whistled silently for a moment. "Spell that out for me, will you, Xave?"

"All right, but you keep this to yourself. One thing that bugs me—that fingerprint. Maubee's no fool. He knows about fingerprints, but he doesn't wipe off the handle of the show-show."

"Maybe he just forgot. After all, he'd just killed a man."

"That's what Searle said. But then there's the little black book. How would Maubee lose a thing like that? He'd carry it where everybody does, in his hip pocket. And everybody wears jeans tight around the ass. He'd have to stand on his head and shake himself for the book to fall out."

"Just might be he was different—carried it in his shirt pocket."

"Nobody does that. Another thing. He knows what will happen if he kills a tourist, but he goes for his head with a machete. You never saw Dave Maubee swing a machete. Back when we were kids, eighteen or so, after I finished high school in the States, he and I knocked around the island for a couple of months. We had a game—toss big green coconuts in the air and cut them with a machete on the way down. You know, when they're green that outside layer is like stone, and you got to go through all that hard fiber before you reach the nut. When it's falling you got to be pretty good just to cut a slice off the outside. I ruined two machetes trying that trick. But Dave, he'd bring his machete up, kind of an underhand slice, and split the coconut right in half every time." He illustrated with a gesture. "There's a good edge on that show-show. With Dave's arm behind it and intending to kill, it wouldn't have stopped at an inch or so. It would have gone right through the neck."

Ted looked doubtful. "He might have checked his swing purposely. If he'd cut off Lattner's head there would have been blood all over the place, on him too. He wouldn't want that."

"Maybe so. The way it stands, I've got to find Maubee, but there's something wrong. What are you smiling at?"

"Somethin' wrong," Motley crooned. It was the name of a famous topical calypso, which was continually brought up to date by island singers. Current lines were: "Astronaut come out of space with female lipstick on his face—somethin' wrong, somethin' wrong." "President Nixon he promise peace, but that ol' war it just won' cease—somethin' wrong, somethin' wrong." Ted improvised a couplet for the occasion:

"Chief Brooke agree that Lattner dead
But wants to know why he kept his head—
Somethin'—"

The look on Xavier's face made him stop abruptly. In a reporter's voice he asked, "You got a plan to find Maubee?"

"He could be anywhere between Gracedieu and Port Cambo, and he's too smart to let himself be cornered by a few policemen. He's got a thousand places to hide. I could waste a year rushing around looking into houses. Only way is to outsmart him. Figure out where he would go and be there at the right time. Take him by surprise."

"How you going to do that?"

An investigative officer who prematurely confides in the press exposes himself and his assignment to the possibility of serious outside interference. But Xavier regarded Ted as a friend and ally—and more than that, as the only white on the island with whom he felt a bond of brotherhood. "If I know Dave, he's not going to be far from some woman he likes. I got his little black book, tells which ones he likes best. He'll want to keep off the roads by day. Might be walking, might use a bicycle after dark. Where would he be today? Sleeping in a bed, is my guess, and whose bed? A girl he felt wouldn't give him away. He's had to think about that for years, with the police after him all the time. I figure he wouldn't rate a girl A-1, no matter how it was between them, if he didn't respect her and feel he could trust her. So the best chance of finding him is to try an A-1 girl, and if he's not there, try the next. There are only three of them in his book. I'll tell the constables to keep an eye on the other girls, but the A-1's are the best bet."

Ted grinned satirically. "You keep the A-1's for yourself, is that it? Toinette will be interested."

"You want to be put in jail for disturbing the peace? I'm telling you that's where Maubee's likely to be, and I don't want anybody to try to bring him in except me. Those constables, if they go to lay a hand on him, they'll get hurt."

"You think you can handle him?"

"Dave and I, we understand each other. He wouldn't want to kill me, I don't want to kill him. I got a better chance than anyone else to put handcuffs on him."

"It makes a kind of crazy St. Caro sense. You driving back to Gracedieu now?"

"No, several things to do first. Right now I'm going to Mangotown, check up on something."

"How about my going with you? Long time since I've been in a village, time I got some new pictures. I'd like to see the way you work, too."

"People I got to talk to, they'd clam up if a white man was around."

"Any place you think I ought not to show, I'll stay outside."

After a moment's reflection, Xavier nodded. "All right. You could get pretty bored waiting around, but if you want to risk it, come along."

7

IT was only a mile or so from the inn to Mangotown, a collection of perhaps fifty houses, a church, and two or three shops, all scattered haphazardly near the road. Xavier had passed through the village often, but had never stopped there. Occasionally a constable from Whitecap Bay, a larger town some miles away, dropped into Mangotown, without ever having found trouble worth reporting. There were many such villages in the island, where local opinion dealt with such wrongdoing as might occur without bothering the authorities.

Most of the houses had once been painted yellow, inside and out, harking back to a distant time when a freighter had struck a reef off the nearby coast and Carovian fishermen had brought ashore as much of the jettisoned cargo as they could carry, including many five-gallon cans of yellow paint. Streaked yellow was still the dominant color of the village. The typical house was a flimsy, two-room affair, not much more than a shack, and the shops were merely houses in which the front room had been given a counter and shelves. One of these, a little more pretentious than the others, had a faded sign which spoke of forgotten ambitions: "MEGGS. Shoes. Shirts. Pants. Pillows and Carpets. Agent for Nine Companies." A few chickens wandered freely in and out of the open door.

Xavier got out of the car to speak to an old man who was dozing on a chair just inside. "Ho, gumpa," he said, using the Carovian term of respect for old men.

The ancient sat up with a start. A battered shade pulled down over the single window made the room almost invisible to eyes adjusting from the bright sunlight. "Don't get up,

gumpa. Just want to know where Reverend Meggs lives.
Jenny's father. He your son?" The old man's eyelids
dropped. "Don't worry. No trouble."

Piled goods dimly discernible on shelves in the rear of the
room looked as if they had been there for centuries. Meggs
blinked and muttered toothlessly, as Xavier bent down to
hear. "Which house?" The old man muttered again. "Oblige
to you, gumpa. Go back to sleep, now."

Outside Xavier found Motley busy with his camera, photo-
graphing a small naked boy who was trying to persuade a
bored goat to let him climb on his back. Heads peered from
nearby doorways, watching them. "Better wait here, Ted,"
Xavier said. He walked a hundred yards down the road to a
small box of a house next to the church, which was itself no
more than two houses joined together with a tiny cross atop.
It was evidently a school as well, for childish voices were
coming from it, raised in song. "Stuck a feather in his cap
and called for macaroni." Xavier chuckled at the thought
that "Yankee Doodle" was the only patriotic song really
popular among Carovians—perhaps because it seemed to them
to describe the typical tourist.

A carefully lettered sign in front of the house said, "Rev. A.
Meggs. Minister and Licensed Teacher. Carpenter. Photog-
rapher." The door was open and Xavier could see within a
plump brown girl of seventeen or eighteen, sewing a skirt.
Behind her a small radio was playing American rock music.
He called softly, "Jenny?"

The girl put down her sewing and came to the door. She
was short, with a pretty but petulant face. "You want me?"

"Just to talk to you for a minute, Jenny. I'm Chief Brooke,
from Gracedieu."

"Maybe you want my papa. He's teaching now." Her
diction was better than was usual among village girls, the
result perhaps of having a teacher for a father.

"No, I just want to ask you a question or two, Jenny. Mind
if I come in?"

The room was clean and agreeable, with net curtains on the
windows, and several chairs. Electric wiring had been strung
neatly to a bare bulb in the ceiling. Although transmission

poles lined the road, few village houses anywhere on the island could boast of an electric light. Prominent on the wall was a framed certificate declaring that Alfred Meggs was qualified to teach in the schools of St. Caro. Tacked on another wall were photographs of a young couple in wedding finery and two laughing girls with a baby. One of the girls was Jenny. There was also a print scissored from an old magazine—Toussaint L'Ouverture, the Haitian patriot who freed Santo Domingo from Napoleon's rule. Blacks in St. Caro who knew what was going on in the world felt strong sympathy with the peoples of the less fortunate islands. Xavier immediately liked Alfred Meggs without having seen him.

Xavier said, "I'd like you to tell me what happened this morning, up at the inn."

"I found the body." Her voice held a faint note of pride, and she spoke with the fluency of repetition. "Me and Mrs. Searle. We went in and the man was on the floor. We were scared. I yelled and ran out, and Mrs. Searle too."

"Had you ever seen Mr. Lattner before?"

"That dead man? No, sir!" For a girl surprised by a visit from a policeman, she was quite self-possessed.

"They tell me you yelled real loud."

For an instant she hesitated. "I guess I did. I was scared. Hand shook like that." She held out a hand and made it tremble. "Mrs. Searle she say—she said I can go home."

"First dead man you ever saw?"

She paused to consider. "I saw my gumma dead. I saw a drowned man once."

"Did you yell then?"

"That's different. I wasn't scared."

"All right, Jenny. This was your first day at the inn, wasn't it? They tell me you took Carolla's place after she got fired."

The girl nodded, but her eyes slid sideways.

"Let's see, when did they fire her?"

"Yesterday."

"And when did you get the job?"

"Last night."

"You went up to the inn last night? About what time?"

"Maybe eight o'clock."

"Who did you see?"

"Mrs. Searle. She knows me. She say—said I come in, start today as maid."

"How did you happen to go to the inn? You knew Carolla had been fired, is that right? How did you know?"

The pause lasted several seconds before she said, "Carolla told me."

"You saw Carolla last night? What time?"

"Maybe half after seven. I was listening to Trinidad calypso on the radio, so it must have been about then." She glanced at the radio and turned it off.

He thought a break in the questioning might help. "Trinidad calypso—that's good music."

She nodded indifferently. "Old stuff now. I like rock better."

She was not precisely resisting his questions, but he felt as if there were a gauze curtain between them. "Did Carolla tell you why they fired her?"

She shook her head—a way, he thought, to avoid putting the lie into words.

"All she said was that she had been fired?"

"And for me to go get the job if I wanted it." A maid's wages, with tips, could make her affluent among the youngsters of Mangotown.

"Where does Carolla live?"

"No use going to her house. She not there."

"I'd like to know where it is anyway."

Reluctantly she said, "House after the flamboy tree." She meant the huge spreading tree, with orange blossoms, that French settlers on the island had long ago called *flamboyant*. Xavier had noticed one some distance from the main road.

"She live with her parents?"

"Her gumma. Her mother dead, she don't know her father. I tell you, no use goin' there." The quality of her speech had begun to slip, as if the effort of grammar was too much for her.

He said, "How do you know she's not there?"

"She tol' me she goin' away."

"Where?"

"I don' know. She just say—said she goin'."

"When did she go?"

"Maybe las' night. Maybe this morning. I don' know."

As he left the house, a hand bell tinkled in the school-church next door, and the sunlit road was suddenly full of capering, laughing children, most of them under twelve years old. Among them walked a smiling man, dressed in neat tan work clothes. He turned toward the house, his glance at Xavier speculative but amiable. Xavier waited for him in front of the door and held out a friendly hand. "Reverend Meggs? I'm Chief Brooke from Gracedieu. Just stopped by to ask Jenny a few questions. Nothing to worry about. That killing up at the inn—have to get all the facts, and she found the body."

"I know. Too bad." Meggs was a slim man in his forties, with an intelligent face and an educated voice. A wisp of black beard at his chin added to his air of authority. "They say Dave Maubee did it. That right?"

"Seems so. I'd like to find him."

"Hard man to find, they say." Meggs' eyes crinkled.

Xavier accepted the innuendo with a smile. "Maybe we'll really try now. Way it works out, bad luck for one can be good luck for another. Guest dies, Jenny gets a job at the inn." Jenny had come to the door and was standing there, listening. "I'm going over to Carolla Peters now."

"I told you she not there," Jenny said sharply behind him.

He turned and smiled at her. "Maybe her gumma knows where she is."

With a flounce, Jenny turned back into the room. "I get the feeling," Xavier said, "Jenny doesn't want me to go to the Peters house. Why would that be?"

Meggs looked at him thoughtfully. "You walking up the road? I'll walk with you a piece."

The sun was moving to the west, and the tree shadows were growing longer on the dirt road. Meggs said, "Got a little problem. Maybe you can give me some advice. Reason Jenny acts that way, she's scared of Francie Peters. That's Carolla's gumma."

"Why is she scared?"

"Superstition. Worries me. The kids around here, I try to teach them, but Francie Peters is the real teacher. The kids get to be twelve, fourteen years, they go to her, get their fortunes told, and pretty soon she starts telling them about the old days, the old magic."

"Obeah?"

Meggs nodded. "We don't have an obeah man in this village now. My father used to be the man, a long time ago, but when I grew up and came back from school in the States I got him to stop. Nearest obeah man now is up at Bamboula. Francie, she used to be a midwife, and now she is the local witch-woman. A lot of people are scared of her, and not only kids. I must admit, she has made some pretty uncanny predictions. She's got a lot of the young people, like Jenny, believing in magic. Once when I talked about it at the village council, she sent word she put a small fix on me. Right after that I got sick. Only a bad cold, but everybody said it was Francie's magic. The old woman hinted she would have put a worse fix on me, but for Carolla and Jenny being good friends. Of course, that made Jenny all the more anxious to believe her. It's a hard thing to stop."

When Xavier silently nodded, he went on, with a note of bitterness in his voice. "A lot of the kids have stopped coming to church. They say Christian religion is white, no good any more, obeah is black and stronger. You know?"

"I know."

"I'm not asking you to do anything officially—I don't want to make trouble. But what would you do in my place?"

"Government policy is to keep hands off obeah unless we can prove a crime. Let me think about it. I suppose Jenny's afraid she might get the old woman mad at her if I go to see her after stopping at your house."

"That's right." They were nearing the Meggs store. Ted Motley had moved the car to a shady spot, where a dozen youngsters were watching him with intense, unwavering interest from every side. The teacher said, "Even my walking up here with you might make trouble. People see us, some are sure to tell Francie. Probably she knows already." He shook his head with a wry smile. "Sometimes I almost believe in obeah myself. I guess it's in the blood."

"Question I'd like to ask you," said Xavier. "When Jenny found the body this morning she screamed and screamed. Would you say that was a natural way for her to behave?"

They stood in the shadow cast by the store. "That's a pretty good question. Don't know whether I ought to answer it or not."

"Why not?"

The teacher passed a hand over his face. When he was not smiling the deep lines in his cheeks and his pensive eyes gave him the look of a man who was suffering. Xavier had the impression that for all Meggs' controlled manner he was in a state of great agitation—possibly at the end of his emotional rope. For anyone aware of the workings of obeah, it was easy to understand why. When a victim was fixed by the obeah man or the witch, the word soon spread in the community, and he found his friends and neighbors looking at him queerly, withdrawing from him, until he felt himself almost an outcast. To a member of a small closed society nothing was more frightening than silent ostracism. A small fix could be endured, but the atmosphere created by a big fix often produced intense depression and prolonged illness, even death, thus tending to confirm the magical powers of obeah.

Even so intelligent and educated a man as Meggs could not cope with the village fear of obeah. He took a deep breath before he said, "Night before last, Jenny told me Francie Peters had put a big fix on a guest at the inn. She was frightened. I told her for the hundredth time that was stupid, magic don't work. Then she gets Carolla's job, walks into that cottage this morning, and sees the dead man. For her it was the big proof that Francie can kill people with obeah. That's why she screamed. She was scared silly."

"How did she know Lattner was the man Francie fixed?"

"Carolla told her, but Jenny would have guessed anyway.

Late last year Carolla had an outbaby, almost white. The other maids who work at the inn said the father was a rich guest, Lattner. Said she was in his cottage all the time. Said she was lucky, he would take care of her. But this year Jenny told me Carolla is angry at Lattner, he wouldn't pay for the baby. A mean man. She needs money—she has her gumma to take care of and her other son, as well as the baby."

"How old is the other son?"

"Maybe six. David. She had him when she was only fifteen. A bushbaby." Meggs took another deep breath, as if by his words he was committing himself beyond recall. Xavier understood and sympathized—the man was risking much. There was a powerful unspoken constraint on every villager to keep the secrets of the community from outsiders. But Meggs was putting his obligation as a teacher and minister first. He was staking everything on a dream of freeing his people from primitive superstition. It was a dangerous gamble—he might end by being hated by those he was trying to help.

Even before he asked his next question, Xavier felt the thrill of intuitive certainty about the answer. "Who was the father of Carolla's older child?"

"Dave Maubee. Everybody in the village knows that. Carolla is proud of it."

Xavier looked at Meggs gratefully. A link between Lattner and Maubee had finally emerged—possibly a motive for Lattner's murder. "All right, Reverend. Thank you. You've helped a lot. I won't forget what you asked me. I'll try to help." As they shook hands, Xavier added with a smile, "Your class sings real good."

The teacher chuckled. "Best thing they do. Not much good at arithmetic or words, but they sing all day if I let them." He turned back toward his house.

Ted Motley, looking hot and restless, stepped out of the police car. "My god, I need a drink."

"Might find some Coca-Cola. Not your kind of drink."

"Forget it, then. You ought at least to carry a pint in your car for medicinal purposes. Did you get anything?"

Xavier took pity on him. "Yes, something." He briefly summarized the facts gleaned from Meggs. "Now Carolla has gone away. Left her baby with the grandmother. Thought I'd better drop in at her house and see if I can learn anything more. No reason why you can't come along this time, if you feel like it. We better take the car—otherwise these kids will be all over it the minute we go."

8

THE faint sound of a steel drum, discordantly beaten, became louder as they bounced over a narrow track toward the *flamboyant* tree. A boy of five or six, wearing a ragged pair of drawers, sat on the ground under the tree attacking the instrument with enormous concentration. He barely glanced up as the car passed by. Near him was a goat with a full udder, munching grass. The boy reminded Xavier of his own son, who was about the same age, similarly black, slender, and intensely serious about his play.

The sound of the motor brought a woman to the door of the house, which stood a few yards beyond the tree. Without being exceptionally tall, she gave an impression of hugeness, partly because of the corpulence that filled out her long blue cotton dress, partly because of the red and green island turban that covered all of her hair and rose a good six inches above the top of her head. The glare in her small black eyes from within the fatty folds of her face had the impact of a whip. "What you want here, mon?" she said in a hoarse arrogant voice. She was probably not more than sixty years old but looked older, her skin having taken on the peculiar grayish surface tone characteristic of the aged of the islands. An especially grotesque note in her appearance was the ill-fitting set of large false teeth that someone had provided for her. The teeth forced a perpetual grimace on her mouth, reminding Xavier of Lattner's *rictus sardonicus*. Her glance darted swiftly from him to Motley and back again.

"Just want to talk to you for a minute, gumma." Xavier got out of the car, and Ted hastily followed. "You Francie Peters?"

"That me. Me know you, p'liceman. 'Bout what you wan' talk?"

"Just a question or two."

"Ask, then, mon." At that moment the sound of the steel drum rose to a painful crescendo. "Davy," she called. "You stop that now." After an instant the boy rose, lugging the shiny red drum, which was half as big as he, and walked purposefully away from the house into the open country.

Motley said, "If he goes on practicing like that he'll be a good drummer some day."

The words did not soften her. "Drummer in a band," she grumbled. "They all wan' be drummer in a band. As if that so great. That boy, he got royal blood in him."

"Royal blood?" Ted had one hand on his camera case.

"Royal *French* blood. On my side of the fam'ly." She put a palm in front of Motley's lens. "You wan' take picture of me, it cost you."

"How much?"

She looked at him carefully and disparagingly. "Two dollar."

"Too much," he said. "I'm from the newspaper in Grace-dieu, gumma. Might print your picture in the paper. Wouldn't you like that?"

"Maybe. Maybe not."

"One dollar."

"Okay. One dollar each picture."

He grinned. "You drive a hard bargain, gumma. Okay." He snapped a picture of her and gave her a dollar bill, which she tucked into a pocket of her dress.

"It would be easier to talk inside," Xavier said.

"We talk here," she retorted. "Baby asleep. Don' wan' wake him."

"That's all right. Babies don't wake up so easy. We'll be quiet. Better if we all sit down."

She did not budge from her stance in front of the door. Arms akimbo, she said, "My house, me no let you in if I don' feel like it. We talk here, mon."

Xavier put on an official scowl. "How you like to be arrested and go to jail, gumma?"

"You can't arrest me. Me don' do nothin'.."

"The government says, you make obeah, I can take you to jail."

Her face changed. "Who say me make obeah? That Meggs?"

"Listen good, gumma. We go in your house, now, and we talk, or I take you to Gracedieu. Maybe you think I'm joking. Look at my eyes, and tell me."

She stared at him for an instant, then stood silent, reflecting. "You can't take me away when baby is in the house."

"We'll find somebody to take care of the baby. And the boy."

"You try take me, I tell you, mon, me knock you back. You goin' fight ol' woman?"

"I won't have to fight you. In the trunk of my car, gumma, is a big piece of fisherman's net. I use it to tie up people who try to fight me." This was true. He also carried a pressure can of tear gas, provided by the American government, but he disliked the idea of using it on unarmed people. His attitude toward the use of muscle in making arrests was similar. In his youth he had learned from a Marine instructor six ways to break a man's neck quietly, and ever since then he had been afraid that in a fight some day he might forget himself long enough to use one of them. Nothing was better than a heavy net, he had long ago discovered, for overcoming the struggles of the belligerent and the berserk. "You want to be tied up like a big fish, gumma, I'll oblige you."

"You do that, mon, I yell, and people help me. They fight you, mon."

"No they won't. I tell them you are wanted as material witness in a murder case." At the word her expression lost some of its defiance.

"Me didn' witness no murder."

He pursued his advantage. "You have information. If you don't give it, that makes you an accessory." He waited for the impressive word to sink in. "Anybody tries to help you, he is an accessory and can go to jail for ten years. People won't help you. They will help me. What you got inside you don't want me to see?"

She was sullen now. "Nothin' inside. Jus' my house."

"I'll see for myself. Well, gumma, do I get the fishnet, or do we go in?" Again she studied his stern face. Finally she spat and stood aside. It was a two-room house, with the doorway to the second room covered by an old blue curtain. The front room, with three small cots, a crudely made chest of drawers, a table, and some rickety wooden chairs, was crowded, but it was clean. A fat baby, light in color and naked except for a diaper, lay fast asleep on one of the cots. From a pot, simmering on a small charcoal brazier in a corner of the room, came a faint aroma familiar to Xavier. "Smells like good kalliloo," he said. The island soup, consisting mostly of okra, spinach, and spices, was standard fare for black Carovians.

Ignoring the remark, Mrs. Peters shooed a chicken out of the house, sat down at the table, and waited, with anger in her eyes. A deck of old playing cards near her hand attracted Xavier's eye. "Tell fortunes, gumma?"

"Don' have to tell yours, mon. Bad luck comin' your way."

"Worse luck coming yours, gumma, if you talk like that. That Carolla's boy in the bed? What's his name?"

"Napoleon. Napoleon Peters." After most of two centuries, Napoleon was still one of the most popular names for boys on St. Caro. For everyone who, like the Reverend Meggs, remembered Toussaint, there were ten who thought Napoleon was the greatest man who ever lived. Myth had it that as a young emperor he had visited the islands and fathered a number of bushbabies on St. Caro—through the veins of whose descendants ran the Napoleonic blood. Xavier had met old women like Mrs. Peters before—strong personalities, feared by their neighbors, maintaining self-esteem with the aid of delusions, the most popular of which was descent from famous whites.

"That boy out there, with the drum. He Carolla's too?"

"Her first." With a burst of pride, she added, "A real man-child. He goin' be king of St. Caro some day."

"Maybe governor would be better."

"Governor! Any fool can be governor! He be king."

"You talk like a queen all right, gumma. They tell me you used to be a midwife."

The remark triggered a spate of bottled-up resentment.
"Thirty years. I take out over two hundred babies, right here
in Mango. Then doctor come to Whitecap and guv'ment say
he got to deliver babies. Deliver! He don' deliver no more
than me. Mama delivers, he jus' helps. Me see him when he
take out Carolla's babies—he jus' do what I do. But she say he
cleaner than me, baby don' die. That a lie! They die jus' as
much. What he know? Las' baby he take out here in Mango
come out upside down, and the mama nearly die. Me could
tell that goin' be arse-first baby, 'cause the girl, she use to
cross her legs when she sat, after she pregnant. That sure way
to get upside-down baby. But you think doctor know that?
The guv'ment, they tell everybody go to doctor, he and nurse
take out baby in hospital. Hospital!" She made a spitting
mouth and sound. "Take away my bread."

"But with Carolla working at the inn, I guess you got along
all right."

Mrs. Peters clicked her false teeth scornfully. "You ever try
feed a family on what a maid make, mon?"

"But she gets an allowance from the papas for her outbabies, don't she?"

The old woman darted a suspicious glance at him. "She get
nothin'. Them bushbabies."

"Too bad. But you make something, telling fortunes."

She shrugged. "People here can't pay much."

"Then with Carolla losing her job, how you going to eat?"

Another sharp glance. "She get another job, send me
money."

"Where did she go, gumma?"

Mrs. Peters made a vague gesture. "She no tell me. She look
for job, some other inn. She not sure where. Maybe Bamboula."

"When did she go?"

"Maybe las' night. Maybe this mornin'. When me asleep."

"She go on the bus?"

"Maybe. You got too many questions, mon. Carolla, she
got right to go where she want."

Xavier smiled pleasantly. "I don't tell you how to make

kalliloo, gumma, you don't tell me my business. You know what happened at the inn last night?"

The old woman hesitated before saying, "That got nothin' to do with us Peters. That Meggs, you been listenin' to him?"

Xavier leaned forward, until his face was only a foot from Mrs. Peters', and spoke softly. "I tell you something. I got ears everywhere on this island. If I hear even a whisper, you put a fix on Alfred Meggs or anybody else, you going to stay in jail for a long time. Just remember, gumma. I'm watching you."

The menace of his words meant less to her than the look in his eye. She said angrily, "You don' got to watch me."

"Just remember." He rose abruptly, nodding at the curtain that hung over the doorway. "You sleep there?" As she began to rise, protesting, he lifted the curtain.

"That my bedroom! You stay out!" Moving with surprising speed for her bulk, she tried to interpose herself between him and the room beyond, but he reached it first. His eyes ignored the sagging bed and threadbare carpet and went directly to the yellow wall. His guess was right. A hasty effort had been made to erase the red chalk drawing—perhaps when Francie first learned there was a police car in the village—but traces were still evident of the outlines of a face, the eyes, and the hair standing on end. Closer inspection revealed what Xavier expected—a thin incision in the wooden wall, where a knife evidently had been jabbed between the eyes.

"You paint pictures, gumma?" he said sardonically.

"My wall, me paint what I like."

"Picture of who?"

For the first time, she appeared flustered. Her eyes wavered away from him. "Nobody. A man. I make him up."

"You fix somebody—a big fix. Who?"

"Nobody. Me no make obeah."

"Knife in a man's face. Last night at the inn a man died. Mr. Lattner. You know him?"

"Not me. Carolla work in his cottage. She tell me his name. That all."

She started at a flash of light behind her. Ted Motley had

taken out his camera and, using a flashbulb, had snapped a picture of the chalk face. Glaring at him, she held out her hand and kept it out until he put another dollar bill in her palm.

Xavier surveyed the room again. A small wooden chest in the corner caught his eye, and he guessed at its contents. As practiced in St. Caro, obeah had much in common with Haitian voodoo, except that it relied less on group rites and more on the powers of the sorcerer alone. In a big fix the death sentence was supposed to be carried out by a zombie called from the dead. Haitian voodoo cultists believed zombies were visible, but in St. Caro they were regarded as disembodied spirits. An obeah fix called for a seething-pot in which various symbols of death, known as "deadies," were brewed together—the blood and entrails of a white cock, the feathers of a black bird, a dead toad and, above all, manchineel apples—while the proper incantations were muttered in front of a picture intended to represent the victim with a knife plunged between the eyes. Ritual demanded that this sinister liquid be sprinkled around his house or on an article of his clothing, in order to guide the avenging zombie to his destination, while as further instruction to him the bloody head of the slain cock and various other deadies were left on the doorstep.

The seething-pot was an essential adjunct of the ceremony, and the chest in the corner struck Xavier as the natural place for it. The fact that Francie was standing solidly in front of the chest increased his suspicion. He said to Motley, "I'd like to get a picture of that baby in the other room."

After a surprised moment, Ted caught the idea. "Sure, Chief," he said, and went into the front room, camera in hand. Instantly Francie Peters followed, full of sulphurous indignation. "You goddam no take picture of my baby, mon! That bad luck! I smash your camera!" Leaving Ted to protect himself, Xavier lifted the lid of the chest, where a small black pot gave off a faint but peculiarly nauseating smell. In it were some chicken feathers, a dead mouse, a few small rotting manchineel apples, and an empty bottle. Francie, he surmised, was preparing another big fix—against whom? Alfred

Meggs? From its shape and the encrusted residue, he guessed the pot to be very old. Obeah pots were usually handed down from one obeah man to another in the same family, sometimes over hundreds of years, and if a pot's record of success was high, it was considered a priceless possession, opening up great possibilities of power for its owner.

Xavier wondered whether the pot had belonged to one of Francie's ancestors—or whether perhaps old Meggs, when his educated son persuaded him to give up obeah, had donated it to her. They were about of an age, and the probabilities of village life suggested that they might have been lovers. It could even be that Carolla was old Meggs' granddaughter and a cousin of Jenny—that would account for the resemblance and close friendship between the girls. Thus the pot might still be in the Meggs line of descent.

He was tempted to take the pot away with him, so as to put an end to Francie's obeah practice, but the law gave him no such authority—not until Francie had been arrested for a crime. Moreover, he had no wish to destroy the old woman. It seemed to him that she was already dangerously close to the borderline of madness, and outrage at losing her most prized possession could break her heart and mind together. He compromised by removing the manchineel apples and carrying them away in his handkerchief.

In the other room, Mrs. Peters had won her battle with Ted, who had retreated outside the house and was standing warily on the far side of the police car. "All right, Francie," Xavier said. "I know what you got in that chest in the bedroom. Who brought the manchee apples?"

Her eyes widened before they dropped. "Nobody. Me find 'em in the road."

"That's a big lie. You listen to me. You make obeah again, even a little fix, I will take your pot away and you will never see it again." He was not sure that this threat was effective— she could always hide the pot—so he went further. "I will tell the circuit judge your house is no good for children, and he will send Davy and Napoleon to the children's home in Gracedieu. If you want to keep the children, no more obeah. You understand?"

She still looked at him with more hate than fear, and he tried again. "If you try put a fix on me or anybody else, I will tell the big obeah man at Bamboula that because of a woman in Mangotown the government is going to get tough with all the obeah men in St. Caro. I know him. He will be very mad. He will put a bad fix on you. Maybe the blind fix." Instinctively she put her hand to her eyes. "You make trouble for him, he will make bigger trouble for you. You want that to happen?"

At last he had reached her. She shook her head sullenly.

"You promise. No more obeah."

After a long pause, her face changed. The passion went out of it and she let out a whimpering sound. She sat down, looking very old. "No more obeah," she muttered.

"One more thing, gumma. When did Davy get that drum?"

The question surprised her. She hesitated before saying, "Me forget."

"No, you don't forget. He got it yesterday."

A touch of the old resonance returned to her voice. "If you know, why you ask?"

"I know who gave it to him."

"Me gave it."

Xavier smiled. "Not you, gumma. That's no toy drum. That's a big band drum. Cost thirty dollars, maybe more. You telling me you bought it? I'm telling you Dave Maubee gave it to Davy. Stole it someplace. Was Dave here yesterday?"

Her mouth closed tightly and she averted her eyes. "That's what I wanted to know," said Xavier.

9

"MY God, what a story I could do about that old woman!" Ted, from the moving car, took a final shot of Francie Peters' house. " 'Black Magic Still Alive in Caribbean Resort Isle.' " When no reply was forthcoming, he glanced at Xavier's set profile. "Why so grim, Xave? Seems to me you have just about what you need on Maubee."

"You think so?" Xavier stopped the car and dumped the apples from his handkerchief into a thorny bush, where they could rot undetected. Glancing at his watch, he switched on his two-way radio and waited for Peter Obee's voice. "Gracedieu headquarters. Over."

"Brooke talking. Just leaving Mangotown to drive back to the inn. Marco there?"

"No, Chief."

"I don't suppose you've got that autopsy report yet?"

"No, sir."

"Listen, Peter. I want you to call Dr. Evans at the hospital right away. Talk to him—nobody else. Say it's a police emergency—that way he'll come to the phone himself. Give him a message for me. Tell him I want him to examine the contents of the stomach for manchineel juice. Got that?"

"Wilco! Manchee juice!" The excitement in Peter's voice made the radio wheeze.

"Then tell him to compare the blood type of the corpse with the blood type of the stain on the coat."

"Roger! Compare blood on coat with blood from corpse!"

"Say I'll telephone him at his home this evening."

"Wilco."

"All right. Call him right away. Don't mention this to anybody else. Over and out."

Ted pursed his lips in a silent whistle. "What's that all about?"

"Ask me again after I hear the autopsy report."

"Oh, come on, Xave. You think Lattner was poisoned?"

"Maybe."

"Let me get this straight. You mean, since dead men don't bleed, the blood on Lattner wasn't his. So the wound was inflicted after death."

"Maybe."

"Dr. Richardson didn't suggest anything like that, did he?"

"No."

Ted stared. "I don't get it. Why look for poison when you've got a cut spinal cord, the machete that did it, and Maubee's fingerprints on the machete? You suggesting that Carolla fed manchineel juice to Lattner? How would she do that? Seems pretty farfetched to me."

They said nothing more until Xavier pulled up alongside Ted's battered little car, in front of Lattner's cottage. Across the compound a few guests were ambling toward the main building: the bar would soon be filled with early evening drinkers. The way American tourists consumed hard liquor had never ceased to amaze Xavier. They drank as if their nighttime happiness depended on booze. Perhaps it did. A stout woman with platinum hair, wearing inadvisable white slacks, waddled out of a nearby guesthouse and headed in the same direction. As she moved, the afternoon sun caught the glint of gems on her fingers and lighted them up like flares. Xavier felt a sudden liking for Francie Peters. In her own way, without benefit of diamonds, she had made a place for herself. A midwife, a mother, a grandmother, a witch, a real human being, maybe a little crazy but full of life. Better to have her spirit, better to put up a fight, than to be a ridiculous old woman with dyed hair and tight slacks around her fat ass, getting drunk at a bar.

"You sore about something?" Ted asked.

After a while Xavier said evenly, "You think Maubee killed Lattner, no doubt about it, and I'm just making the thing complicated."

"But Xave—you've got his motive now. He must have heard Carolla's story and hated Lattner's guts as much as she did. So he decides to rob Lattner and get her the money she was entitled to. And when Lattner came into the cottage at the wrong time, Maubee picked up that machete. All right, I know he can split green coconuts, but maybe this time it wasn't a full swing."

"Thinking that way, you must believe I've got some private reason for not going right after Maubee."

"Now wait—"

"Because I knew him from way back? Because we're both black? Or, maybe, because I'm afraid of him?"

"For God's sake, Xave. You know I don't think anything like that."

Xavier took a deep breath, but his voice was still tight as he said, "I see how it looks to you. To me it looks different. That's all."

The silence that fell between them had sharp edges. Finally Ted pushed his way through it to say, "You're offended. Sorry—didn't mean it that way." He got out of Xavier's car and opened the door of his own. "You going to be at the station tomorrow morning?"

With an effort, Xavier said, "Probably be starting out around eleven, after I report to Chalk." The words came out strained and lifeless. With a churning of self-reproach, he watched Ted drive away. Something was working in him, something he could not put into words. A sense of inadequacy? A feeling that he was out of his depth? He came to the conclusion that he was in fact angry at himself and had used Ted as a whipping boy. A lousy thing to do.

He did not want to leave the inn before talking to Barbara Keys. If she had anything useful to tell him about Lattner's movements prior to his death, delay would be an error; she might decide to cut short her visit to St. Caro at any time and fly home. From a distance he saw that there were lights in her cottage and that the drapes over the picture window were closed. His knock was answered by a contralto "Yes?" He identified himself and the voice said crisply, "One moment."

When she opened the door, she was wearing a loose blue silk housecoat that swept the floor. "You've caught me at a bad time," she said. Her speech had a precision and assurance that he associated with upper-class British women he had observed, but her accent was cultivated American. "I'm getting dressed. Can't it wait?"

"I'm sorry," he said. "This won't take long. Just a question or two."

"Mr. Searle told me you already know who committed the murder. In that case, why ask questions?" She was not so much hostile as coldly unconcerned.

He kept his tone formal and his words vague. "In a murder case we have to try to get the whole picture, Mrs. Keys. I would appreciate a few minutes."

Her eyes watched him from behind ivory-framed spectacles, which contrasted strikingly with her deeply tanned skin. The eyes were a chilly gray, which together with sharp well-proportioned features above a long patrician neck gave her an effect of challenging whatever she looked at. The way in which she wore her reddish-brown hair, drawn back over the ears into a loose knot, accented the impression of a no-nonsense personality. It was not easy to imagine such a woman sleeping with the man Xavier guessed Lattner to have been; but was any normal woman indifferent to a combination of high sexual drive and great wealth in a man?

He could see clearly enough why Lattner was interested in her. The light behind her, through the thin fabric of her housecoat, suggested a figure as classical as her features. She may have realized the extent to which she was silhouetted, for she suddenly stood aside, saying, "All right. Come in. But make it brief, will you?" She sat on a chair, motioning him to the sofa.

He took a moment to survey the room, chiefly remarkable for the picture on the easel and a dozen similar water colors mounted on cardboard and propped against the walls at floor level. All of them portrayed larger-than-life tropical plants and foliage, painted with great exactitude, and so far as he could judge, with considerable skill. "Well?" she said. "What do you want to know?"

Meeting her gaze, he could detect no sign of grief in her, such as a man's mistress might be reasonably expected to feel at his violent death. "I'm trying to learn something of Mr. Lattner's movements last night. When did you last see him?"

She considered. "If you literally mean 'see,' after dinner
last night. In the card room, playing bridge. I was playing
too, at another table."

"You had dinner with him?"

"No. I dined with the others in my bridge party."

"You did not see him after the bridge game?"

"No."

Her terse resistance made him sharpen his attack. "Had you
quarreled with him?"

The plucked arch of one eyebrow rose. "Not at all."

"Wasn't it unusual for you and him to go through an entire
evening without speaking? My information is that you were
very good friends."

He thought her cheeks colored a little under their tan. "I
don't know who you've been questioning about me, and I
don't propose to discuss my friendships with you. I didn't
talk with Mr. Lattner last night. That's what you want to
know, isn't it?"

"That's right." The sparks between them were almost visible
now. "Mr. Searle thinks that Mr. Lattner may have intended
to go to the dance pavilion after the bridge game. Were you
there?"

For the first time she hesitated. "Yes, I was."

"Perhaps you planned to meet him there."

This time the pause was longer. "Yes, I did."

"How late did you remain there?"

"Until about two o'clock. The band stopped playing at one,
but I stayed on to have a bite to eat with my friends from the
bridge party."

She would have asked herself, of course, whether Lattner
was ill, or had fallen asleep—or was with another woman. Her
affair with Lattner was by then two or three weeks old, and
she could hardly fail to know his reputation. "When Mr.
Lattner did not appear, you surely must have wondered
why."

She allowed her spectacles to slide down her straight nose
and frowned at him above them, as if she were seeing him
clearly for the first time. "That's really none of your
business."

"I wouldn't have asked if it was none of my business. Seems to me you would have said something to the people you were with about his not showing up."

"I may have."

"You must have been annoyed." All at once the explanation for her reticence stared him in the face. "You would have gone to his cottage to see if he was there." When she did not immediately reply, he said, "The other people in your party might know. It would be simpler, Mrs. Keys, if you would tell me. That way I won't have to question your friends."

The quick narrowing of her eyes showed that he had touched a nerve. "Ask whom you like," she began to say, and then shrugged. "All right, I started to go to his cottage. I thought if he had fallen asleep it would serve him right to be waked up. But I changed my mind and came back here instead."

"That was a little after two?"

"Yes."

"How close did you go to his cottage?"

"Do you think I measured the distance?"

"Close enough to see a light in the window?"

"Yes, I saw a light."

"Yet you did not go to the door. Why?"

She shrugged. "That's a stupid question. I decided to turn back, that's all."

A shadowy picture formed in his mind—the handsome, angry woman marching across the compound in the dark night. Curiosity to know whether Lattner was alone must have been very strong in her. "Did you see anyone else?" he asked.

The fraction of an instant that elapsed before she said "No," and a slight overemphasis made him sense a lie in the word. He tried again.

"Perhaps you have forgotten. Wasn't there someone else—"

"I've told you everything I know." She stood up, drawing the housecoat around her. "I really can't give you any more time. I'm late now. You had better go."

He realized he was not going to budge her from her story.

Rising slowly, he looked again at the watercolors. One painting showed a thrusting cluster of shiny leaves, partially concealing a number of small green apples. "A fine picture of manchineel," he said. "Painted from life?"

"Of course."

"You had the branch here? What did you do with it when you finished the painting?"

"I told the maid to burn it."

"Which maid?"

"A girl named Carolla. What's all this about?"

"Did you realize when you cut the branch from the tree that if even a little of the sap gets on your skin it can produce bad effects?"

"I'm aware of that, naturally. We were very careful. It was my husband actually who cut the branch down."

"Was there anyone else with you at the time?"

"Why, yes. The Searles and one or two other guests. We gave them a sort of botanical tour."

"Who were the other guests?"

"Of all the superfluous questions! If you must know, a Mrs. Dillon and a Dr. Richardson."

"No doubt you explained the poisonous properties of manchineel to them?"

"Naturally."

"Where is the tree?"

"What on earth do you want to know that for?"

"The government is trying to get rid of manchineel."

"Ridiculous! Eliminating any species of tree is a crime against nature. I certainly won't tell you where it is."

He felt his anger rising. It would have been a pleasure to warn her that she must not leave St. Caro until his investigation was completed, but he had no way to enforce such a request and in fact no clear idea of what he was looking for. When she opened the door pointedly, he said merely, "Good night." Walking to his car he felt scratched, as if he had been holding an unwilling cat in his hands. Behind him he heard the door slam.

10

HIS first words to Toinette were, "What happened?"

Their children, a girl of seven and a boy of six, were clutching him and asking to be picked up. Toinette said, "Later," and then added teasingly, "maybe I called you home just because I was thinking about this morning."

With a child on each shoulder he retorted, "Don't nothin' ever satisfy you, woman?"

They smiled at each other in the conspiratorial way of loving parents, but he had to wait until the children were in bed and the supper dishes washed before she would satisfy his curiosity. With a serious face, she said, "We got trouble with Marco. That's why I called Ted. I didn't want to send a message from the station, where Marco would know. That devil, late this morning he come here, riding his motorcycle, making a big putt-putt. I went to the window and saw him park in front of this house. It scared me. I thought maybe you had an accident. When I opened the door, he say—said, very serious, 'Can I talk to you a minute, Mrs. Brooke?' I said, 'Yes, come in, is anything wrong?' " Her voice began to take on the depth of anger. "He beat around the bush. He say what a nice house. He ask about the children. I say, 'Marco, what is it?' Then he say, 'I want your help. For your husband as much as for me.' That don't sound right to me. I say, 'What kind of help?' He say, 'How you like it if Xavier is elected Councillor at the next election?' "

The story poured out of her. Marco said he did not want Xavier to think he was an enemy. No, he wanted to be his friend. Governor Chalk thought the time had come for a change in the police department. But Marco did not want to push Xavier out of a job, and if Xavier would run for Councillor—after all, a post of high honor—Marco and the governor would support him. Personally, Marco said, he had great respect for Xavier. He went on talking about the fine career Xavier could have in politics. A lot of the Councillors made plenty of money on the side.

While Toinette fought to conceal her indignation, Marco talked and talked, as if making a political speech. She thought he would never stop. He kept repeating himself, until looking at his confident, smiling face, she got the feeling that he did not mean a word of it. Then why was he there? For a minute she wondered whether he was going to make a pass at her, but she decided he was not such a fool as all that.

Suddenly she realized that many of her neighbors must have observed Xavier's earlier departure and Marco's arrival. Then she knew. He wanted people to think that he was her lover—make them laugh at Xavier, take away their respect for him. She could hardly restrain herself from striking Marco, scratching his eyes out, but she kept a calm tongue. She told him she would think about his idea. He didn't have to say anything more—she understood. Now she had to get back to her housework—she had a lot to do.

Even then he lingered, finding small things to talk about. How old were the children now? Were they doing well in school? Did Xavier read all those books on the shelf? What a fine thing to go to college! She edged her way to the door and opened it, and he finally picked up his helmet, but he managed to stay on the doorstep, where everybody in the neighborhood could see, and told her a story he had heard, laughing all the while as if they had been having a good time. At last he left, but not on his motorcycle. He walked. It stayed there in front of the house for several hours, so people would think he was coming back to see her, or was still there. When he finally came to get it, he made a big noise again. Nobody could miss him.

Toinette was in tears when she concluded. "He trying to make trouble between you and me." The fury in Xavier burst out in a few brief but eloquent comments on Marco's ancestry and habits. At the same time he felt a grim appreciation of the fellow's cleverness. He had not done or said anything that he could be called to account for. He could protest that he had been acting in friendship and goodwill. But he had dealt a cunning blow at Xavier's standing in the community. Gossip in Gracedieu, especially about marital infidelity, was merciless and swift. It would be only a matter of time before some of the Councillors themselves would be whispering the story behind their hands, laughing at the presumed horns on Xavier's head—and in politics men who laugh at you are not likely to back you.

He was determined not to let Toinette perceive the depth of his concern. Experience had taught him that for an anxious wife the best tonic is the quiet confidence of the husband. In a strong voice, he said, "Good girl. You did just the right thing. Leave it to me."

"I don't want you to hit him," she cried. "I think that's what he wants. Then he could tell Chalk you had no reason, you must be losing your mind. Or maybe he shoot you or stab you and say he was only defending himself."

"Don't worry. I won't do anything foolish. You are a wise woman and I love you."

She looked at him with relieved eyes, and he wiped away the tears on her cheeks and kissed her. As yet he did not have the faintest notion of how to deal with Marco, but he was not going to brood about it. It was his habit, when depressed, to do something—use his hands or work. He kissed Toinette again and said, "Now I must make a phone call."

The operator got him Dr. Evans' home on the second try. The moment he heard the doctor's gruff, friendly voice, his heart lifted. "Brooke? I've been waiting for your call. I thought I'd finished the autopsy when I got your message this afternoon. What made you think of manchineel?"

"A girl who hated the man had some manchee juice. And I saw a couple of people, years ago, who died of manchee poisoning. Both of them had big death grins like Lattner's. Only the white of their eyes showed, like they fainted before they died, and it took quite a while for the rigor to set in."

"That happens sometimes. Anyway, you were absolutely right. I didn't spot the manchineel the first time round, but it was there, all right, together with a good deal of alcohol. The manchineel wasn't in his dinner, otherwise he would have collapsed much sooner. It may have been in a drink taken shortly before he died. From the amount present I'd say it would account for his death. Especially since the cut on his neck was inflicted after he died."

"Blood not his?"

"That's right. Another good guess on your part. The wound didn't bleed much, if at all. That mess on the clothes isn't human blood. Animal—a dog, from the way it tests. I'd say somebody knifed a dog and spilled the blood around to make it look like Lattner had been killed by the machete. Could have got by me if you hadn't called for a blood check. I was taking the thing pretty much for granted."

"How long would the manchineel take to kill him?"

"Hard to say. We haven't had much experience with it. What we know comes mostly out of cases recorded a long time ago. The stuff acts pretty fast—sort of a distant cousin of cyanide, but not so strong. No antidote that we know about. After drinking it he'd have a burning sensation in the throat and esophagus, followed by bad stomach pains. If it was a strong dose, he wouldn't be able to speak or to stand up."

"I've been wondering why he didn't yell for help or stagger outside. That explains it."

"Yes, once the convulsions set in, he'd be helpless. Then there would be severe cardiac irregularity, and he might faint. But death—I'd say that might take anywhere from twenty minutes to an hour, depending on circumstances."

"Thank you, doctor."

"If you ever want a testimonial as a good guesser, Chief, ask me."

"Got a lot more guessing to do now. Will you send over a report tomorrow morning, doctor, early as you can? I want to show it to Governor Chalk. He's going to need a lot of convincing."

"Yes, I will. Fill me in on the story one of these days, will you? And say hello to your lovely wife for me."

Xavier rose from the telephone and took Toinette into his

arms in a bear hug. "Dr. Evans says you are lovely. He is so right."

"What he tell you?" she asked when she could breathe again.

So many new thoughts were churning around in him that he seized the opportunity to talk them into some kind of order. He respected Toinette's judgment, her knowledge of the ways of St. Caro, and her discretion. "Sit down," he said. "Forget Marco. I'm going to tell you about this case. If I say anything you don't think is right, you stop me. If I can convince you, maybe I can convince myself."

As she sat, his eyes took pleasure in her slim grace and gleaming femininity. She looked happy and at the same time intensely serious—a wife who felt needed in her husband's work as well as in his house. "I want you to get the whole picture," he told her. "Dr. Evans says this dead man Lattner was poisoned by manchineel. After he died, someone sliced his neck with a machete and spilled blood around to make it look like he was killed that way." Toinette drew in an excited breath. "That somebody must have been Dave Maubee because his fingerprints were on the machete. Also we found his little black book near the corpse."

"Oh," she cried. "Then Maubee, he must have been covering up for whoever poisoned the man."

He nodded approvingly. "That's the way it looks to me, too. I think the poison was put into the man's drink by a girl from Mangotown named Carolla Peters. Maid at the inn—looked after Lattner. Last year he gave her a baby, almost white, and refused to pay her out-money. Then he reported her to the Searles for stealing and got her fired. Likely she did steal something—felt she was entitled to it. Anyway, she must have hated him."

"And Maubee is a friend of hers?"

"More than a friend. Years ago she was his woman and he gave her a son, about the same age as our boy now. From her picture she's a pretty girl, the type Dave always liked. Looks like he was at her house last night. Brought a present for his boy—a steel drum. Probably stole it some place."

Toinette smiled. "If he do that for all his children, he would have to keep pretty busy."

"That's for sure. But listen, now. This girl Carolla had manchee juice. We know that because her gumma made it. She is an old witch. She put a big fix on Lattner and used manchee apples in her obeah pot. Carolla brought her the apples—I know where she got them. The gumma is too fat to walk much, so I figure Carolla took the obeah juice and went up to Lattner's cottage at night to sprinkle it so the fix would work. Only thing is, I don't know how she got him to drink it."

In an uncertain voice, Toinette asked, "You think he had to drink it?"

For a moment the question astonished him. Then he laughed. "You still believe in obeah? Honey, you know better than that. He drank it, all right. He had an open bottle of rum in his house, but the rum is good, and anyway, if she had put the juice in his rum he would have noticed it."

"How you mean, noticed?"

"The color. I've seen manchee juice—a kind of milky green. Cloudy. If she put that in the rum, Lattner would see something was wrong as soon as he lifted the bottle."

"What did he drink his rum with? "

He looked at her for a long moment, and his eyes widened. "What did you say?"

"I say, maybe she put the manchee juice into something else."

He rose from his chair, bent over, and kissed her hard. Surprised as well as pleased, she said, "What for?"

A weight was lifting from his brain. At last he knew what had been troubling him ever since he left Lattner's cottage. "Toinette, you are a better detective than I am. I should have seen it before."

"See what?"

"You put manchee juice into a bottle, it's pale green and cloudy. What else looks like that?"

She thought for only a moment before saying, "Green coconut water."

"Right! Now I tell you something. Lattner was big on rum and green coconut water. Kept rum in his bar and every day had a bottle of green water sent up and put in his refrigerator. But when I looked in the refrigerator it was empty. Should have been a bottle of green water somewhere in the house, or at least an empty bottle, but there wasn't. Never thought what that means till just this second."

Frowning, she shook her head. "I don't get it."

"It's easy, now. Carolla goes to sprinkle the cottage and leave the deadies on the doorstep. But the manchee juice reminds her of the green water in Lattner's refrigerator. She gets the idea to switch bottles. Maybe she feels her gumma sent the idea to her."

Toinette reflected. "Yes, she might think that way."

"So instead of sprinkling and leaving the deadies, she goes into the cottage—the door isn't locked. She takes the bottle of green water out of the fridge, puts in her bottle of manchee juice, and runs out again. No, wait. First, she turns down the bed. That way, if Lattner drives up to the cottage while she is there, she has an excuse. Doing her job right to the end of the day. All right, she is out of the cottage with the green coconut water in her hands. And the deadies too—she doesn't want to leave them because now they would make Lattner suspicious. So she throws them and the bottle into the bushes somewhere."

"But what happened to the manchee bottle? You said there was no bottle like that in the house."

"That's right! And if I had any sense, I would have asked myself right away, who took away the bottle?"

"Dave Maubee?"

"Who else? The way I see it, Carolla goes home and tells her gumma what she has done. The old lady is scared. She smells trouble coming. Too many people know Lattner is the father of Carolla's baby and she hates him. So gumma Peters tells Carolla she's got to go away until people forget about Lattner."

"You don't know she said that."

"It stands to reason. If anybody asks about Carolla, her

gumma would say she had just been fired from her job and went somewhere else to find work. I know Carolla went to the house of a girlfriend in Mangotown, Jenny Meggs, told her she was going away and to ask for her old job at the inn. But she couldn't leave until morning—the bus doesn't run at night."

"Where does Dave Maubee fit in?"

"I'm coming to that. I got a picture in my mind. He likes to travel at night. All right, he comes to Mango after everybody is asleep. Maybe on a bicycle—he steals bicycles like they were coconuts. He sneaks into Carolla's house. She sleeps in the front room with her two kids. He wakes her up."

"How you know he wasn't at the house earlier? Before she went to the inn?"

"Because then he would have stopped her. He don't like obeah and the old foolishness, any more than me. He used to say, 'Obeah means people on their knees, got to obey. Education means people stand up, got aspiration.' " Xavier shook his head regretfully. "Dave had a lot of good ideas. Anyway, I figure he arrives late and takes Carolla outside. Wouldn't be surprised if he'd been coming around to see her pretty often lately. Didn't see her name in his little black book, but some of the pages were missing. She tells him she is going away, and he finds out what she has done.

"That would get him mad. Not so much because she left obeah juice for Lattner to drink, as because he doesn't want her to be arrested for murder. He would ask her, did she wipe her fingerprints off the bottle of juice. She would say no. He sees she is in big trouble. He has got to help her. He would figure, maybe Lattner isn't home yet. Or maybe he is already dead and, if the door of the cottage is still open, it will be easy to get rid of the bottle. The danger would come if Lattner had drunk enough manchee to make him sick but was able to telephone for help. But Dave had to take the chance. Otherwise Carolla would go to jail, her gumma too."

"You sound like you're on his side."

He felt a twinge of guilt at the words. "Just being fair. My picture is, Carolla tells him how to find Lattner's cottage and

he goes up there. Now comes the big risk. He opens the door
a little—a little more—finally slips inside, and sees Lattner's
corpse on the floor."

Toinette's concentrated frown made him pause. She said,
"Why didn't he just take the bottle of juice and slip out
again?"

"Maybe that's what he started to do. Then he thinks, the
doctors are going to cut Lattner up and find the poison that
killed him. As soon as they know it is manchee, the finger
points at Carolla. Plenty of people know she hates him, and
why. It would be easy for the police to find out gumma
Peters put a big fix on Lattner. The next thing, I would have
them both in jail, and his son Davy would not have anybody
to look after him. So Maubee had to make it look like
Lattner died some other way, that somebody else killed
him."

"But he wouldn't want you to think he killed the man."

"Why not? He knows this island better than anybody else.
He figures he can hide out so the police will never find him,
and pretty soon everybody will forget. That's the way he
would think. All right, how is he going to make people
believe he killed Lattner? He looks around, sees the show-
show that Lattner has bought somewhere. He gets the idea of
putting a good thumbprint on the handle, and making a cut
in the back of Lattner's neck, the kind of cut that would
have killed him."

"Why the back? Why not the front?"

"Because Lattner is dead, and Dave knows dead men don't
bleed. If his throat had been cut while he was still alive, there
would have to be lots of blood all over the place. If the
wound is in the back of the neck, there wouldn't be so much.
Anyway, he needs an animal, a chicken, or something. He
goes out of the cottage, probably plans to rob the chicken
coop back of the inn, but then he sees a little dog. Belonged
to one of the guests at the inn and it's missing. My guess is
that Dave got hold of it and—"

"If he's the man you say, he wouldn't want to kill a
harmless dog."

"Didn't have much choice. Suppose he cut himself—unless

it was a deep cut, there wouldn't be enough blood to make it look real. No, he had to have an animal, and there was the dog. He wasn't going to argue with a break like that."

Toinette, he saw with annoyance, was looking more and more dissatisfied. She said, "But even if he killed the dog, why would he leave his little black book? He wouldn't want to lose that, surely."

"That's what I thought too, at first. But what does he need it for? He knows where his A-1 girls live, and the rest don't matter much. Mostly it's habit that makes him keep the book out there in the bush. Anyway the book is almost filled up. First he tears out the pages with Carolla's name on them, and then he leaves the book near Lattner's body. That way he makes sure we will go after him, even if we miss the fingerprint." When Toinette did not respond immediately, he added, "You see something wrong with that?"

Her smile had a touch of apology. "It's an awful lot of suppose."

Indignant, he said, "It's a theory. A theory always has a lot of suppose, but if it fits the evidence, it gives you something to go on. Seems to me that's what must have happened. You got a better idea?"

She shook her head. "You think Dave and Carolla went off together?"

"No, not together. She probably is looking for a job, like she would if she was innocent. And he wouldn't want to have to worry about a woman while he is on the run. My guess is Carolla took a bus early this morning and we'll find her working someplace."

She went to him and stroked his head, as if to let him know she was sorry that he had not convinced her. All at once he was tired of the sound of his own voice. "Let's go to bed," he said, and reached for her in a significant way. Firmly she removed his hands, saying, "Who you think you are, Dave Maubee? You got to keep your strength."

He laughed. "Best way to keep it is to use it. Difference between me and Dave, I concentrate mine on one woman." But he saw that she was not in the mood for love; her mind was elsewhere; so he did not persist.

11

ACTING Governor Chalk threw himself back in his big armchair, looking indignant—an expression natural to him, for his small mouth, with a protruding lower lip, was made for indignation. He was a short man who looked shorter because his office, his chair, his desk, and the gold-fringed American flag on its standard behind him were all oversized. "You telling me Maubee didn't murder Lattner?"

Xavier said carefully, "I've got Dr. Evans' report right here. It shows that Lattner was killed by whoever put manchineel in his drink. That would more likely be the girl than Maubee."

"Doesn't sound reasonable that Maubee would try to frame himself."

"Only if you figure he cared enough about his son to protect the mother."

"I don't believe it. Anyway, that business with the machete, cutting the spinal cord and planting the blood—that's too sophisticated for a type like Maubee."

"I'm not saying that's the way it was, Governor. But on the evidence we've got so far, I don't see any other way to account for the facts."

"Well, even if Maubee only tried to fool the police, that makes him an accessory. And you haven't got any real proof that the girl poisoned Lattner. Anyway, she won't be hard to find. First thing is to bring in Maubee. As I told you yesterday." His tone implied that Maubee ought already to be in jail.

One of the walls of the office was crowded with photographs—the President of the United States, smiling affably,

Chalk in a Naval officer's uniform, Mrs. Chalk and their children posed for the camera, Acting Governor Chalk addressing the annual banquet of the St. Caro Council. It occurred to Xavier that Chalk would fight like a tiger to keep that office.

"We're looking for Maubee, Governor," he said. "I decided not to fool around with roadblocks or a harbor watch, but I have a plan for tracking him down—"

"I don't want to get into the details. Just bring him in, that's all."

Xavier left the room in time to conceal his rising wrath. He did not have to be told why Chalk, ordinarily insistent on knowing all, was now refusing to hear anything. He did not want to be put in the position either of approving or rejecting the police strategy; to do either might relieve Xavier of a measure of responsibility, and he wanted no doubt as to where the responsibility lay if Maubee was not found.

From Government House Xavier turned down a side street to a frame building where the *Sentinel* had its offices. In a rear room Ted Motley swiveled away from a typewriter to grin at him. "Feeling better?"

Xavier said, "This is an official diplomatic mission. The police department offers its apologies to the press. I was feeling a little frustrated yesterday. Didn't mean to take it out on you."

"Forget it. Listen, overnight I got a great idea. You're going out after Maubee. Let me come with you."

"What for?"

"Might be a big feature in it. Something I could sell to one of the big mainland magazines. 'On the Trail of a Killer in Beautiful St. Caro. A Firsthand Report.' With pictures. I'm serious. This could be big stuff. *National Geographic* might go for it. Or even *Life* or *Look.* I don't remember ever seeing any article about police work in a resort island. You'd be a celebrity. You could thumb your nose at Chalk in public, and he'd never dare fire you. Come on, Xave, react."

"You've got a newspaper to run."

"I put this week's issue to bed last night, and a lot of the

stuff for next week is at the printer's already. I can take a
few days off."

It occurred to Xavier that Chalk would be annoyed if Ted
accompanied him. That ended his hesitation. He said, "A
policeman isn't supposed to take a newspaperman along on
official business. So stand up."

"What?"

"Just do it. As chief of police I have the right to appoint
any citizen of St. Caro as a temporary deputy with remunera-
tion of three dollars a day to assist me in the execution of my
duties. Raise your right hand and repeat after me: I, Theodore Motley, do solemnly swear that while serving as special
temporary deputy I will faithfully obey and carry out to the
best of my ability all orders given me by the chief of police in
accordance with the Constitution of the United States. So
help me God. Very good. You are now my deputy."

"What about the three dollars?"

"You have a materialistic outlook. My first order is, change
those clothes. No deputy of mine is going to travel around St.
Caro looking like a refugee from a comic strip. Plain pants
and shirt."

"You're asking me to give up my uniform as a free agent of
the press. By this costume am I known and my credit
respected in all the bars of Gracedieu."

"That reminds me. Another thing. You are to keep reasonably sober while you are with me."

"My God, you're a hard man. You're attacking the spring of
my journalistic inspiration. Don't you realize that the booze I
take in is transmuted in my veins into the ink I write with?
Well, you said 'reasonably.' On those terms, all right. Do I
wear a shield?"

"I'll look in my desk drawer. I may have a spare."

"How about a gun? I've got one around somewhere."

"I've no objection to your wearing it for show as long as
you don't use it. Meet me at the car in an hour and we'll get
under way."

At the station, Xavier called Marco and George into his
office and briefed them on the evidence against Carolla Peters
and Maubee. "First thing is to cover all the inns and

guesthouses and see if Carolla has applied for a job. She might be using another name, so I'll give you her description. Write it down, George, and distribute it to all the constables. About twenty-two, five feet three, black skin, broad cheekbones, wide-apart eyes. Black hair, curly. In the picture I saw she was wearing it loose, down to her shoulders. Good figure, plenty of curves."

"She looks like that, I hope I find her," Marco laughed.

Xavier ignored that. "You will also be in charge of the station, Marco. You will have to work up a complete written record of all reports as they come in, so we will know where we stand. I will keep in touch by radio.

"George, I want you to instruct the constables in the other towns to check every place where Carolla might be working. And I'm leaving it to you to talk to the bus driver on the Mango Beach road. Find out whether he picked up Carolla Peters at Mangotown any time recently. If he did, we want to know where she got off.

"Now about Maubee. As I told the governor, I think Maubee is still on the island, and the best way to find him is through his women. Even if he heads for the hills, he won't stay there long. He likes his food, he likes to bathe and shave, and most of all he likes girls. Sooner or later he'll come down to the beach or one of the towns, and if we keep an eye on the right places, we'll spot him.

"I've told Peter Obee to copy out the names and addresses in Maubee's little black book. He evidently didn't visit Gracedieu much, because he only has a couple of girls here. You can assign a constable to cover those addresses, Marco. The ones in the rest of the island George and I will assign to the constables or will handle ourselves. We'll divide up the names as soon as Peter finishes his list. If we're lucky, we'll soon pick up Maubee's trail." He paused before adding, "One more thing. I have deputized Ted Motley to assist me personally for the next couple of days. He'll be with me."

A sudden glint came into Marco's eye. "Keeping in with the press?"

They stared at each other steadily. "I expect Motley to be useful," Xavier said quietly.

"Governor Chalk know?"

"He will very soon. You'll tell him. Don't fail to do that, Marco."

Marco smiled mirthlessly. "I'll take care of my part of the job." George Michelle looked from one to the other, bewildered.

As they were leaving the room, Xavier called Marco back, rose, and shut the door to the outer office. At the moment, he did not quite know what he was going to do or say. Marco leaned against the desk with exaggerated nonchalance, his hands casually thrust into his trouser pockets, and they faced each other, their eyes locked in challenge. With an effort, Xavier kept his fists unclenched and walked back to his desk chair, compelling Marco to stand erect and turn around. Toinette was right, he thought. If he began a fight with Marco, the resulting gossip would be personally disastrous, and might even create bad feeling between the Puerto Rican and black communities. Moreover, most people would sympathize with Marco, because although he was strong and tough, he was several inches the shorter and twenty pounds the lighter man. But if not a blow, then what? It would be folly to mention Toinette's name and allow Marco to put on an act of injured surprise at her reaction to his visit. It came to Xavier that the best way to deal with such a man was to make him mad, get him to do something foolish. Xavier sat in his chair, put his hands flat on the desk before him, and said lightly, "Marco, I just want to tell you, better watch out where you park your motorcycle. You leave it in the wrong place again, and I'll have to fine you for illegal parking."

Margo first looked taken aback, then he smirked. "I can explain—"

"No, don't explain. But I'll give you a piece of advice. You're a very clever man, but it's dangerous to be too clever. They say sometimes a lamprey can get twisted up so much it bites itself."

The smile on Marco's face vanished, and he took his hands out of his pockets. To be called an eel, even indirectly, is a considerable insult on St. Caro. Before he could answer, Xavier went on, "I worry about you, Marco. Don't like to see a clever fellow like you make people spit when they hear his name."

"Nobody spits at my name!"

"I spit, Marco. Now what you going to do about that?"

For an instant, Marco was so close to violence that the touch of a feather would have pushed him over the edge. His eyes glittered, and his words came out throaty with rage. "You'll find out what I do, nigger man." He stood for a moment more, staring at Xavier's unmoved face, before turning on his heel, opening the door, and slamming it behind him.

12

SEVEN times in the previous three months, Maubee had noted in his little black book the name of one Elsie James, in Morganstown, with an A-1 rating. His several gifts to her, including "a ring with a reel dimond," had been impressive testimony to his feeling for Elsie; and on one page he had put after her name the mark "!"

"A woman who could make Maubee use that kind of punctuation must have something," said Ted Motley. "I'll bet she's no kid. Not likely you'd find a girl under twenty who would have exclamation point technique."

"That shows you don't know much about St. Caro girls. I'll take that bet," said Xavier. "One dollar."

Morganstown sprawled along the south coast of the island, twenty miles from Gracedieu, an active market town with seven or eight hundred inhabitants. A word with the constable on duty in front of the town office revealed that Elsie James was the daughter of the woman who owned the main grocery store, which was also the post office. Elsie, said the constable, assisted her mother at the cashier's desk, sorted such mail as came in or out of the town, and sang in a church choir. This last bit of information struck Motley as a happy avocation for an A-1 girl. He was bitterly disappointed when Xavier pointed out that it would be easier to talk to Elsie if he entered the shop alone.

Xavier left the car some distance from the grocery and walked up the narrow sidewalk at a casual pace. People stared at him as he passed, and a couple of small boys saluted. He returned the salutes in due form. Where a sign said SUPERMARKET, he entered. The word was a good deal larger than the store, which, like all food stores on the island, had a musty but not unpleasant smell compounded of spices, bananas, and coffee. Two small windows and a few weak electric bulbs offered just enough light to permit customers to distinguish the labels on cans and bottles. The stout, formidable woman at the single check-out counter had her eye on him from the moment he stepped inside, and he went up to her at once.

"Mrs. James? I'm Chief Brooke, from Gracedieu. One of my men and I are driving through and we're a little thirsty. Like to buy a couple of cans of root beer."

She permitted herself a smile and directed him to a row of shelves in the rear. He knew at once that Maubee would never entrust his safety to such a woman, whatever he felt about the daughter. Propriety and righteousness were written all over her face. Walking through the store he saw a girl whom he took to be Elsie, standing inside a small barrier selling a stamp to a customer. He was a little surprised. She was a tall, ample girl, with a nose too broad and a mouth too wide for beauty. A second glance made him think again. The sparkle of her eyes and the radiance of her smile suggested a personality; and her flawless dark brown skin had the luster of youth. Her age he guessed at eighteen. When she was alone, he went to her and said, "Can you tell me what time the mail car from Gracedieu gets here?"

" 'Bout noon," she replied. "You missed it. Expecting a letter?"

He smiled at her. "Just wanted to start a conversation."

She returned the smile but shook her head reprovingly. "Bet you got a wife. No way for a married man to act."

The vibrant quality of her voice prompted him to say, "Way you sound, you must be a singer."

She had a bubbling and infectious laugh. "Who you been talking to?"

"Bright, too," he said. "I bet you're popular with the boys."

Shrugging, she retorted, "Boys don't interest me much."

"Men?"

"A real man might, but I never met but one."

"I'd like to talk to you a little about him," he said, lowering his voice.

" 'Bout who?"

"Dave Maubee."

She caught her breath and, with a darting glance at her mother, said, "Don't tell me you're looking to arrest him." The laugh came again. "Nobody ever arrests him."

"Not up to now, but he's in bad trouble."

"Oh, my." Her forehead wrinkled. "Why you come to me?"

"I know you're a friend of his."

"Who told you that?"

"Never mind. Your mother know?"

She shook her head in quick anxiety. "You goin' to tell her?"

"No reason to do that. I want to talk to you. Might be a help to Dave. Where can we meet?"

"You better buy a stamp," she said, with another peek at her mother. "Five cents. The Methodist Church, where I sing."

He put a nickel on the counter and took the stamp. "Can you meet me there in fifteen minutes?"

"What can I tell my mother for an excuse?"

"Maybe you have choir practice. Maybe the minister asked you to do something. You're smart. You make up the lie."

The mirthful chuckle welled out of her again. "I'll try."

At the check-out counter Mrs. James looked disparagingly at his two cans of root beer and took his money unsmilingly. He could read her problem in her unfriendly eyes. A girl as attractive as Elsie, and with a prosperous mother, was bound to be sought in marriage by local men. If she persistently refused them, as Elsie must have, the mother would wonder if she was in love with someone else, and any strange man who talked to the girl, even the chief of police, would be an object of suspicion.

He stopped at the car to say to Ted, "She ought to be coming out of the store and heading this way soon. Big girl. Looks about eighteen to me, but make up your own mind. I'm going to wait for her at the Methodist Church. I spotted it as we drove in, a couple of streets down. If you get tired of sitting here, you can kill time shopping. Meanwhile, here's a couple of cans of warm root beer." Ted was not grateful.

A neat sign outside the white church said, "Come in and pray at any hour." The door was wide open and the deep shadows within were cool and inviting, but no one else was there. Rows of hard backless benches looked as if they demanded genuine zeal from worshipers, the old plaster walls were cracked and the wooden floor warped, but everything was spotlessly clean—always the sign of a devoted congregation, with women willing to get down on their knees to scrub as readily as to pray. The only decoration was a gilt crucifix at the plain altar. At one side a railed section with hymn books and loose cushions on the benches showed where the choir sang. Xavier sat on the bench nearest the door and considered. Now that he had observed the mother's protective attitude toward Elsie and the girl's straightforward style, he wiped out the possibility that Maubee was concealed in their home. He might, however, have a hideaway nearby where he and Elsie met on his visits to Morganstown. A good deal might depend on her willingness to talk.

When the girl arrived, her first words were, "I don't get it. You're a policeman but you say you're a friend of Dave's."

"Not a friend exactly, but we grew up together."

"Yes, he once talk about you. Xave and Dave, he says the other kids called you, and nobody ever wanted to fight either of you. He tell you about him and me?"

"In a way. He thinks you're quite a girl."

She was more puzzled than ever. "How come you and he talk and you don't arrest him?"

They were speaking in low tones, almost in whispers. As he took in her tall, handsome shape and caught the young, fresh scent of her, he began to understand Maubee's enthusiasm for this warm and spirited girl. "Suppose you let me ask the questions, Elsie. Come on, sit down."

"Can't stay long. Told my mother I had to deliver a box of cornflakes to the minister." She sat, putting a brown paper bag on the bench next to her.

"How long have you known Dave?"

She thought briefly. "Four months next week."

"How did you happen to meet?"

A flash of white teeth as she smiled suggested that the memory was a happy one, but she said, "None of your business, man!" Xavier smiled too. He could make a reasonable guess about the first meeting. A restless, romantic girl, unable to sleep, walking on an empty road, late at night—a big dark figure moving alongside and striking up a conversation, saying things to allay her fright. Maubee, he felt sure, was no rapist. He had always been a lively talker and had a gentle way with women. A spark struck, a sudden flame, and the chance encounter had turned into a passionate love affair. It could have been like that.

"Has he ever been at your house?" Xavier asked.

"My house?" The mirthful look came back to her face. "I tell you, man, you ask a question like that, you don' know my mother."

"When he comes to town, what does he do—throw a pebble at your window? And you sneak out after your mother is asleep?"

"He tell you that?"

"It's not important. Now listen, Elsie. You're an intelligent girl, I can see that. Dave is wanted in a murder case."

She gasped. "Murder! Who he kill?"

"I'm not sure he killed anybody. But a tourist was cut with a machete and it looks like Dave was there at the time. My men are looking for him all over the island. Sooner or later, they'll find him, and then somebody could get hurt. Dave might even be shot. But if I find him, he and I could talk man to man. It's the best way for him. If you help me, you're helping him."

She gave him a long, searching look, as if to estimate his sincerity. After a while, she said, "What you want to know?"

The diamond on her right hand, he noticed, was perhaps one carat—large enough so that if it were of good quality it might have cost a thousand dollars. He hoped that the woman from whom it had been stolen could afford the loss. "How did you explain that ring to your mother?"

It took a moment before she absorbed the question. With a

sidelong glance, she said, "Oh, it's just glass. I found it in the street. Some tourist must have lost it."

He grinned. "Just remember that. Now Elsie, I want to know when you saw Dave last."

"Three weeks ago." There was a hint of a sigh in the words.

"There's some hideaway where he takes you. I want to know where."

She laughed and looked embarrassed at the same time. "I'm not telling you that, man."

To put pressure on her, he felt, would only increase her resistance. "Elsie," he said, "let me give you a little advice. Dave is a remarkable man, but it isn't smart for any woman to take him too seriously."

The girl gave him another appraising stare. Finally she said, "He tol' me the same thing himself." Her voice, while still low, became charged with feeling. "You think I don' know he's got other women? I wish he didn't, but if that's the way it's got to be, I'd rather be Dave's part-time woman than some other fellow's wife. And not just because he knows how to make love. He's a man. Do you understand? He teach me to be brave. He's got soul."

Xavier said, "You couldn't say much better than that about any man. But it must have been taking a big risk, your going off to him in the night. Where did you meet him? The place couldn't be too far away from your house."

Another quick change of mood made her face suddenly mischievous. "You wouldn't believe me if I told you, so I won't tell you."

Perhaps it was the slight embarrassment he had detected in her, perhaps a momentary flicker of her eyes toward the far end of the church, but he knew instantly what she was concealing.

"Here?" he said incredulously.

"Nothing wrong in that," she retorted. "It not big sinning, man. Dave and I talked it over. He says sex with real love is beautiful in the eyes of the Lord, and I would be forgiven. There's no other place we could go, here in town. He never stays long."

"But weren't you taking a big chance?"

"Not after midnight. Whole town goes to sleep early."

Come in and pray at any hour. Well, perhaps there was a kind of unspoken prayer when Dave Maubee held this girl in his arms, with the choir cushions to make them comfortable. No wonder she sang lustily at the services. Hers was a rejoicing nature. "Don't worry," he said. "I'll never tell."

As if she had just made up her mind about him, she said, "I think you're a good man. You won't hurt Dave?"

"Not if I can help it."

"You think he'll come back?"

He hesitated before saying, "I don't think so, Elsie. He's got to hide, and when I get him I will have to put him in jail."

"I hope you never get him." She put her face in her hands and wept. He did not attempt to comfort her. When she could speak again, she said, "Last time he kissed me good-bye, he tol' me he might go away from St. Caro. I knew then he wasn't ever coming back. He didn't say so, but I knew. So that's the end."

Xavier said, "Would you like to be alone, Elsie?" When she nodded, he rose and put a hand on her shoulder. "You're a fine girl and I wish you well," he said, and went out of the church.

13

FROM Morganstown, Xavier turned the car toward the range of blue-green hills, some almost entitled to be called mountains, that dominated the center of the island. As they climbed, he said, "I'd better bring you up to date on the case. See what you think." When he had reviewed the facts so far uncovered by his investigation, Ted's first comment was, "You must be enjoying yourself. Marjorie Searle. Mrs. Dillon. Barbara Keys. Elsie James. Just one good-looking woman after another."

"Naturally. You start with men like Lattner and Maubee, and there are going to be women on all sides."

Ted snapped his fingers. "Good point. I can use it in the article. On the surface, these two men are entirely different, but when you get right down to it they have a lot in common. Both of them strong, dynamic, intelligent, hard, and determined to have their own way. If Lattner had been born black in St. Caro he might have turned into a famous outlaw. If Maubee had been born white in Cleveland, he'd have wound up at the head of a big corporation. Both with the same weakness—if it is a weakness—a need for lots of women. The Don Juan complex."

"That might be right as far as Lattner is concerned," Xavier conceded. "I think he got pleasure out of making women love him, and then more pleasure out of humiliating them. Strong element of cruelty there. Dangerous man for a woman to mess with. But unless Dave Maubee has changed a lot, he's not like that. I don't see him as a Don Juan. More like Solomon with a thousand wives. He really likes women. Likes their company. He wouldn't want to hurt them."

Ted laughed. "Headline. Chief of police praises murder suspect as Solomon. How does that sound?"

"A little more of that and I'll take away your star."

Although the sun was strong, the air was distinctly cooler than on the coastal plain. The rising road staggered around a hairpin turn, skirting a deep ravine. Below them the dense green jungle growth looked still and ominous. When a shadowy gray shape darted across the road, Ted started. "Just a mongoose," said Xavier. "Every time I see one it makes me think that nothing the human race ever does comes out quite right."

"What do you mean by that?"

"It's nearly a hundred years now since the British brought the mongoose over here to get rid of the snakes. In those days, fer-de-lance and coral snakes all over the place. The mongoose goes to work, breeds like crazy, and pretty soon no more fer-de-lance, no more coral snakes, no snakes at all. Everybody says that's good. But now he's everywhere, the mongoose. No more snakes to eat, he eats chickens and even little goats. People all over the island complaining about him. And everybody says that's bad. Which is worse, some snakes around, or losing your chickens? Same question goes all through life."

"I'm not sure I follow you."

"Sure you do. Americans are all proud of their industrial production. Biggest in the world. Everybody says that's good. But I read in the magazines, pollution caused by industry is ruining the air and water all over the country, spoiling everything. Everybody says that's bad. Which is worse, not having much industry, not having a car, or having too much pollution and being sick half the time?"

"You've got a point. That's why I'm not married. Never been able to figure out which is worse, not having a woman to share your life, or having one who takes it over."

"A smart husband just lets her think she's taken it over."

"Ever say that to Toinette?"

"You think I'm that foolish?"

Presently Ted said, "Pretty lonely part of the world. Why

would a woman who gets an A-1 from Maubee live way up here?"

"She owns a coffee plantation. Small one. She and her two brothers run it. I looked her up before I left Gracedieu. Inez Dardo."

"Puerto Rican?"

"Probably, to judge from the name. There are five or six Ricanas in Maubee's book. He didn't seem to have a racial problem there."

"What about white American women?"

"None, far as I can tell. Funny thing, though, about this girl Inez. The other two A-1 girls he gave gifts to and got back to regularly, but not Inez. He never wrote a word about her. Just a big A-1. And it looks like he only saw her a couple of times."

"Maybe he didn't feel like climbing these hills. But it might be different now. A house up here could be just what he wants as a hideaway."

"That's what I've been thinking. He could spot us coming a long way off and wait in some cave until we're gone. Lots of caves up this way. If the Dardos are willing to risk helping him, and if Maubee stays in this vicinity, it might take months to dig him out. Somehow, though, I don't see Dave doing that. Not enough to keep him interested, even with an A-1 girl at hand."

High up on the next ridge they could see the blaze of a window catching the afternoon sun. A narrow rutted track took off from the road, and rising among small, dark green coffee trees on either side, pointed them toward the house. As the car jolted upward, Ted spotted a figure moving down the hill at a fast pace. "Man running," he said excitedly. "Think that's Maubee?"

"I doubt it. He's heading our way."

They saw him standing in the middle of the track as they came around the final turn leading to the house. "Who does he think he is—Che?" Ted muttered. The man who barred their progress had unmistakably modeled himself to the guerrilla ideal. He was young, possibly not yet twenty, dark, black-bearded, hot-eyed, and his aggressive pose, legs wide apart, thumbs thrust into his wide belt, suggested that he was prepared at any moment to use the holstered pistol next to his right hand. He was wearing blue jeans and a half-buttoned tan shirt. "What do you want here?" he demanded in a loud voice, as the car braked to a stop.

Xavier stepped into the road and said, "Police. I'm Chief Brooke." He added in rapid Spanish, "I would like to talk with Señorita Dardo. You are her brother? Which one? Enrique or Pablo?"

"I am Pablo. What do you want of my sister?"

"I'll explain to her. Be good enough to tell her we are here."

The Spanish words, the use of his name, and Xavier's quiet assurance made the young man hesitate, but he still sought to assert himself. "Who is that with you?"

"A special deputy. Mr. Motley."

"He looks like an American."

"He is."

Dardo spat in the dirt. "So they are moving into the police force, even in St. Caro. Naturally. Well, you and he can turn around and go back to Gracedieu. I'm not letting you through."

Xavier stared at him steadily and said in English, "Listen carefully, man. I am looking for a murderer. If you interfere with me, I'll handcuff you and put you in jail. Take your hand off that gun, or I'll ask the judge to make it a year."

"You said a murderer. Who?"

"I'll tell that to your sister. I have no time to waste. Will you call her or do we have to drive over you?"

The young man surveyed Xavier's set face and powerful build, turned wordlessly, and began to walk up the hill. They followed him in the car. The house, painted gray, was one of the sturdy old plantation houses, part stone and part solid wood, built by the British in their heyday on St. Caro. As they reached it, the door opened, and a woman stepped out. At first sight of her, Ted Motley had to restrain himself from whistling. They saw her first in profile, as she faced her brother. She was small in stature, but the way she held

herself and the slim elegance of her figure in blue shorts and a
white cotton shirt made her seem half a foot taller. Her
beauty was island Spanish, tawny skin contrasting with soft
dark hair loosely pulled back from her high forehead. It was
only when she turned toward them that they saw the long
disfiguring scar, perhaps a knife slash, that ran across a cheek
from ear to lip.

"These men are police, Inez," Pablo said. "You want to
talk with them?"

"Why not?" Her voice was low-pitched and resonant. There
was intelligence in her dark eyes, sensuality in her full mouth,
and pride in the tight curl of her nostrils. High cheekbones
and flat facial planes made her face look sculptured. She
might have been close to thirty. Scar or no scar, Xavier found
himself marveling at Maubee's luck. "Well?" she said.

He knew without being told that she would respect only
plain, direct talk. "Señorita, we are looking for David
Maubee. He is implicated in a murder. Information has
reached us that he has visited this house in the past. I have
come here to ask whether you have seen him in the last few
days."

Her eyes widened slightly and narrowed again. "How do
you know he has ever been here?"

"That's another matter. Perhaps you will answer this
question. Why did your brother feel it necessary to block our
path with a pistol in his belt? Does he have a permit to carry
a gun?"

She threw an annoyed glance at Pablo and shrugged. "He
enjoys playing games."

"What is this game called?"

Her frown deepened. "I will answer your first question.
Maubee is not here. I have not seen him for some time. Is
that all?"

"Not quite." He turned to look at Pablo, still maintaining
his militant stance. "What I have to say is for your ears only,
Señorita. Perhaps you will be good enough to let me talk to
you alone. I will then tell you how I know you and Maubee
are friends."

He was glad to see that she was feminine enough to find

this offer tempting. As she hesitated, Pablo said, "It's just a trick, Inez. Don't do it."

"I know what I'm doing," she answered curtly, and with a nod to Xavier, led the way into the house. The windows of the room to which she brought him were so heavily curtained that he could tell little more about it than it was sparsely furnished. He wondered if she liked to sit in shadow in order to conceal that terrible scar. In some strange way, it enhanced his awareness of her beauty. With such a woman the best way to learn the truth was to tell it. He decided to continue in Spanish. "I know, Señorita, that you and David Maubee have been lovers. He kept a diary and I have seen it."

That shocked her. "The fool!" she cried. She did not seem embarrassed, only angry. "The vain fool!"

It occurred to Xavier that if he could get her to talk about Maubee as a personality he might learn more than if he asked for specific information. "Yes," he agreed, "David has always been a little vain. I used to know him well. When he first turned outlaw I think he saw himself as a romantic figure, standing alone against society. Does he still feel that way?"

A slow shake of the head suggested that she was seriously examining his question. "It is an old-fashioned idea. In a crowded world the man who stands alone can do nothing." She pulled herself up sharply. "If you know he has come here, you must also know that he came seldom."

"Yes, it puzzles me that he did not visit you more often, especially since he was evidently fascinated by you."

"How do you know that?"

He did not think she would appreciate even a top rank in Maubee's rating system, so he said, "He wrote something, I forget the exact words, that left no doubt about his feeling for you."

Somewhat to his surprise, she did not demand to know what Maubee had written. The pause that preceded her next remark and the care with which she phrased it, put him on his guard. "It's true that I was greatly excited by David. He is a remarkable man in many ways. But I was not eager to become deeply involved."

"How did you meet in the first place?"

With a shrug, she said, "He happened to come this way and stumbled on our house."

Xavier grunted. "Señorita, that cannot be true. You certainly did not fall into the arms of a wandering stranger. Who brought him?"

Without being able to see her eyes clearly, he knew that she was searing him with a glance. "I don't like your tone."

"I am paying you the courtesy of frankness. If you prefer to be questioned in a police station, I can arrange that. Someone brought Maubee here. I want to know who, and why."

"I shall not tell you, either here or anywhere else."

All the impressions gathered in the few minutes since he had arrived at the house suddenly came into focus. "We will go on," he said quietly, "to another matter. The immigration records at Gracedieu show that you and your brothers came here from San Juan four years ago. But your accent, if I am not mistaken, is Dominican, not Puerto Rican."

A few seconds passed before she said, "We are from Santo Domingo, yes, originally. But my brother and I were allowed to come here under American permits."

"Of course. Do you sell your coffee in Gracedieu?"

Again that significant pause. "No. It is a very small crop, but excellent coffee. We get a better price for it in the export market."

"Where is it shipped?"

"At Port Cambo. One of the small merchant freighters picks it up and sells it in some of the islands that do not grow coffee of their own."

"You go to Port Cambo often?"

"Seldom." A finger touched the scarred cheek. "My brother Enrique takes care of that part of the business."

"You are not lonely?"

He felt her staring at him. "A little, sometimes. But I have my books, the radio, and my plantation."

In the same conversational tone, he said, "Was it Enrique who met Maubee in Port Cambo and brought him to you? You might as well tell me. Otherwise I will inquire in Port Cambo. They would certainly have been seen together."

She was quick to change her tactics. "There is no reason to make a mystery of it, after all. If you must know, for a time we considered hiring someone to help us with the coffee. Enrique came across Maubee in a bar and thought he might be the man. He stayed here for a few days. But after we became acquainted, we decided it would not be a good arrangement. That was months ago."

"Señorita, the idea that anyone would believe Maubee might take a job on a plantation, even to be near you, I find incredible. However, you say you dropped the idea. Then when he came back again, nearly a month ago, no doubt it was simply to see you. How long did he stay then?"

"Two days, as I recall."

The investigating officer is fully justified in making an assertion that he cannot prove in order to extract essential information from a reluctant witness. "And his visit this week. I suppose he has left by now?"

"He has not been here. If you wish to search, go ahead, Señor."

"No, I think not." He came to his feet and sketched a little salute. Maubee was right, he thought. A superior woman. "I shall not trouble you any more just now."

The abruptness of his departure surprised her. "You have not told me," she said. "What has Maubee done? Why are you searching for him?"

"He has evidence we need, in a murder case."

"Who was killed?"

"A tourist."

She sniffed, as if such a casualty was beneath notice. "I am sorry I cannot help you," she said formally.

At the front door he turned to her and said, "I hope you and your brothers will not violate the laws of St. Caro, Señorita."

A hint of irony touched her lips. "No, no, never, Señor. We are content, my brothers and I, with our life here. We are grateful to the United States and to St. Caro. Why should we violate your laws?"

He smiled at her in the same spirit. "Good-bye," he said in English. She stood framed in the doorway, motionless, watching him walk to the car. There was no sign of Pablo.

As they bounced downhill back to the road, Ted said, "You mean to say that woman slept with Maubee? What's his secret?"

"I've often wondered."

"You're sure he's not up there somewhere?"

"Pretty sure." As Xavier put the car on the road running south through the hills to Port Cambo, he said, "Put a few facts together and see where you come out. Fact one, she's not Puerto Rican. Comes from Santo Domingo. You know the conditions there. A girl as beautiful and high-spirited as that in a city run by strongarm boys—you can imagine. It's a pretty fair bet she and her brothers are refugees."

"You could be right. It would be interesting to know how she got that scar."

"Fact two. It stands to reason a woman with her brains isn't going to be satisfied with the life she's leading if that's all there is to it. She says she has enough to content her, but I don't believe it. A woman like that, without a husband or children, needs purpose in life. Has to be a pretty strong purpose to make her isolate herself on a hilltop."

"I see what you're getting at. Political stuff?"

"That's it. Nothing to do with this island, or I'd have heard about it. The independence movement in St. Caro you could blow away with a sneeze. It's not like Puerto Rico. No, I'd make a small bet she's tied up with the underground Dominican refugee organization."

"I didn't know there was one."

"Yes, there's one for Haiti and one for the Dominican Republic. The rumor I hear is that the Cubans have been training refugees as commandos, looking to the day of revolution."

"She's a Communist?"

"Not necessarily, but these refugee patriots have to take help where they can get it. It would make sense for them to have stations on the island and pick up young fellows who are looking for adventure or want to help change the world. That place of hers would be ideal for recruiting."

"That accounts for Pablo's Guevara imitation."

"And also perhaps for Maubee."

"How do you figure that?"

Xavier outlined the idea that had taken shape during his talk with Inez Dardo. He could see one of her brothers—probably Enrique, Pablo was too juvenile—going into a bar, say in Port Cambo, and getting into a conversation with Dave Maubee, who would certainly have heard rumors of the beautiful girl up in the hills. Enrique would say to himself, here's a possible recruit for the commando camp. Maubee would say to himself, here's a chance to meet Inez Dardo.

"Next thing, he is at the plantation and the Dardos work on him. Is he against the bullies and the bastards of the world? Wouldn't he like to help free an island people from terror, torture, and misery? Doesn't he know what happened to the Dominicans under Trujillo and those who came after him? All the islands have to stand together if they are ever to be really free. Why not give up a life of crime and become an officer in the commandos, a man with a cause worth fighting for?"

"It's a movie!" Ted snapped his fingers half a dozen times. "The handsome black outlaw gambling for high stakes with the tragic Spanish beauty. She playing for his body in her cause—he for her body in his. Followed by the big bedroom scene. In Technicolor."

"Something like that. No doubt she told him what she told me: 'In a crowded world the man who stands alone can do nothing.' Join us and be the new Guevara, a hero to the world. Maybe he was close to saying yes. Maybe he just encouraged her to think so. Chances are, she was lonely, needed a man, needed love. To judge from that A-1, it was a big thing for him, so it probably was for her too. He stays for two, three days more. I can see him promising, or half-promising to return soon and sign up. But once he is back in the old groove, the idea of fighting for justice in some other country doesn't appeal so much. Other women come into his life—Elsie James, for one. So months go by and the Dardos don't see him."

"But you said he finally went back to Inez."

"Yes—and as far as I can see there's only one explanation

for that. Look at it this way. Let's assume the memory of her stayed with him and he wanted her again."

"Safe assumption."

"All right—but can he go back to her except on her terms? Not to a woman like that. She would never accept him merely as a lover who turns up when he feels like it. To me that second visit means he was prepared to join whatever setup she is recruiting for."

"It's hard to picture Maubee taking orders and standing at attention."

"Yes, but maybe it isn't so strange. He's been an outlaw, knocking around the island, living a pretty meaningless life, for a good many years now. He's my age—no kid any more. How long is he going to go on like that? Even if the police don't catch up with him some time for petty robbery, even if some jealous woman doesn't put a knife in his back, what does he have to look forward to? He's bound to want something more out of life. To fight in a big cause—be a celebrated guerrilla who helps bring off a revolution—that could appeal to him a lot. Something like that had to be going on in his mind. Otherwise Inez would never have welcomed him back."

"Maybe he tricked her again."

"I doubt it. If he did, those brothers of hers would never rest until they had his blood."

"But didn't you say that was a month ago? If he joined up, what's he still doing in St. Caro?"

"That's not hard to explain. How are they going to get him to Cuba, or wherever their camp is? I don't believe they have a plane—all the private planes at Gracedieu airport are registered, and we know who owns them."

"How about a small boat?"

"Pretty risky. If he tried it alone, heading for Cuba, it's 500 miles to Manzanillo. And if he made it, there could be plenty of problems for him after he landed. No, if they are running a recruiting system, it has to be better organized than that. It's likely they have radio contact with Cuba—that would be easy. Suppose every so often a Cuban boat flying some other flag stops by and picks up the recruits. Inez told me they export their coffee. Ship it out by merchant freighter. That could be the transport for the recruits too."

Ted looked amused. "That's a pretty big story you've built out of a couple of little facts."

"Call it a working theory."

"It's all right with me. I like it. About Inez, though. If you're right, if she's really trying to knock over some crummy dictatorship, I don't see anything wrong with what she's doing. On the contrary, I say more power to her. You going after her?"

"On what grounds? I'm not the CIA. Far as I know, she is not the agent of any foreign power and I have no evidence that she has committed a crime. Probably Pablo has in carrying the gun, but men on these isolated plantations often carry hand guns and the government doesn't bother them. It would be a good lesson for Pablo if he has to pay a fine and apply for a permit, but as for Inez—" Xavier shrugged. "Maybe she is helping men leave the island without emigration permits. If I could prove that I would have to arrest her, but I might have a lot of trouble finding proof."

"Don't look too hard."

14

IN the late afternoon, with the sun sinking toward the horizon, they came down toward Port Cambo. The undulating terrain around them looked out on a broad expanse of the sea and was a favorite location for the island homes of wealthy Americans. There was brilliant color everywhere— white or pink houses against the green of the surging hills and frequent splashes of hibiscus, wild orchids, and bougainvillea. The dreamlike quality of the landscape moved Motley to say, "Why don't I come here more often? If I were rich, I'd build a house up here and publish in Port Cambo."

"Don't think you could stand it," Xavier said. "Just two bars in the place."

"An unworthy gibe. Which reminds me. This girl, Isabel Cannon, sings in Mac's Place, doesn't she? I remember hearing about her in Gracedieu. She must be pretty good. Someone told me she had offers to work in Jamaica and in St. Thomas, as well as in Gracedieu, but she said she preferred to stay in Port Cambo."

"Might be so she could see Dave Maubee. She's the biggest thing in his book, after all."

Ted scratched his nose thoughtfully. "Xave, are you convinced about the little black book?"

"Meaning what?"

"I mean your idea as to why he left it behind." When Xavier did not reply, he went on, "Seems to me he'd realize that once the police had the book, they'd go after his women. Would he let that happen?"

The pause that followed extended itself into significance.

Ted turned to study Xavier's profile. "You bothered by something?"

Xavier said, "I am so bothered that I am beginning to think I'm not fit to be chief of police."

"What's eating you?"

"Stupidity. I went off half-cocked. That's stupid for any-body, but for a policeman it's a disaster."

"Suppose you explain that."

"It's not only Maubee's black book. I let my imagination run away with me. Toinette was right. Too much suppose."

"Wait a minute, Xave. I didn't say your theory was wrong. I just raised a question."

They had reached the flat coastal plain. A few miles away the low buildings of Port Cambo were visible on the horizon. "The blood on Lattner's clothes," Xavier went on. "That bothers me. Soon as Maubee had the idea of covering for Carolla by slicing Lattner, he'd know he would have to find a lot of blood somewhere. In my picture I had him going out to steal a chicken and then seeing Mrs. Dillon's Mexican hairless wandering around. But that would have to be a damned convenient coincidence. I don't like it."

"Yes, that stops me too."

"Another thing. Those missing pages at the end of the little black book."

"I thought your explanation was reasonable. If Maubee had just started visiting Carolla again, he'd have destroyed those pages to keep her name out of it."

"I can't make myself believe it. He's got plenty of other women. Why would he suddenly start up with her again?"

After a moment, Ted said, "But when you come right down to it, nothing else makes sense. His fingerprints are on the machete, after all. It has to be the way you said. If Maubee didn't frame himself for the murder, who put the thing in the room?"

"If I could answer that, I'd probably know everything. No point in trying to find out who bought the show-show. Those things are imported from Puerto Rico by the hundreds and sold in maybe fifty little shops around the island. Whoever sold the one in Lattner's cottage isn't going to remember which tourist bought it. Lattner might have had it in his cottage since last year. No, I tell you, Ted, I'm just about back where I started."

The police station at Port Cambo was housed in a neat frame building close to the docks. Xavier stopped for an instant to survey the craft in the harbor—perhaps a dozen sailboats, a few expensive motor-powered cruisers and, tied up at the dock, a small dingy freighter flying the Panamanian flag. A wisp of smoke trailed from its single stack. "The ship that takes the Dardos' coffee probably looks like that one," he said.

Skepticism put an edge on Ted's voice. "You suggesting that particular ship, which just happens to be here, is the one Maubee intends to make his getaway on? When you don't even know he's in Port Cambo? I thought you weren't going to suppose any more."

"I didn't say that. You've got to suppose in my job, but you've also got to know where to stop. How many freighters put in at Port Cambo? I'll bet not more than one or two in a month. Right now I think I'm justified in suspecting any merchant ship that flies a foreign flag at this dock of having a connection with the Dardos. And if it loads their coffee it could also be the ship Maubee would sail on if he was planning to start a new life somewhere else. He could have been waiting for it. It makes me feel good inside to say that, so I believe it must be right."

"Is that intuition or wishful thinking?"

"We will soon know."

The sergeant in charge of the station, Pedro Melendez, was in Xavier's estimation one of the best men in St. Caro's police force—a thin, wiry veteran of about twenty-eight, with the spectacled look of an earnest student. He looked relieved at seeing Xavier and launched into his report. It was totally negative. Gracedieu had radioed that the bus driver on the Mangotown road had not seen Carolla Peters, and no one answering her description had asked for a job in any inn or guesthouse. Dave Maubee similarly had not surfaced any-where. No missing boat had been reported. The only woman in Port Cambo whose name had been assigned to Melendez for investigation by Deputy Chief Michelle had gotten married and moved away six months earlier.

Xavier said, "Thank you, Pedro. A question. That ship at the dock. What do you know about her?"

Melendez answered instantly, "The *Corinto*. Tramp freighter. Thirty-five hundred tons. Panama registry. Came in this morning. Sails tonight at ten." He consulted a record on his desk. "Out of San Juan for New Orleans with a cargo of pineapples. Stops here every few months to load some native coffee or coconuts and maybe buy a few stores. Never stays long. I know the captain, a Venezuelan, Morino. Anything wrong? Smuggling?"

"No. Something else entirely. Whose coffee do they buy, do you know?"

"Yes, comes from the Dardo plantation. Enrique Dardo was in town today, loading it."

Xavier threw a triumphant glance at Ted. "Call it a hunch," he said, "but it wouldn't surprise me if Maubee tried to board that ship."

Melendez controlled his astonishment like a good policeman. "Going to hold her?"

"Not so easy. For that we would have to ask the circuit judge at Gracedieu to sign an order. Even if he went along with us and was willing to interfere with a foreign vessel on my hunch, by the time somebody got here with the order, the *Corinto* would probably be gone."

"Then what are you going to do?"

"We'll forget about the order. If it comes to the worst, and Maubee hasn't shown up before the ship sails, I'll get the harbor master to go on board with me and try to soften up the captain so we can make a search."

"That could be difficult." Melendez shook his head. "He's a proud man, Morino. He would stand on his rights."

"We'll have to do our best with him. Anyway, my feeling is that if Maubee is in Port Cambo and planning to get away, he's still on shore. He wouldn't want to be cooped up in a cabin sooner than he had to. And he would be taking an unnecessary chance if he showed himself by daylight. I think there is a good chance he will try to go on board tonight. Probably late."

"Want me to watch her?"

"No, I need you for something else." Xavier glanced at a burly young constable who was listening to them avidly. "Can you assign Ford here to patrol the dock for the next couple of hours, until we relieve him?"

The acknowledgment of his authority in the station brought an appreciative note to Melendez' voice. "Ford, you heard what the Chief said. Do you have any special instructions for him, Chief?"

"Yes. Listen, Ford. Take your position near the gangplank and put a flashlight on everyone who starts to go on board. If anybody asks what you're doing, just say you are looking for a friend. If you see a really big man, three inches taller than me and broader than you, that's Maubee. My guess is that if he sees you on the dock, he will back off. That's all right. We'll be watching for him."

"Maybe he'll try to knock me over," Ford said hopefully, as he buckled a pistol holster onto his belt.

"Yes, he might figure that if he got on board, the ship would sail before we could stop her. I notice she's got steam up. The second you see him, fire two warning shots in the air. If he attacks you, you'll have to shoot in self-defense, but I've never heard of his using a gun or even carrying one. Unless he pulls one on you, aim low, at his legs. If he doesn't attack, if he runs, follow him and keep firing in the air. We'll be close by, and as soon as we hear the shots we'll start moving. Don't try to lay hands on him by yourself. Wait until we catch up with you. Got that?"

"Yes, sir. Shoot first in the air. Don't shoot him except in self-defense, and then aim at his legs. If he runs, I follow him and keep firing in the air until you catch up. Big thing is to keep him off the ship."

"Good. Just stick to that."

Ford's sepia face broke into a white-toothed grin of delight. "Me and Maubee! Just wait till my girl hears that!"

Before he could leave the station, Motley stopped him,

saying to Xavier, "How about my going along with Ford? You've got me half convinced now that Maubee's going to show up. If he does, I'd like to be around."

"You could have a long wait before that drink you've been dreaming about."

"In the service of the St. Caro police no sacrifice is too great. I could keep Ford from getting lonely."

"Just so you don't distract him. All right with you, Pedro? Ford? Okay, Ted, go ahead."

When they were alone, Melendez said, "Chief, what makes you think Maubee is in Port Cambo?"

"It's just a theory at the moment. I happened to find out his favorite girl lives in Port Cambo. If I'm right about his deciding to leave St. Caro, it would be natural for him to want to spend his last nights with her."

"Who's the girl?"

"A singer named Isabel Cannon. Know her?"

"Everybody knows her. The big attraction at Mac's Place. I never heard she was Maubee's girl, though."

"He probably sneaks in at night and doesn't show in the daytime. I want to check her house right away. Brought along a search warrant, got it signed in Gracedieu before I left, so she can't keep us out."

"She probably won't be home. Starts work at Mac's about now."

"We'll go to Mac's afterward and get something to eat. Know where she lives?"

"A little house on Poco Street. Only a couple of minutes' walk."

"Then we'll take the car. I want to be able to get back to the dock fast if we hear shots."

15

MAC'S was an unpretentious, high-raftered restaurant situated on the waterfront. A well-stocked bar on one side, a small stage on the other, and some twenty tables in between offered enough hope of entertainment to attract a nightly throng consisting mostly of tourists staying at nearby inns, with a sprinkling of prosperous Carovians and estate-owning Americans down from the hills with their house guests. The stout, pink-faced proprietor, Mac, presided over the bar with a beaming smile, a bogus Irish brogue, and a shrewd eye. The eye picked out the tan shirts of Xavier and Melendez as they entered, and he came around the bar to greet them with the excessive hospitality displayed by restaurateurs all over the world when startled by unannounced visits from high police officers. "This is a pleasure, Chief. Haven't seen you for a long time. You, too, Sergeant. Don't see you often enough. You gentlemen must have a drink on the house."

"Thanks, Mac," Xavier said, "but we'd like something to eat—not on the house—and our time is limited."

"I'll have a waiter at the table in a minute. But you've got to have something for the thirst. Now what will you be drinking?"

They told him and he went away. Immediately Melendez, continuing an interrupted conversation, said, "You think that clothing in the drawer at Isabel's house has to be Maubee's?"

"From the size, I'd bet on it. I always figured some of his girls must keep a change of clothes for him and look after his laundry."

"She must really care about him." Melendez thought about that for a moment and allowed himself a smile. "Being a

131

married man with a wife who knows everything I do before I
do it, I only know about Isabel from what they tell me, but a
lot of the men in the town say she must be a Lesbian or
something, because she stands them off. Keeps them away
from her house. Now I see why."

"No Lesbian could make Maubee give her an A-1."

"I guess he's all the man she wanted. Think we ought to
arrest her for harboring him?"

"She could always deny those clothes are his."

"I'd like to see this Maubee," said Melendez. "He gets a
woman like Isabel to keep her bed warm for him only. Not
only that, she hides him out. She takes care of his laundry.
How does he do it?"

"That's what a lot of people wonder. Ted Motley says he
wants to write a book called 'Dave Maubee's Secret, or How
to Make Willing Slaves Out of Your Women.' He says it
would sell a million copies."

A waiter produced rum punches for them and took their
orders for the specialty of the house, curried chicken. They
had scarcely begun their dinner when Melendez said, "Here
she is." A girl had come through a door at the rear of the
room and was walking toward the stage with an elegant and
precise step that reminded Xavier of an antelope. The effect
that she created in the simple black shirt and narrow black
slacks that she wore was of a creature designed for speed,
with eager, wind-swept lines. A red band around her forehead
kept her long black hair from falling over her eyes. If the
guitar that she carried had been a hunting bow, she could
have posed as a dark Diana.

She bowed to the applause of the room, sat down on a
plain wooden chair, and checked the tuning of the guitar. Her
face, tilted slightly to one side, seemed to Xavier to have
more charm than actual beauty. Toinette was better-looking
and so was Inez Dardo, yet he recognized something irresist-
ibly attractive about the wide humorous mouth and glowing
eyes of the girl on the stage. When she looked up and smiled,
everyone became still. She struck a soft chord or two and
said, "This is one of Pete Seeger's songs. It's big in the
States." Her voice was deep and strong, and she played with

authority. When at the song's end the audience clapped lustily, she offered them "an old Trinidad song from way back. It's called 'Nobody Tell Me Nuthin'.' It tells of an old slave's puzzlement at the attitude of his white master." Xavier had heard the song before. The refrain, which never failed to touch him, went:

> ". . . Look like he willin' to let me die—
> Wouldn' mind so much if he tell me why—
> But nobody tell me nuthin'—
> Nobody tell me nuthin'."

"She sings a lot about poor people," Melendez said, "but the rich people who come here like it."

"Maybe it gives them the feeling they are being democratic. Nothing so democratic as poverty."

They watched her pluck a few chords from the guitar as if she were making up her mind what to sing next. Somebody called, "Big Change," and she nodded with a smile that lit up the room. To an erratic tune, with strong staccato, she sang,

> "I'm not just strummin' to amuse—
> I'm a serious woman—listen to my news.
> Got a message from someone who knows what's the score—
> There's a big change a-comin'—
> Big change a-comin'—
> You can hear the drums drummin'—
> People gettin' sore. People gettin' sore!"

After another stanza, she broke off suddenly, saying, "That's enough about social problems, folks. We now move into a more interesting subject, namely, sex." She sang a bawdy calypso, "Drillin' for Oil," that was enjoying a burst of popularity in the islands. The crowd loved it. Xavier applauded, but his mind began to drift back to his own problems. Where was Maubee? Not at her house—then perhaps not in Port Cambo at all? Or already on the freighter? Ought he to have forced his way on board without delay and searched, captain or no captain? As if reading his mind, the girl on the stage announced, "Here's a little thing I wrote myself about a certain man. I hope you like it. I hope he likes it.

"Been hearin' 'bout this man call' Dave Maubee.
They say he never pretend to be honest.
But what could be more honest than that?
He steal a little here and he steal a little there—
Somethin' to eat or somethin' to wear—
An' if anybody's hungry he's willin' to share—
But he never pretend to be honest.
What could be more honest than that?"

As the song went on, she lifted her head occasionally and her eyes looked around the room as if gauging the response of the audience. It seemed to Xavier that they lingered for a moment on the gold star pinned to his shirt and that for the fraction of an instant her voice faltered. She recovered quickly, but not before her glance flickered to the rear of the restaurant, behind Xavier. He turned and saw that the door through which she had come was open and that two men were standing in the doorway, listening. One of them wore the white uniform of a ship's officer; the other, a slender, bearded young fellow, looked familiar. An instant later the reason came to him. The resemblance to Pablo Dardo was unmistakable. This had to be his brother Enrique. With that realization came another. Isabel Cannon in a strident voice was singing lines which he would have sworn were impromptu:

"Here's a message for Dave Maubee—
Go fight for the people and peace.
Just got one bit of advice for you—
Look out for the police!"

The rising last word evoked a roar of laughter. As Xavier pushed back his chair, the two men in the doorway vanished and the door closed behind them. Even if the door was not bolted, he guessed, before he could open it the men in the room behind it would be out of the building through a rear exit, and he did not stop to discuss the point with the startled Melendez. "To the dock! Fast!"

As their eyes adjusted to the darkness outside, they saw against the yellow glow of the dock lamp and the lights of the *Corinto* the silhouettes of three men a hundred yards in front of them running for the freighter, and the man in the middle was huge by comparison with the others. As one of the smaller figures broke away and took off in another direction, Melendez checked his stride. Xavier rapped, "Dardo! Let him go!" and put on a burst of speed. The two men ahead had reached the dock and the white uniform of the ship's officer was plainly visible. Someone shouted, two shots were fired, there was the smack of a blow and the thud of a fall, another shot, and a yell. In the seconds that it took Xavier and Melendez to cover the remaining distance, they saw Ford standing on the ship's railed gangplank, pistol in hand, barring the way to the white uniform, while the dark faces of several members of the crew peered down at them from the freighter's side. Sitting on the dock were Ted Motley, holding his jaw with one hand and rubbing the back of his head with the other, and Maubee, clutching the inside of his thigh with blood streaming over his hands and demanding of Ford, in a deep voice tight with pain, "You crazy, man? What you trying to do, shoot my balls off?"

Xavier said to Motley, "You all right?"

"Not sure where my head is, but I'll live."

"All right, then. Hello, Dave."

"I should have known. If anybody got me, it had to be you, Xave."

"How bad is that wound?"

"Bad enough. Lucky he didn't hit me a couple of inches higher."

"We'll take care of it. Search him for weapons, Ford." He turned and spoke in Spanish. "You are Captain Morino? Tell one of your crew to bring down a bandage for that leg."

The captain, whose face was chiefly distinguished by a

mustache of extraordinary ferocity, was still panting. He said, "Very well," and called an order to one of the faces above. "Now get away from my gangplank. I want to go aboard."

"I advise you to cooperate with me, Captain, if you don't want to be arrested."

"Arrested? For what? I have done nothing wrong." His flow of words gained momentum as his breath returned. "It is your policemen who have shot my passenger and now prevent me from boarding my own ship. I shall report this to the government of Panama and to my own government in Caracas. You will hear more from me."

"Listen carefully, Captain. You were aiding a known criminal to escape. That is a serious offense."

With an air of outrage, Morino waved a hand in the air. "If that man is a criminal, I did not know it. As far as I am concerned, he is just a passenger. He has paid his fare. He is entitled to board this ship."

"Is that why you ran from Mac's Place?"

"We ran because—because the other member of our party remembered he was late for an appointment. An appointment with a lady. Yes, that's it. He was in a hurry so we hurried too." Seeing the expression on Xavier's face, he added hastily, "Also the tide is turning and I wanted to catch it."

Xavier laughed. "Not very good, Captain. I recognized Señor Dardo, and I know what he was doing here."

"Why should he not be here? He sold me a cargo of coffee beans."

"No doubt. And made certain other arrangements, did he not?"

"You have no proof of what you say."

"I could get proof, but the important thing is that we have Maubee. He's the man we want, not you. So I'm not going to hold your ship—not this time. And since the tide is turning, as you say, I advise you to cast off and be on your way." He took a first-aid kit from the crewman who had come down the gangplank and passed it to Melendez. The captain, he noticed, was looking hard at Maubee, and it seemed to him that some enigmatic message had flashed from eye to eye. "Is there anything to prevent you from leaving at once, Captain?"

"Nothing." Morino was all at once calm and courteous. "I am sorry, Señor, that you have misinterpreted my actions. What is between you and that man—that is none of my affair. I will go now." He ascended the gangplank with dignity.

Melendez cut away the upper leg of Maubee's trousers and began to wind a tight bandage around his thigh. "He's bleeding a lot. Flesh wound but the bullet went through at a long angle. Ought to get him to a doctor."

"Don't need a doctor," Maubee growled.

Xavier said, "Remember you're under arrest. If we say doctor, that's it."

"You always liked telling people what to do, Xave. How about my human rights?"

"Don't try to be funny. Ford, what happened?"

"Just obeyed orders, Chief." Ford, holding a sheathed knife he had taken from Maubee's belt, stood at attention. "Mr. Motley and I were in front of the gangplank when they come runnin'. So I fired two warnin' shots in the air like you said. The captain, he stop, but Maubee, he keep movin'. Mr. Motley try to get in his way and got knocked flat. Then he was comin' at me. So I jump back on the gangplank and shot him. Like you said, I aim low at his legs. Reason he got hit so high up, his leg was lifted to climb the plank. Shot knocked him off balance."

"You did the right thing, Ford. Now here are the keys to my car. It's parked in front of Mac's Place. Bring it around. Feeling better, Ted?"

Motley was on his feet, still rubbing his head. "Bump on the head, but no permanent damage. This guy's another Muhammad Ali. With a wallop like that, just the back of his hand as he passed me, we ought to book him into Madison Square Garden."

With a chuckle, Maubee said, "Didn't mean to slam you so hard but I was in a hurry. Xave, you say you're arrestin' me. What for?"

"Suspicion of being accessory to a murder, and about eighty-seven acts of robbery and theft. You're entitled to a

lawyer and I'm supposed to tell you that anything you say
may be used against you in court."

Maubee stared. "Murder! You crazy, man? I never murdered nobody."

"We'll go into that later. Melendez, is there anyone in
attendance at the hospital at this hour?"

"Yes, sir, ought to be a night nurse. We could take him
there and get Dr. Jeffers to come over. Ought to do it pretty
soon. Bandage is tight but his leg is still bleeding a lot."

"Let's go direct to the hospital, then. Can you walk to the
car, Dave?"

"Sure. But I don't get that murder thing at all." He rose
slowly and stood looking at Xavier with a puzzled frown.
"You and me got to talk, man."

Melendez had taken a pair of handcuffs from his pocket
and Maubee made no resistance as they clicked around his
wrists. In the years since they had last met, Xavier thought,
he had changed hardly at all. His broad-nosed, full-mouthed,
strongly structured face, with the gleaming chocolate brown
skin tight around the cheekbones, still had the look of a man
who enjoyed life; one corner of his mouth quirked upward,
as if he were remembering some private joke. But there was
some contradiction between the mouth and his wide-apart
eyes, which were thoughtful and even a little sad. Standing
about six feet four, with powerful shoulders and a narrow
waist, he looked like a sculptor's model or the prizefighter
that Motley saw in him; the bandaged leg from which the
trouser had been removed had the smooth balanced muscles
that mean speed and endurance. Even the blood running
down it seemed redder than other men's. Xavier could
imagine the thrill of anticipation that any woman would feel
at an advance gently made by a man who looked like that.

He was conscious that Maubee was giving him the same
kind of scrutiny, and had to swallow an impulse to say
something that would reestablish the old bond between
them. Instead, he said curtly, "Let's go."

Port Cambo's little one-story hospital had no X-ray ma-
chine, and its sterilizer consisted of a kettle of boiling water
poured into a tin tank, but the self-respect of its staff,

consisting of one doctor and two nurses, was conveyed by the sparkle of such equipment as they had and the spotlessness of their starched professional gowns. The doctor, a very black native Carovian with the confident manner of a man who knew that he could at any time move to the States and multiply the income he was getting in Port Cambo but who nevertheless chose to stay, examined Maubee in one of the hospital's six rooms and dressed the wound efficiently. "Not serious," he told Xavier and Melendez in the corridor outside, "but he's lost a good deal of blood. He ought to stay here overnight."

"I'd feel safer if we had him in jail," Melendez said.

"You do that and the wound starts bleeding again, you would have a problem. Another thing. You'll have to take off those handcuffs so he can turn over and get some sleep and use a bedpan. If you're worried, put a constable in the corridor outside his door."

"What about the window? It's open, with just a jalousie over it."

Dr. Jeffers raised his eyebrows. "We've taken away his clothes and he's wounded. Think he's going to escape in a nightgown? I can give him some pills and put him to sleep."

"Not yet," said Xavier. "I want to talk to him first. Don't look so concerned, Melendez. We can always handcuff him to a bedpost, and we'll keep a guard in the corridor round the clock, with the door to Maubee's room open."

Melendez relaxed. "That ought to do it."

"That's settled, then. I'm glad you brought him here." The doctor took off his white gown. "Finest physical specimen I've ever seen. If it's true he has produced bushbabies all over the island, I say he's a valuable citizen. He's doing a fine thing for the race. Did you see the way the nurse looked at him? And she's no chicken."

"He seems to have that effect on women. Thank you, doctor, for your big help." Xavier beckoned to Motley and Ford. "The sergeant and I are going back into the room to talk to Maubee. You must be hungry. Better go to Mac's Place and get something to eat. Settle my bill at the same time. We left without paying."

Motley said, "Do you think Mac knew Maubee was in the place?"

"Probably, but we can't be sure. My guess is he came to the rear door with Dardo and Morino to say good-bye to the girl before going on board the ship, and she put him and the others in the back room to hear her farewell song to him. Something like that. She's probably in a state, waiting to find out what happened to him. If she or Mac asks you about the shots, say that Maubee is under arrest and has a wound in his leg, not serious. Don't say where he is or what charge we're holding him on. When you get back we'll work out the shifts for guard duty."

Melendez said, "You going to do anything about her tipping him off?"

"We wouldn't look very good in court trying to prove that. No, we won't bother her."

16

"SOME questions to ask you, Dave."

"Got some to ask you, Xave. What's this thing about murder?"

"You telling me you don't know?"

"That's what I'm telling you. Who got murdered?"

"Man named Lattner. Guest at Mango Beach Inn. His cottage was robbed."

The white hospital gown was too small for Maubee's frame, and he pulled at the neck with his free hand. "Why you think it has to do with me?"

"When you find a corpse and his neck has been cut, and the machete that cut it is lying next to the body, and on the machete is a fingerprint, and the fingerprint is identical with one on the card of a man who used to work for the Gracedieu post office, and that man is Dave Maubee, it's reasonable to suppose you had something to do with it."

The incredulity and bewilderment that first registered on Maubee's face might have been faked, but not the rumbling chuckle that followed. "Machete with my fingerprints at Mango Beach!" He laughed again. "The joke is on me."

"Let me in on it. The sergeant and I would like to laugh too."

Earnestly this time, Maubee said, "Xave, there was a show-show up that way in somebody's house. One night I picked it up to show off a little for a woman. Splitting green coconuts. Remember that trick? Later I put the show-show back in that somebody's house. That's about all I can tell you."

"You're going to tell me more than that. You're in big trouble, Dave. Governor Chalk gave me orders to bring you in dead or alive. The man who was killed was a big shot in the States. If you didn't kill him, we need to find out who did and find out fast. There's another thing you got to explain too. Your little black book was on the floor near the corpse."

Maubee chuckled again, but this time on a sardonic note. "So that's where it was. I guess she's out to get me."

"Who you talking about?"

"Hate to tell you. I'm kind of sorry for her."

"You trying to make me think you don't like talking about your women? Don't forget, I've read your little black book."

"That's different. That's just so if there's a baby I'll know it's mine. I never showed it to anybody. Anyway, if you read it, you know who I'm talking about."

"No, I don't. Somebody tore out the last few pages."

A few seconds elapsed before Maubee said, "That figures. Man!" He shook his head ruefully. "She must have gone through my pockets while I was asleep that last night and found the book. Trouble was, I only gave her a B-3. When she saw that, I bet she must have wanted to kill me."

"Looks like that's what she's trying to do. Come on now, Dave. You talking about Carolla?"

Maubee looked amazed. "Carolla! What does she have to do with it?"

"Never mind that now. I know you were at her house the other night, the night of the murder. You brought Davy a drum."

"Hey, man. You know a hell of a lot. But Carolla, I'm not talking about her. She and I, we don't play around together no more." He said this so simply as to compel belief. "I never even saw her the night I visited Davy. She wasn't home."

"Do you know her old gumma, Francie Peters, is a witch? Puts fixes on people?"

Amusement came and went in Maubee's face as he said, "Sure I know. She's been making obeah for years."

"Did you know she was putting a big fix on somebody that night?"

"She didn't say anything about it, and I didn't stay long

enough to look around. Just dropped in, talked a minute with Davy and Francie, and then went back."

"Back where?"

Maubee's luminous eyes looked doubtfully at Melendez. "I want a chance to think. Not going to mention her name now."

A burst of insight, like a tropical sunrise, poured into Xavier's mind. He tore a sheet out of his notebook, wrote a name on it, and passed it to Maubee, who read it with lifted eyebrows. "Hey, man. You don't miss much." He crumpled the sheet and passed it back.

Xavier said, "I heard she's been going out by herself late at night." He turned to Melendez. "You might as well know now as later, Pedro, but keep it to yourself. We're talking about Mrs. Searle, at Mango Beach. Dave, you certainly didn't pay her any visits there, so she must have a hideaway near the inn. Where is it?"

The chain of the handcuff on Maubee's wrist clinked against the metal bedpost as he shrugged his shoulders. "You know her name, you might as well know the rest. It's on the far side of the first little hill north of the inn. You would hardly see the road unless you were looking for it. House looks like any old shack, but fixed up nice inside. Right in the middle of a coconut grove."

"How did you happen to meet her?"

Maubee ran his hand through his kinky, resilient hair, which he wore much in the style of Xavier's, close to his head; and he smiled at the memory. "Happened to be in the neighborhood, three, four weeks back—"

"Casing the inn?"

"You expect me to say I was?"

"No, you don't have to answer that. You just found the house by accident?"

"I was looking for a place to sleep. Saw this track going up the hill and thought I'd see what was up there. The house was dark, looked empty, but it turned out she was there. Alone. In bed. She was scared, tried to pull a gun on me, but we got talking, and after that one thing led to another."

The scene was almost as vivid to Xavier as if he had been

there. The handsome frustrated woman, her blond hair falling around her, sitting up in bed in the dark room, turning on the light, gasping as she saw the big, black man, reaching for a pistol and having it wrenched from her hand, expecting him to try to rape her, only to find that he was soft-spoken, intelligent, and not disposed to use violence on her. Presently she would begin to see him as a human being, magnificent to look at, and discover that he was the famous Dave Maubee. A swift decision to take him as her lover would be entirely in keeping with her nature as he sensed it. "And you only gave her a B-3?"

"That woman, she's too confused to make love like it meant something. Got knots in her mind."

"But you went back for more. Must have gone back several times in the last few weeks for her to rip all those pages out of your black book."

"That's right, I did. You find a woman who looks like that and wants it, you keep thinking you can teach her how to relax and enjoy it. If I had more time with her, maybe I could have. But the last time she made a mistake. Offered me money. That spoiled it. I don't mind taking somebody else's money, but not that way. I told her I wasn't coming back. She was pretty upset. That was the night she must have taken the little black book out of my pants."

"So she had the machete and the little black book. You have any idea how things were between her and this dead man, Lattner?"

"Never even knew there was such a man, alive or dead, until you told me."

"She never mentioned his name to you?"

"Wait a second. She said there was a man at the inn making a big play for her, but she despised him. Could that be the one?"

"Sounds right."

Maubee shook his head. "I don't see her hitting anybody with a machete. But who knows what a woman will do if she's mad enough?"

Turning to Melendez, Xavier said, "Think we ought to believe him, Pedro?"

The sergeant considered. "He has to be a pretty good actor to tell it like that if he is making it up."

"I agree with you. Couple of things puzzle me, though. That hideaway of hers, Dave. How could she be going out that way at night without Searle knowing?"

"I asked her the same thing. He knew, all right. She had the place for months. If she met a man and liked him enough, she would bring him up there, she admitted that, but sometimes she'd go there alone just so she wouldn't have to sleep near Searle. Seems he snores. She told me he didn't object to her sleeping out. He couldn't, I guess. She has the money."

Xavier said, "Any questions you'd like to ask, Pedro?"

"No, Chief. I think you got the story."

"Then see if you can find the nurse, will you?"

As Melendez went out, Maubee looked pensively at Xavier and said, "Answer me a question, Xave. How'd you know where to find me?"

"You told me."

"What you mean by that?"

"Three A-1 girls in your little black book. Thought I'd find you with one of them."

The rumbling chuckle came again. "Guess you know me better than I know myself."

Studying Maubee's alert and formidable features, Xavier wondered why the man had chosen to waste all that magnetism on petty thievery and casual sex. It was not surprising that he had come to feel a need for something worth doing, something to believe in. Big change a-comin', and he wanted to be part of it. "After I talked with Inez Dardo, I got the idea you were going away to find a different way of life."

"She didn't tell you that!"

"No, she didn't tell me. I heard enough, though, so I wasn't surprised to find Enrique Dardo with you and that freighter at the dock. I could even make a guess where you were going, but I don't think I will."

The click of Maubee's tongue was a respectful sound. "Man, you have to be good to get all that out of Inez. I wouldn't want her to come to harm on account of me. She's a great woman. You going to make trouble for her?"

"Not unless she committed some crime. Like helping a known criminal escape. Right now I don't see a case against her."

Maubee let out a breath of relief, but his expression remained anxious. "Does that go for Isabel too?"

"I like the way she sings."

The remark tickled Maubee. "That sounds like the Xave I used to know. Tell you something. I think a lot about you when I'm off by myself."

"I think about you too."

"People tell me you married that beautiful girl with the French name and you got two kids."

"That's right."

"Sounds like a good way to live. But that's not for me. I got to go my own way."

"You're entitled to do that, but I wish it wasn't a way that made me have to arrest you."

"Even though I didn't commit no murder?"

"That's right, Dave. Long record of suspected theft."

Maubee grinned. "Suspected. Anything you can prove?"

"I've got to try."

"Well, that's the way it goes." He held out his free hand, Xavier gripped it, and they looked at each other soberly, without saying anything more.

When Melendez and the nurse returned to the room, she carried a paper cup containing two yellow capsules in one hand and a thermometer in the other. "First I'm going to take your temperature, big man," she told Maubee, thrusting the thermometer between his lips, "and then I've got something to make you sleep."

"No pills, honey," he mumbled out of the corner of his mouth. "I sleep like a baby without 'em."

She was a middle-aged, maternal woman, with a sturdy body and a humorous mouth. Her frown was unconvincing. "You do like I tell you, big man." Catching Xavier's eye, she looked significantly at the door, and he took the hint. "She's in charge, now, Dave," he said. "You better know, there will be a guard outside in the corridor all night. Don't give us any trouble. Leave the door open at all times, please, nurse. Good night."

It was not long before Motley and Ford returned from their dinner, but it was long enough for Ted to have acquired a breath and a glaze in his eyes that told of more time spent at the bar than at the table. Xavier felt too exhilarated to take the lapse seriously. The only task that remained at the hospital was to organize the watch in the corridor. This he proposed initially to divide between Melendez, Ford, and himself, exempting Ted on the ground that the fracas at the dock had made him a casualty. The vehemence of Ted's protest took him aback.

"Bump on my head don't matter a damn. Lemme get a li'l sleep and I'll be good as new. I may be in a slightly spiritual state, but I'm not stoned. I could drink twice what I had and keep guard over a man who was handcuffed to his bed. You telling me I'm not man enough to sit on a chair out here for a couple of hours?"

"Take it easy," Xavier said, laughing. "If you're so sensitive, here's the way we'll arrange it. Melendez, you take the first watch, so you can get home to your wife. Ford will relieve you at midnight, and Ted, you relieve Ford at two. The nurse tells me there's a vacant bed in the hospital you can have until then—and don't argue with me. I'll come in at three or four and stay until the doctor arrives. If he says Maubee is okay, we'll drive him to Gracedieu right after breakfast."

He was aware that his own feelings were strangely mixed. There was a policeman's professional satisfaction in having anticipated Maubee's presence in Port Cambo and his move to leave the island. At the same time his recollection of that final friendly handclasp with Maubee, as he lay there wounded with one wrist chained to a bedpost, gave him a dispiriting sense of the tricks played on men by the passage of time. In the ways that really counted, Maubee had been the best friend he had ever had, and as good a man as he had ever known. No murderer, no rapist, and he had never been accused of using those mighty fists of his to hurt anybody seriously. A thief, but not a crook, not a gangster. What had been accomplished, after all, by arresting him? An amiable island legend had been destroyed and many a woman would weep. Only Governor Chalk would be pleased. It was in a mood of considerable self-doubt that Xavier left the hospital and crossed the street to the police car. One of its seats reclined to make a tolerable place to sleep.

17

HE was asleep in the car when he was awakened by a nearby gunshot, followed immediately by another. Both sounded muffled. Automatically he switched on the inside light of the car, glanced at his watch, saw that it was nearly three o'clock, and came fully awake with the thought that Ted Motley was on duty in the hospital corridor. As he jumped from the car and ran across the street, he heard a woman's scream. Racing down the hospital corridor he saw Ted Motley pushing vainly against the closed door to Maubee's room, while the agitated nurse scurried toward him with another scream half-checked on her lips. Xavier caught Ted by the arm. "The shots! Did they come from inside?"

"He must have had a gun!" Ted cried.

Without another word, Xavier turned and ran back the way he had come. His intention was to circle the building to the window of Maubee's room, but before he reached it he saw he was too late. Ahead of him were two figures running in opposite directions. The night was brilliant with stars and he could plainly see Maubee's white nightgown no more than fifty yards in front of him. The other runner he glimpsed only as a black shadow. The nightgown fluttered to the ground, but the white bandage on Maubee's leg made him a visible target. Sprinting in pursuit, Xavier drew his gun and fired into the air. It was a waste of ammunition. Maubee was heading for the dock, with glints of metal at his side. A pistol? The handcuff, with the chain shattered by two shots? The distance between them shortened, and he had the impression that Maubee, always a fast runner in spite of his size, was limping, but he retained a short lead as he reached the dock and sped to the end. There he dropped something on the dock and unhesitatingly plunged into the sea. Xavier yelled, "Come back, man! Don't make me shoot you!"

A second later he heard Maubee's voice. "You're not going to shoot me, Xave." It was not a taunt, not a plea, but a plain statement of fact. The revolver in Xavier's hand was meaningless, and they both knew it. He glanced at the object that Maubee had dropped and saw, as he expected, that it was a hand gun, no doubt the one that had been brought to him in the hospital. Maubee was swimming powerfully and soundlessly, his direction revealed only by the shimmering movement of the star-studded water. He seemed to be heading for one of the small boats moored in the shallows of the harbor on the far side of the ship channel. Xavier called, "You try take a boat, Dave, I'll shoot it and sink it!" This time there was no reply. At the sound of running steps on the dock Xavier turned and saw Ted Motley.

"My God, Xave, I—"

"Not now!" Xavier had just become aware that perhaps half a mile out in the harbor a black bulk showed motionless against the sky, and it came to him with a shock that this must be the *Corinto*. Instantly, as if to confirm his thought, a searchlight blazed from the side of the ship onto the water. He shouted again. "Don't be a damn fool, Dave! There's shark and 'cuda out there. You'll never make it with that leg!"

Maubee's voice floated across the water. "Don't you worry 'bout me. You take care of yourself, hear me?"

Just to stand there was intolerable. Moored close to the dock was a small boat with a single mast. He had kicked off his shoes and taken off his gunbelt, when he heard a sudden sound of distant splashing, and Maubee cried, "Shark! Shark!" The splashing continued for a few seconds, after which there was a nightmare silence.

"My God!" Ted muttered. Xavier dove off the dock and swam to the boat he had picked out. As he pulled himself over the edge he saw the pair of oars that he had guessed might be there. He hauled himself in, found oarlocks, cast off the mooring line, and began to row toward the spot from which he thought Maubee had called out. There was no sign of him. Blood would not show on the night water. He continued to row, in a widening circle, staring into the night. The impressions of the last few minutes were coalescing in his mind. Who had brought that gun to Maubee? Dardo? But there was something in the lithe grace of that black trousered running figure outside the hospital that made him think of a woman, of Isabel Cannon. She could have spied out his room in the hospital and risked bringing him the gun. Whose gun? Hers or Dardo's—it made no difference. Probably the plan for the ship to wait overnight in the harbor had been prearranged, in the hope that Maubee, if arrested, could find a way to escape.

How could he have been so stupid as not to consider that a first-floor window might be got into as well as out of? A woman psychoanalyst from the States whom he had known in the old days had once told him that a lapse of foresight was often the result of an unconscious wish. Was that why he had left loopholes in his security measures, allowing Ted to stand a watch with too much alcohol in him, shrugging off the danger of the window? Had he in his heart wanted Maubee to escape? In a way, his incompetence had been responsible for what had happened to Maubee.

Listlessly he rowed back to the mooring post, fastened the boat, swam to the dock ladder, and climbed up to rejoin Ted. The only sound as they stood peering out over the harbor was the gentle lapping of the sea below the dock. The searchlight from the motionless ship in the harbor still threw its futile beam on the rippled surface of the sea. Abruptly Ted took Xavier's arm and said, "Come on. Nothing you can do now. Let's go."

Xavier stopped and picked up the pistol Maubee had thrown away. Without, he thought, having used it to hold off pursuit. The gun was a Colt .45 automatic. He stood weighing it in his hand for a moment. Aloud he said in an angry voice, "Guns." On an impulse he hurled the pistol as far as he could into the harbor waters. It made a faint gleaming arc in the starlight before it hit the surface with a small plop. He did not know why he had thrown it—unless as a kind of tribute to Maubee? They walked away slowly.

As they neared the hospital, Ted said, "I know how you must be feeling, but Maubee—"

"I don't want to talk about it." Xavier stopped to pick up the nightgown Maubee had shed. "What's done is done. Except that I'll have to make a report about what happened at the hospital."

He guessed Ted's story before he heard it. "I dozed off, and the first thing I knew I heard the shots. I jumped up, saw the door was closed. It wasn't locked, you can't lock those doors, but it was wedged so tight I couldn't open it. I think they had a chair against it and somebody was pushing back. I tried to bust it open." He rubbed a shoulder ruefully. "On TV it looks easy, but maybe I'm not the type. God, I'm sorry, Xave."

Xavier gave him a wry glance. "Doesn't help. My fault more than yours. I had the responsibility. Whoever climbed in the window and gave Maubee the gun must have wedged the door and held it until he shot through the links of the chain. With a big caliber pistol two shots would have been enough. Well, let's get some rest. Nothing to be done until daylight."

18

MELENDEZ held out the telephone to Xavier and said, "Governor Chalk wants to talk to you." Xavier took it with an expectation of disaster. "Brooke speaking." He wondered what had made Chalk call so early in the morning, and personally.

After a moment the governor came on the line. "What's the word, Brooke? Getting anywhere?"

"Yes, Governor, I found Maubee last night and arrested him, but—"

"You did? That's a pleasant surprise."

"Maybe not so pleasant, Governor. He was arrested while trying to board a ship, wounded in the leg, and taken to the hospital. During the night he escaped and—"

"You mean to say you let him get away?"

"I didn't say that." Xavier had no intention of exposing his lapse to Chalk if he could help it. "Maubee managed to get away by jumping out of a hospital window. I chased him. He ran down to the waterfront, dove into the sea, and started swimming. He hadn't gone far before we heard him yell, 'Sharks! Sharks!' Then there was a lot of splashing and he disappeared. I took a boat and rowed out to make a search, but there was nothing to be seen."

"Sharks! Well, I'm damned. Best thing that could have happened. Saves us the expense and nuisance of a trial." Chalk sounded almost affable. "Now he's out of our hair once and for all. That closes the Lattner case."

"How do you figure that, Governor? We haven't found the girl yet, and we—"

"Oh, yes we have. That's what I called about. She's dead.

Couple of kids near Bamboula found her body lying in a cane
field late yesterday. Dr. Evans says she was killed by some
kind of pressure on her neck. I can't recall the technical term.
I suppose we could say strangled. Makes the whole thing
simple. Maubee must have killed her."

"Why would he do that?"

"Any number of reasons. Keep her quiet so she wouldn't
involve him in the murder. Doesn't matter why. Then he
obviously headed for Port Cambo, and the sharks got him. As
I said, that closes the case."

Anger began to reanimate Xavier. "I have to tell you,
Governor, the case is still wide open."

"What's that? You challenging me on this, Brooke?"

"I'm stating a fact, Governor. With the evidence I've got—"

"Whose evidence?"

"Maubee's. He explained—"

"You take his word for anything? You're pretty confused,
aren't you, Brooke? You yourself pinned Lattner's murder
on the Peters girl and said that Maubee was covering for her.
That made him an accessory—"

"I know I said that, but I was wrong."

"No, I think you were right, for a change. She did it and
Maubee decided to shut her up, that's all."

"Not a chance, Governor. I know enough now to be
reasonably sure neither one of them had anything to do with
Lattner's death, and Maubee had nothing to do with Carolla's."

"Then who did?"

"I've got some points to check, but I think I'll be able to
identify the real murderer in a day or two." Xavier hoped
that he sounded more confident than he felt.

"I've had just about enough of your theories, Brooke. Now
hear this. I want this case settled and out of the way. You be
here this afternoon for a meeting in my office. I've got a full
schedule—better make it five o'clock. We'll review the whole
situation then. I tell you now, you better be able to convince
me. My patience is running short." He broke the connection
with a growl.

As Xavier hung up, he became aware of the anxious

expressions on the faces of Ted, Melendez, and Ford. He said, "The governor just told me that Carolla Peters has been murdered. He also would like my head served up for dinner tonight."

Melendez said, "Would it help if I sent the governor a report? You handled the whole thing, guarding the ship, the arrest, everything, better than anybody else would have."

"Thank you, Pedro." The island grapevine would long since have told Melendez that Marco Ferrer was trying to get Xavier's job, and the fact that he was not letting ethnic ties dictate his loyalties meant much. "But don't stick your neck out until we see what happens to mine." Xavier glanced at the three intent faces, the Puerto Rican, the Carovian, and the American, and was oddly comforted by the thought that these men were his friends. "I've got to get started," he said. "Not much time to do all the things I've got to do. Come on, Ted."

As the car moved onto the narrow coast road to Mango Beach, Xavier switched on his two-way radio and asked Peter Obee to read Dr. Evans' preliminary autopsy report on Carolla's corpse. In spite of Peter's difficulty with the longer words, which he had to spell, the facts came through. The only significant marks on the girl's body were a contusion on the lower maxillary and unmistakable pressure marks over the carotid arteries. Her hands and fingernails showed no signs of having been used in self-defense, blood analysis showed no trace of any narcotic, hypnotic or anesthetic, and the stomach contents indicated that she had not eaten for some six hours prior to her death.

"Thank you, Peter. I expect to be at Mango Beach Inn all day. Is George Michelle there? Well, as soon as he gets in, give him a message for me. I want him to come to Mango Beach in a hurry. Got that?"

As soon as Xavier put up his transmitter, Ted said excitedly, "That bruise on the jaw! Whoever it was must have knocked her out. That's why she didn't put up a fight."

"You got the message. Evans is telling us somebody slugged her and squeezed her neck in the right places. Somebody with powerful hands and scientific knowledge."

"Sounds like a medical man. Dr. Richardson?"

"Not necessarily. Could be anybody who has taken lessons in unarmed combat. Strike or press hard at the right spots and you can produce stupor almost instantaneously and death in a few minutes. It's the karate principle."

"What are the right spots? Might be useful to know sometime."

"I'll show you. There. Feel it? I hardly pressed at all."

"Wow! Yes. I get the idea." Ted shook his head to clear it. "For a man who doesn't like violence, you certainly know how to apply it." He rubbed his neck. "Why aren't more murders committed that way?"

"Maybe they are. Sometimes I think a lot of murders in the States get passed off as natural deaths because nobody noticed the squeeze marks over the carotids. A man who has had commando training and who wants to kill doesn't need any weapon but his hands."

"Was Searle a commando? He doesn't seem the type."

"Wouldn't need to be. These days plenty of others learn the trick. Women too."

"Why don't you ask the FBI for a check on the Searles? Find out whether either of them has a military background or went to karate school."

"Not so easy. My request would have to go through the governor's office, and you can bet that Chalk won't call Washington with questions about a prominent local business-man unless I can show a lot more evidence than I've got now."

Ted was silent for a worried moment. "The meeting this afternoon. You think Chalk is going to make it the show-down?"

"Looks that way from what he said."

"A rotten break. I'm afraid I've messed things up for you, Xave. Me and my dreams of glory."

"Forget it. We both did what we thought was right."

"It was a sorry day when Washington decided to foist Chalk on St. Caro."

"Got to remember a lot of people on the island think he's just fine. Like the Searles. The money people."

Ted squinted thoughtfully at the sunlit sea and said, "You say that like a man with a class prejudice."

Xavier considered the accusation. "Maybe so. It's bad for a policeman to feel that way, I guess, but to tell you the truth, every time I have anything to do with rich people, I find myself preferring the poor."

"Xave, in all the years we've known each other, I don't think I've ever heard you talk about your political beliefs."

Xavier smiled reminiscently. "I've had a lot of trouble finding out what they are. When I was a kid, I was all for independence. We would have a republic of St. Caro. When I grew up I realized that wouldn't help us much. Look at Haiti. Look at the Dominican Republic. And they're a lot bigger than we are. We don't have enough educated and trained people to run a government. We don't have enough natural wealth, and the United States naturally isn't interested in giving us money unless they tell us what to buy with it. So what's our choice? Russia? Well, they helped Cuba make herself independent, more or less. For a time after Castro came in, I went through a Communist phase. But the thing that stuck in my throat was the idea of all that regimentation. The Communist bosses cracking the whip. You take ex-slaves like us Carovians, and personal freedom means an awful lot. We wouldn't want a dictator, black or white, Communist or Fascist, Castro or Trujillo."

Ted laughed. "You sound like a lot of Americans I know. So you decided to put up with colonialism, capitalism, and tourism after all."

"When Governor Roberts was running things, I thought I saw some hope there. But now the government takes the tax money the tourists bring in and uses it to attract more tourists. Chalk tries to run the island as if it was a business that had to earn a profit."

"In a businessman's world, profits have to come first."

"Yes, and look what that point of view has done to a lot of the other islands. If we once started to imitate Nassau or St. Croix, soon we would have gambling casinos, a horse track, a TV station, and night spots featuring strippers and stand-up comedians. The gamblers and gangsters would be all over the

place. They would teach our people to do anything for a
buck. The best land would be owned by American million-
aires. It would be a misdemeanor for a boy to climb a tree
and shake down a few coconuts because all the trees would
be owned by the North American Coconut Export Corporation, or somebody. And in another twenty years there would
be filling stations every five miles, an oil refinery, and air
pollution. Instead of the kids smoking a little marijuana the
way they do now, they would learn to use heroin. And
perhaps express their frustrations in an occasional race riot.
You like that picture?"

"You're exaggerating. But where does that leave you? So
far you have rejected independence, Communism, and the
American way of life. What would you have instead?"

"There was a period when I put my faith in education.
More schools. A bigger share of taxes and American aid had
to go to education so every Carovian kid would have a chance
to graduate from high school. One day I asked myself, what
kind of education? You take the ordinary island child, he's
ignorant, but he's not afraid and he isn't greedy. But you put
him in an American-type school for a while, and he's lucky if
he doesn't come out feeling inferior, like most black kids in
the States. And greedy, too."

"I've never been particularly aware that American education makes kids greedy."

"Easy to see you never attended a St. Caro grammar school.
One big message comes through. The more things you own,
the better you are. Happiness is being as much like a white
American as possible."

"Strikes me you're pretty pessimistic about the whole
outlook."

"No, I don't think so. I think I see some hope in a balance.
I mean a balance between tourism—not enough to swamp us,
but enough to provide a reasonable revenue for the island
and, at the same time, careful development. Guided by people
who really know. Educators who can help us improve our
schools. Agricultural experts who can show us how to
improve our crops. Economists who can help us plan the

right kind of local industries and services. The trouble is, the only chance we have of getting the kind of help we need is if the government is run by competent and honest men who have a genuine desire to do something for the Carovian people."

"You remind me of Benjamin Franklin," Ted said with a grin. "He once said any form of government can be a good government if it is well administered."

"He was a wise man. That's why Chalk worries me so much. He could make any form of government look bad."

"Maybe we can get rid of him."

"Right now it looks like he's going to get rid of me."

"We can't let that happen."

"It will happen, all right, if I don't solve this case in a hurry. Ted, instead of talking about politics, which just gets me hot and bothered without making any real difference, let's talk about the case. Listen. I'm going to tell you what Maubee told me last night." With no interruption other than an occasional long whistle from Ted, he recapitulated Maubee's explanation of the fingerprints on the machete.

"You buy that?" Ted asked.

"Yes. I'll check it out, but if you had heard him, I think you'd accept it too."

"Where does that leave you?"

"It gives us a general picture of the murderer. We've got two murders, Lattner and Carolla, but for the moment let's concentrate on Lattner. We know this much. Whoever killed him had to want him dead, had to be capable of poisoning him, had to have access to manchineel, had to know that the machete was at the hideaway with Maubee's fingerprints on it, had to realize the need for plenty of blood, and had to find Mrs. Dillon's dog. Show me anybody who meets those specifications and I'd say you had the murderer."

"That makes sense. What about Margaret Searle? She knew where the machete was. That seems to me the crucial fact. She also had the little black book."

Xavier shook his head. "Why would she want to kill Lattner?"

"Didn't you tell me that the kid at the inn, Percy, said Lattner was making a play for her?"

"If that was a reason for a woman to commit murder, no man with balls would be safe."

"No, but wait." Ted was warming to his theme, and his eyes shone with enthusiasm behind his spectacles. "Think for a minute about the kind of man Lattner was. Everybody agrees he was a lecher, an aggressive, ruthless man. That shows in the way he treated Carolla. Now suppose he learns something about Margaret Searle that he could use to break down her resistance. Blackmail, not for money, but for sex. Do you think he would have hesitated to use a weapon like that? I don't."

The night before, Xavier, between fitful dozes in the car as he waited for dawn, had carefully considered the possibility of Mrs. Searle's guilt, but he did not want to put out Ted's fire. "So far you're doing fine," he said. "What was this weapon?"

"Try this on for size. Suppose Lattner found out about Margaret and Maubee. Now you're going to ask me how he found out. All right. He followed her one night when she went up to the hideaway, spied on her, and saw Maubee with her. How's that?"

"Not bad. Plausible."

The happiness of creation was working in Ted, and his words tumbled out so fast that they almost ran together. "It's a situation he would enjoy. Humiliating a proud woman. Either she sleeps with him or he'll spread the word about what he saw."

"Why wouldn't she just tell him to go to hell?"

"She wouldn't do that, Xave. You know as well as I do, the white residents on this island are a pretty conventional crowd. Get them gossiping, and they could ruin her social status. Also the inn. She has a lot of money tied up there. Spread it around that she has been sleeping with a black criminal and a lot of these rich stuffy people who own cottages at Mango Beach might decide to sell out and go elsewhere."

"I don't see it." Xavier remembered the impression Margaret Searle had made on him. "A woman like that, I think she would thumb her nose at anyone who disapproved. As far as the tourists are concerned, that wouldn't bother her. Some go, plenty more would come. For a lot of them, a rumor like that would even be an attraction."

Ted scratched his head uneasily. "I don't know about that. She could get hurt. Another thing. Maybe she isn't as rich as we have been led to believe. Maybe the inn isn't making much money after all. Didn't you tell me she's doing the housekeeper's job?"

"That's true."

"There you are." Ted's voice was triumphant. "If that's the way it is, Lattner's threat might have scared her into doing something drastic."

"I'm still not convinced, but go on."

"The way I see it, she was damned if she would sleep with Lattner, so she decided he had to die. Now she had to find a way to kill him. Along come Professor Keys and his wife, and they show her a manchineel tree. You did say she was on that walk with them, didn't you? All right, then. She knows the sap is extremely poisonous. She goes back to the tree alone, taps it, and draws off enough of the sap for her purpose."

Chuckling, Xavier said, "You make tapping a tree sound as easy as tapping a foot."

"Maybe she comes from Vermont, like me, and knows all about tapping maple trees for sugar. Or, if not, maybe the Keys told her how to do it. That's it. They probably explained how the natives drive a spike or something into the tree and let the sap run down into a gourd. In Vermont we use a sapper and a pail. She could have done it. All right, then, she goes back to the tree, collects her manchineel sap, removes the spike."

"Where would she get a spike like that? Wouldn't it have to have a channel in it for the sap to run down?"

"A frivolous question. I ignore it. A mere detail."

"Not so mere. But the tree will tell us. If there's a puncture in the trunk where some kind of tap has been driven in, I'll bow to you."

"You do that. Where is the tree, do you know?"

"I don't, and Mrs. Keys won't tell. I don't want to ask the Searles, because if they are guilty the question would just put them on their guard. But Mrs. Dillon would probably cooperate. We'll talk to her. Might save time if you found the tree and examined it while I check out Maubee's story. And time is something we've got to save if I'm going to be able to stand up to Chalk this afternoon."

"We'll do it your way. But assuming I'm right, Margaret Searle got herself some manchineel juice. At that point she may not yet have figured out a way to get it into Lattner's food or drink. But then she puts it in a bottle and she sees it is green and cloudy. Here I am borrowing from your theory when you thought Carolla committed the murder. The manchineel sap looks like the green coconut water that Lattner has in his refrigerator. Doesn't it? All right, then. Now everything is easy. That night Margaret goes into Lattner's cottage. She switches the bottles, leaves the poison, and takes away the green coconut water. Now the deed is done. She goes back to her own cottage, the one she shares with Searle, and tries to relax after the strain. She sleeps. Later she wakes up in panic. She forgot to wipe her fingerprints off the bottle."

"Very dramatic, but why would she forget a thing like that, a woman as smart as she is?"

"People don't act normally when they commit murders. She just forgot about the prints, and when she finally remembers, it is after midnight. She thinks of going back to Lattner's place, but her courage fails her." Again Ted snapped his fingers in elation. "I see it all. She wakes up her husband, tells him what has happened, and begs him to do something."

"I can't see her doing that, not with Searle."

"Why not? His motive for helping her is even stronger than hers for killing Lattner. If she is arrested, the inn is finished and so is his source of income. So he goes to Lattner's cottage, finds him dead, and takes away the bottle with Margaret's prints."

"So now you have Lattner dead and no clue as to who did it."

"Right. Oh, this is great. I haven't enjoyed myself so much since I first read Sherlock Holmes. Sure you wouldn't like to appoint me as your permanent deputy? No? Then I'll have to give you the result of my lucubrations free of charge. As Searle leaves the cottage, he has a fatal piece of bad luck. He finds himself face to face with Carolla."

"Hold it. That had to be after midnight. The way I figured it, Carolla must have been up there before nine o'clock to sprinkle the house. She wouldn't try to do it when Lattner would normally have been there."

"That's right. Wait a second. God, then the whole damn thing falls down."

"Not necessarily. Let me help you out. Could be that when Carolla was there the first time, sprinkling, she failed to leave the deadies. For some reason. Maybe somebody came along and scared her away. When she goes home and tells her gumma, the old woman gets mad. Without the deadies the obeah would be weak. So she tells Carolla to wait until Lattner is asleep and go back and finish the job. Carolla doesn't like it, but she is afraid of Francie and she finally obeys."

"You've got it! Great! And just when she is about to put down the deadies, the door of the cottage opens and Walter Searle comes out. It has to be that way. When she sees Searle, what does she do? She panics and runs away." Ted scratched his head in an agony of improvisation. "Searle stands there, holding the poison bottle, with Lattner dead inside the cottage. He realizes that if Carolla tells what she has seen, the scandal could destroy him even if he wasn't convicted of the murder. But Carolla has gone. What is he to do? He goes home and tells Margaret what has happened. She sees the way out. The important thing now is to make it appear that Lattner died some other way. And she knows how to do it. In her hideaway is a machete that Maubee has handled and that must have his fingerprints on it. Also she has his little black book. All they need to do is plant these things in Lattner's cottage, cut his neck to simulate a fatal wound, pour some blood on his clothes, and make it seem as if he had been robbed. With their influence, they would be confident of being able to prevent an autopsy. Maubee will be the only suspect. If he is found, he will be charged with murder committed in the course of a robbery."

"You think she would do that to Maubee?"

"Sure she would. Remember, she is full of resentment over that low rating he gave her as a lover and for leaving her."

"That's a lot of revenge for a bruised ego."

"Never underestimate the fury of a woman scorned. Her idea would be to do Maubee in. So she and Searle drive to her hideaway—"

"She admits to her husband that she was Maubee's woman?"

"Why not? Feeling about Searle as I think she does, she might even flaunt her lovers in his face, and he wouldn't do a thing for fear she would walk out on him. Bear in mind what Percy told you—they don't sleep together any more. He has got to help her. So he takes the machete and the book and does as she tells him."

"Man, you are supposing like mad. I will never trust anything I read in your newspaper again. But who am I, after all, to criticize anyone else for supposing? All right, where are we? You have now got Searle cutting Lattner's neck with the machete. Which puts him right up against the blood problem."

"The blood. Yes. That's easy. On their way to the cottage they see Mrs. Dillon's dog. Maybe until then Searle has considered cutting himself to supply the blood. He would not want to raid the inn's chicken coop because he might be seen when the chickens squawked. But once the dog crosses his path he doesn't have to worry."

"The remarkable incident of the dog in the night," chuckled Xavier. "I seem to have heard that phrase somewhere."

"You are mocking me," Ted rebuked him. "I admit, the dog happened along very conveniently, but you had the same coincidence in your theory when you thought Maubee was guilty. I've got the right to use it in my theory, too. I say Searle cut Lattner's neck, killed the little dog, and let the blood spill on Lattner."

"Wouldn't there have been a lot of blood on the floor, too?"

"You've got a point. Wait. Easy. He wraps the dog's body in a towel or something to prevent dripping and leaves the cottage. See anything wrong with that?"

"I have the feeling it's out of character for him. He struck me as a weak personality. To do all that he would have to be a lot tougher and more capable than I think he is."

"Don't forget, he's operating under his wife's orders. She's the capable one."

"Well, let's see. You have Searle leaving the cottage. He must have been carrying quite a load. The dog's body. All Lattner's equipment. Also the glass Lattner drank out of—the one that had the manchineel in it. Unless Searle washed and dried it."

"No, I don't think he would do that. He takes it away with the other stuff. His car is there—they have driven from the hideaway. He would put all that stuff into the trunk and they would drive off to dispose of it someplace where it won't be found. On the way they discuss Carolla. Margaret sees that so long as the girl is alive, she will be a threat. She saw Searle at the cottage with a bottle in his hand. If she talks, the police would be a nuisance. They might call for an autopsy and then the fat would be in the fire. Carolla has to die."

"First they would have to get hold of her."

"Nothing difficult about that. Probably Margaret felt sorry for her when she fired her. Asked her what she was going to do. And Carolla told her she was taking the bus to Bamboula early in the morning. Before the bus comes, Searle is there in his car. Perhaps Margaret is with him—I think she is—she wouldn't trust Searle to handle Carolla alone. They tell her they are driving to Bamboula and offer her a lift. She would accept—why not? As yet she doesn't know Lattner is dead and has no reason to suspect the Searles of any murderous intent. They drive toward Bamboula—turn into a solitary road somewhere. Searle knocks her out and does the carotid artery bit. They hide the body in a cane field and drive back to Mango Beach. Nobody has seen them. They are safe. So they think. They have not reckoned with the dogged determination of Chief Brooke and the brilliance of his special deputy, Theodore Motley."

Xavier eyed Ted with considerable respect. "You are wasted in journalism. You ought to be a novelist. With your imagination you could produce a flock of paperbacks with bloody knives and naked women on the cover and make a fortune."

"Thank you, perhaps. You don't agree that was the way it was?"

"Some of it sounds possible. Some I find hard to believe."

"All right. But I can't think of anything else that fits the facts. Can you?"

"No," said Xavier. "That's the hell of it. I can't."

19

AT Mango Beach, they drove directly to Mrs. Dillon's cottage. Next to her little blue MG was parked an identical model in white. Xavier's polite knock was answered after a few moments by an irritated jerk of the door, which revealed the tall figure and stern face of Dr. Richardson. "Well?" he said gruffly. He was wearing a white sport shirt and gray slacks. "Oh, it's you." There was a stethoscope in his hand. "If you've come to see Mrs. Dillon you picked a bad time. She's not feeling well."

A voice behind him, Mrs. Dillon's, said, "Who is it, Jimmy?"

Over his shoulder Richardson snapped, "That policeman again."

"This will only take a moment," Xavier said in a voice loud enough for her to hear.

"Oh, let him come in, Jimmy," she called. "I like him. He watched me get tight the other day and he couldn't have been nicer."

For an instant Richardson seemed inclined to ignore the request but finally, with an annoyed shrug, he stood aside to let them enter. "You ought to be resting, not talking," he scolded her, and then turning to Xavier, "Make it short."

"Thank you, Mrs. Dillon," Xavier said. She was lying on the sofa, wearing a long, frilly, white peignoir. With her dark glossy hair falling over her shoulders and making a frame for her pretty face, she looked like an eighteen-year-old girl, a testimonial to her plastic surgeon. Only the shadows under her eyes suggested illness. She looked at Ted curiously.

"This is Mr. Motley, my special deputy," said Xavier.

"Hello, Mr. Motley. Wait, I've seen you in Gracedieu, haven't I? Oh, yes, I remember. Someone pointed you out to me in a bar one night. You're the newspaperman. You were really tying one on, but who am I to chide you? And you're working for the police? Does that mean anything I say will be published in your newspaper? Would you like to take my picture?"

Ted grinned. "It would flatter the paper."

"Oh, I like you too," she told him happily. She turned to the scowling doctor. "I think this island has the most gallant policemen I've ever met. What would you think of this pose, Mr. Motley, just as I am? Now Jimmy, don't protest. I'm perfectly well enough to talk to these nice men."

"Sad to say," Xavier intervened, "Mr. Motley is on police business now. Assisting me. If he wants a picture, he will have to come back later, on his own time. We're only bothering you in the hope that you can give us a little information." She looked crestfallen, but before she could speak again, he added rapidly, "My recollection is that you and Dr. Richardson were both on that hike you mentioned, with Professor Keys and Mrs. Keys—about two or three weeks ago, I think you said."

"Why, yes. But what a peculiar thing for you to ask about."

"Why are you interested in that?" Even the simplest question, given Dr. Richardson's authoritative manner, became a demand.

"It's a minor matter," Xavier said, "but I learned that the Keys showed you a manchineel tree. The government is anxious to get rid of the manchineels. They are poisonous, you know."

"You mean to say you're taking time from a murder investigation to fool around with trees?"

"No, doctor, I'm not, but Mr. Motley here has taken on the job of helping us locate manchineels. I just came along to introduce him, and to ask you to help find the tree you saw."

"Pretty damned unlikely story," Richardson said. He cocked his strong-boned head at a skeptical angle. "It's got to have something to do with Lattner. Let's see, you ordered that autopsy after all, didn't you? Did they find manchineel in him? Is that what you're getting at?"

Xavier nodded in good-humored defeat. "My mistake, doctor. No use trying to kid you. Yes, Dr. Evans at Gracedieu Hospital found manchineel in the corpse."

Mrs. Dillon looked puzzled. "But I thought—didn't you tell me, Jimmy, that Carl was killed with a machete?"

"He was. That's what I thought at the time and what I still think." His expression said that he was not accustomed to having his professional judgment questioned. "If he had died of poison, the cut couldn't have produced that much blood."

"I'll have to let you argue that with Dr. Evans," Xavier parried. "Our purpose now is merely to locate and examine the tree."

"How odd," said Mrs. Dillon. "What on earth do you expect to learn from a tree?"

"We want to know whether the trunk shows signs of having been tapped. It's a detail, but it's one we have to check."

"Oh," she said, "I see what you mean. You think someone drew sap from the tree and poisoned Carl? How interesting! Awful for him, of course. Poor Carl—and then having his head almost cut off on top of it." She shuddered but went on with, "Not that I can feel very sorry for him. It would be hypocrisy to say I do."

Richardson said, "Why don't you ask Mrs. Keys to show you the tree? After all, it was she and her husband who showed it to us."

"I don't know where she is at this moment. Her car isn't at her cottage. And when I brought up the subject the other day she refused to tell me where the tree is."

"Then why should we?"

"Why not, doctor? Her reason was a botanist's objection to having any species of tree stamped out, even if poisonous. Surely you don't share that feeling."

"I certainly don't," said Mrs. Dillon. "I thought it was a perfectly disgusting tree, with all those ugly little apples leering at one. But I couldn't possibly tell you how to find it. All I remember is we walked and walked. Up there beyond the golf course somewhere. Do you remember where it is, Jimmy?"

The doctor nodded. The blue-eyed stare he turned on Xavier was condescending, but he suddenly smiled. "You've got me interested in this thing. I don't see how I could be wrong about the cause of Lattner's death, no matter what the autopsy report shows. I was going to play golf this afternoon, but I don't want to stand in the way of your investigation. If you think it's important to find that tree, I'll show you where it is."

"That's kind of you, doctor. It's Mr. Motley who is going to inspect the tree. I'll be busy on other things."

"We'll take the car as far as the golf course," the doctor told Ted. "It's all cross country from there on." He turned to Mrs. Dillon. "Now, Andrea, I want you to rest. And I mean rest. Read. Write letters. But take it easy." His eyes, Xavier thought, were saying, "Lay off the booze." "When I get back," he went on, "I'll order some lunch sent in for you, and I'll look in and see how you feel."

"Thank you, Jimmy." She smiled at him. "But you do fuss so."

As he watched Richardson and Ted drive away, a thought occurred to Xavier. He turned back, knocked again at Mrs. Dillon's door, and met her surprised expression with, "Sorry to disturb you again, but I neglected to ask about your little dog, Pepe. Have you found him?"

She shook her head with a deep sigh. "Poor little Pepe. I'm afraid he's gone forever." Her eyes filled with tears. "I hate to think what may have happened to him, wandering around alone."

"How did he happen to get out of the cottage?"

"I've wondered about that, over and over. I had taken a sleeping pill that night and was terribly foggy. I may have opened the door and let him out to do his business. Ordinarily I left the door open and he came right back. Jimmy—Dr. Richardson—thinks I may have forgotten he was out and closed the door, and fallen asleep, and not heard him barking, and then some creature may have come along and chased him away. Perhaps a mongoose. Walter Searle says there are lots of them around. And Pepe was so small, he'd be helpless if he was attacked. I can't imagine how I could have closed the door if he was out, even if I was doped up, but I suppose I must have." A tear rolled down her cheek and she brushed it away, managing a wan smile. "I love that dog. I don't think there's any human being I've ever loved more. I suppose I oughtn't to say that. It's sweet of you to remember to ask about Pepe."

He smiled at her, touched his helmet, and as the door closed, glanced at his watch. It was half past ten. He was reminded of an old calypso:

"Too much work to do, not much time to do it.
So jus' sit back and pretend you never knew it."

But this was no time for sitting back. There was a murderer to catch and a job to keep.

20

THE point of entry to the track that led uphill to Margaret Searle's hideaway was deceptively narrowed by weeds and low bushes, and Xavier passed it twice before recognizing it as a drivable road. The car bumped its way upward for half a mile before reaching a nearly level hilltop, much of it covered by a tangle of trees and wild shrubbery. When the road abruptly ended, he got out of the car and proceeded on foot. A few minutes' walk brought him to a relatively clear area, where coconut palms drooped their long fronds over a small, one-story house. Gray-green paint that nearly blended with the landscape made it look camouflaged. From the front, it seemed to have no more than one or two small rooms, but as Xavier came closer he saw that an extension with wide windows had recently been added to the rear and trees had been cleared on one side to afford an unobstructed view of the Caribbean.

He chuckled aloud as he saw lying under one of the trees the rotting halves of a green coconut that had been neatly split by a single blow. A little farther on there was another half coconut. He looked around for its mate but could not find it. Why only three halves? The answer came to him in a pictorial flash. A moonlit night, with Maubee and Margaret Searle wandering out of the house, he carrying her machete, promising her some green coconut water for their rum. Big as he was, he had always been a fine tree climber. In boyhood contests with the lighter Xavier he had won as often as he lost. His feet were hardened by years of practice, and his powerful shoulder muscles enabled him to pull himself up at remarkable speed, especially if he had a gripper, the knotted rope used by St. Caro tree-boys to do away with the need for handholds on a slippery trunk. She would have stood staring up at him admiringly as he climbed, knocked down a few greenies, and swiftly descended, all in a minute or two.

Then, the toss of a coconut into the air, the underhand swing of the machete, the two halves flying apart as the water spilled out. Evidently he had repeated the trick for her. His huge body gleaming in the moonlight, the wet machete in his hand, he must have epitomized for her the noble savage for whom, Xavier suspected, most women secretly yearn. Then he would have become the sophisticated man-of-the-island. From another whole green coconut he would slice the top in the conventional way. He would pick up one of the coconut halves from which to scrape the soft white beginnings of the meat in the center. Back in the house he would pour the green water into glasses, blend in the white pulp that added smoothness and flavor, pick up the bottle of rum, and concoct the best of all the island drinks. She would praise him, they would laugh, he would make love to her. That was Maubee's way.

The sun was high overhead, and the place was quiet. It was the time of day when well-fed birds take their siestas. The unmistakable sound of a woman's sob, coming from the house, was as startling as a gunshot would have been. Xavier stood stock-still under the coconut trees. He had seen no other car, but someone, he supposed Margaret Searle, must have walked up the hill. He heard another sob, and her voice distinctly said, "Oh, God!" It was a voice of pain. He thought someone might be hurting her. Quickly and silently he moved through the trees until he could look into a window of the room at the rear of the house, where the jalousies had not been completely lowered. What he saw riveted him to the spot. She was alone, lying naked on a white mattress, bathed in sunlight that poured through an open panel in the ceiling directly overhead. One hand was cupped between her thighs. Her eyes were hidden by dark glasses, but her mouth was contorted with weeping. He could see a tear on her cheek. A woman begging the sun for love, he thought. The policeman in him reprimanded the voyeur and made him move out of eye range toward the front door, but not before he recognized the beauty of her long, slender, firm-breasted body. He took a deep breath and waited awhile for the emotion in him to subside before he knocked.

After some minutes, during which he knocked again, she finally called, "Who is it?" He told her, and she opened the match. He waited for her to speak. After a deep pull and puff, she said in a low voice, "Why are you telling me this?"

"When I questioned him at the hospital he told me that the machete we found in Lattner's cottage came from this house."

After another long drag at the cigarette she cleared her throat and said, "That's ridiculous."

"He also believed that you had his little black book, the one we found next to Lattner's body." He waited for a moment and, when she said nothing, added, "With some pages torn out. The pages with your name on them."

In a bleak voice she repeated, "That's ridiculous."

She was no longer looking at him and he leaned forward to command her eyes. "Mrs. Searle, I know Dave Maubee visited you here and I hope you aren't going to make it necessary for me to prove it in court."

Several seconds passed before she said, "How could you prove it?"

He saw that he would have to shock her into the truth. With some reluctance, not knowing whether he was lying or not, he said, "Maubee was seen here, the night he split the coconuts with the machete."

She gasped. "Who saw him?"

That at least cut the knot of her denial. "The name can wait," he evaded, wishing that he knew it. "I don't want to add to your troubles. All I'm trying to get at is this. When you saw the machete in Lattner's cottage and heard Maubee's fingerprints were on it, you must have known it came from this house."

Her silence was all the corroboration he needed. He kept his voice casual as he said, "Was it you or your husband who took the machete to Lattner's place?"

"My husband!" The word came out on a sardonic note. She

paused before she said seriously, "Why do you ask me that? Do you think we killed Lattner?"

"I don't exclude the possibility. Suppose you tell me this. When did you last see the machete here?"

"I don't see why I should tell you anything at all." Her voice was stronger, as if her confidence was returning. door. She was wearing a long, white, sleeveless wrap-around, belted at the waist. Her blond hair was loose around her shoulders. She held her head high, and he could now see no sign of tears, but her eyes were still covered by dark blue glasses. "What do you want?" she said harshly.

"I'm sorry to intrude, Mrs. Searle," he said, "but I need some information."

"About what? Lattner? I've told you everything I know." She seemed ready to slam the door. "How did you know where I was?"

"It will take a little time to explain," he said quietly. "Where would you prefer to talk?"

Hesitating, studying his face, she suddenly made up her mind. "Come in," she said, and led the way through a small living room and bedroom, both unpretentiously furnished, to the larger sunroom behind. The light coming through the roof was a golden column in the room's prevailing shadows. She sat down in a rattan armchair well out of the sun, crossing her legs and carefully covering them with her gown. When he was seated in another chair a few feet away, she said sharply, "I came up here to be alone. I don't want visitors. I insist on knowing who told you about this place."

"Dave Maubee."

She caught her breath, and he could sense the violence of her stare behind the dark spectacles. "I don't believe you."

"You had better know the facts," he said. "I arrested Maubee last night in Port Cambo. He was shot in the leg, not by me." He tried to choose colorless words that would not trigger a hostile response. "In spite of the wound, he managed to escape. When he was last seen he was swimming toward a ship in Port Cambo harbor. I'm not sure he made it. There are sharks and barracuda in those waters."

She picked up a cigarette and lighted it with an unsteady

match. He waited for her to speak. After a deep pull and puff, she said in a low voice, "Why are you telling me this?"

"When·I questioned him at the hospital he told me that the machete we found in Lattner's cottage came from this house."

After another long drag at the cigarette she cleared her throat and said, "That's ridiculous."

"He also believed that you had his little black book, the one we found next to Lattner's body." He waited for a moment and, when she said nothing, added, "With some pages torn out. The pages with your name on them."

In a bleak voice she repeated, "That's ridiculous."

She was no longer looking at him and he leaned forward to command her eyes. "Mrs. Searle, I know Dave Maubee visited you here and I hope you aren't going to make it necessary for me to prove it in court."

Several seconds passed before she said, "How could you prove it?"

He saw that he would have to shock her into the truth. With some reluctance, not knowing whether he was lying or not, he said, "Maubee was seen here, the night he split the coconuts with the machete."

She gasped. "Who saw him?"

That at least cut the knot of her denial. "The name can wait," he evaded, wishing that he knew it. "I don't want to add to your troubles. All I'm trying to get at is this. When you saw the machete in Lattner's cottage and heard Maubee's fingerprints were on it, you must have known it came from this house."

Her silence was all the corroboration he needed. He kept his voice casual as he said, "Was it you or your husband who took the machete to Lattner's place?"

"My husband!" The word came out on a sardonic note. She paused before she said seriously, "Why do you ask me that? Do you think we killed Lattner?"

"I don't exclude the possibility. Suppose you tell me this. When did you last see the machete here?"

"I don't see why I should tell you anything at all." Her voice was stronger, as if her confidence was returning.

"Perhaps you will answer this question, then. Did you know that Carolla Peters was going to Bamboula?"

The question astonished her. She moved sharply in her chair and he saw one hand tighten momentarily into a fist. "I heard she was murdered. Do you think I was involved in that too?"

"Were you?"

"How absurd can you get? No, Mr. Brooke, I didn't know she was going to Bamboula. When I last saw her she was very angry and in no mood to confide in me. I gave her severance pay, a good deal more than I was obliged to give her. And I told her I would not blacklist her with the other inns."

He said nothing, but she caught his unspoken thought. She looked at him moodily and made another restless movement in her chair. "I don't know why I should defend myself to you. It *was* generous of me. I was sorry for her." She hesitated before adding, in a different voice, "Have you ever felt sorry for anyone, Mr. Brooke?"

He thought of her as he had seen her a few minutes earlier, lying on the mattress, sobbing convulsively, and her woman's radar instantly caught his heightened male awareness of her. Deliberately she uncrossed her legs and leaned forward in her chair, her gown loosening with the movement. She said huskily, "You are an interesting man. I wish I knew you better." The deep cleavage between the sleek curves of her breasts was like a path to heaven or hell. "Dave Maubee said you are the best man in St. Caro."

She waited for him to say something. Rising, he gripped the back of his chair as if it was the impulse toward her he was trying to strangle. It came to him that he would never forgive himself if he did not take this woman, or if he did. The controlling thought in him was Maubee's remark—"Got knots in her mind." A woman too confused and wretched to be rescued by the act of love. As if sensing his inner turmoil, she too rose and removed her glasses. There were shadows of misery under her eyes. In a quick supple movement she unbelted her gown, let it slip to the floor, and stood there, tall, erect, her body like carved ivory in the shadows of the room. She looked at him, breathing deeply, the small pink nipples of her breasts already budding with anticipation.

He forced himself to stand still. In a voice that he did not recognize he said, "God damn it."

She made a small movement of her hand. "For God's sake, don't reject me," she whispered in a panic-stricken voice.

He turned abruptly and charged out of the house before the change of mind that was working in him could sweep him away. The memory of her standing there, all that beauty wasted, haunted him as he compelled himself to his car and drove down the hill. It was not until Margaret Searle said, "Don't reject me" that he realized he had done so. Why? As Toinette's husband? As a policeman reluctant to enter into a sex relationship with a possible suspect? As a male unwilling to be bossed? As a black refusing a white demand? He was not sure. He was a fool, he was wise, he had done the right thing, he had failed in a human responsibility. Dave Maubee, he thought, would have laughed his head off.

21

IT seemed to Xavier that Francie Peters had aged ten years in two days. She sat at the table in her front room with the old deck of cards in her hand, occasionally putting a card down and studying it, but listlessly, without conviction. Her face was gray and rutted with sorrow. Without a headdress or teeth she looked shrunken and unkempt. Thin gray hair struggled loosely over her hollow cheeks. The only sound was the happy little noise made by the baby, playing with his toes on a cot. The older boy, Davy, was not there.

She looked at Xavier with dull eyes. "What you want, mon?" she mumbled. There was none of her accustomed ferocity in the question.

"I am sorry about Carolla," he said simply. "I want you to know that we will get the man who did it." The assurance meant nothing to her. She put down another card and stared at it. "Does Davy know?"

Slowly she nodded. "Me tell him this mornin'. He don' cry. He jus' look and then he walk out. Ain't seen him since."

"He'll be back. Listen, gumma. You're going to need money to take care of the children. I will get it for you from the government."

"Guv'ment," she muttered. There was disbelief and disdain in the word.

"The government will help you," he said quietly. "Do you have any money now?"

Her eyes showed neither cupidity nor hope. She said, "Me got four dollar."

"You will need money for the funeral. Tomorrow I will ask the man in Gracedieu who gives out the welfare money to come here right away and make sure you and the children are all right. He will do it if I tell him."

She turned to look at the baby, said something indistinguishable, and resumed her slow play with the cards. "Listen, gumma," he said. "Would you like to know who killed Carolla?"

For the first time she gave him her full attention. "You know who?"

"Not yet, but I will soon. You can help me find him."

"How me do that?"

"Just by answering one or two questions."

She said disappointedly, "Questions. Me don' wan' no more questions."

"If you tell me what I want to know, maybe I will arrest the man who killed Carolla this afternoon." She said nothing. "I promise you will not get into trouble if you tell me the truth. I will not say anything to the government about obeah or the big fix you put on Lattner." Still she was silent. "Look into my eyes, gumma, and say if I speak from the heart."

She raised her head and stared at him hard. Presently she nodded. "You speak from the heart, mon."

"All right. Tell me this. The night you put the fix on Lattner somebody had to sprinkle the cottage. You sent Carolla, didn't you? What time was that?"

She looked so long at the cards on the table that for a while he feared she would not answer him, but she said at last, "Maybe eight o'clock. Maybe nine. Me not sure."

"The bottle she had the juice in. It was an empty soda bottle, wasn't it? A pint bottle?"

Surprise gave animation to her face. "Who tol' you that?"

"I saw one like it in your obeah pot. I suppose Carolla brought the bottles from the inn."

She misunderstood. "She bring me a little soda to drink, that all. Good for my kidneys. You goin' hold that against her?"

"No, gumma. I'm just trying to figure out what happened. Then Carolla went out again. What time was that?"

"Late. Real late."

"She went back to the inn. Why, gumma?" When she said

nothing, he answered for her. "She went to leave the deadies."

Startled again, she said, "How you know that?"

"I guessed. You told her she had to leave the deadies for the fix to work. She was afraid to go back. You and she argued. And after a long time, she went. Am I right?"

"You not such a big fool, mon."

"Thank you, gumma. What time did she come back home?"

The old woman's eyes suddenly filled with tears. "She no come back." Her voice began to break. "She never come back no more. She go to Bamboula and die." Moaning, she moved her head from side to side. "If I die too, what goin' happen to Davy and Napoleon?"

He offered the only consolation he could. "You won't die for a long time, gumma, but when your time comes, I'll see that the kids are looked after. Dave Maubee used to be my friend."

The name had enough meaning for her so that she looked up at him.

"One more question, gumma. Is there any chance that Carolla came back here from the inn after you were asleep and left in the morning to catch the bus to Bamboula before you were awake?"

She shook her head. "Me no sleep that night, mon. Me wait and wait for her to come." She sagged, put her face in her hands, and wailed. "Never see her again."

He stood watching her until she regained control of herself. He thought he was beginning to see a glimmer of light in the dark fog of his uncertainty. If he could find out who it was that Carolla had encountered on her second visit to Lattner's cottage that night, he would know the identity of her murderer and have the solution of the case in his hands.

22

SEARLE was in his office abutting the inn's reception desk—an office so emphatically cheerful in its splashes of bright Caribbean color that it made Xavier all the more aware of the despondency of the man who sat in the green leather chair behind the white-topped desk. Searle looked almost as green as the chair. He made no secret of his agitation. "You've really done your best to hurt the inn, haven't you, Brooke? I tell you frankly, I've complained to Governor Chalk about it. Just as I feared, the Lattner family is raising hell about that autopsy."

"I don't see what they can do about it."

"Don't you! One thing they can do is insist I buy back Lattner's stock. Another thing, they're threatening to sue the inn for criminal negligence, on the ground that the poison in Lattner's stomach was administered by an employee, Carolla Peters. That was what you told Chalk, wasn't it?"

"Yes, but I was wrong about that. Carolla didn't do it. They won't sue you."

"You've been wrong about everything, it seems to me. Why did you insist on that damned autopsy? It was a clear-cut case up to then."

"There's such a thing as getting at the truth."

"The truth! Who knows what really happened? You don't. I don't. It could have been Maubee. The way things stand, my guests are upset. Two more families checked out this morning. One of them hinted they want to sell their stock. And here you are, parking your car outside my office to remind everybody that the murderer hasn't been found. Why couldn't you leave well enough alone?"

Xavier regarded the man with mingled irritation and sympathy. A vivid recollection of Margaret Searle as he had seen her a little while before, whispering her woman's need, flickered across his mind. In his own way, Searle was suffering as much as his wife, and probably for the same fundamental reason, a twisted response to sex, an empty marriage. "I have just a few questions, Mr. Searle. First, did you know the machete found in Lattner's cottage belonged to your wife and came from her house on the hill?"

The shock in Searle's eyes might have been due either to the revelation that the machete was his wife's or to Xavier's awareness of the fact. He said angrily, "I don't have to answer that!"

Xavier eyed him steadily. The man was almost sure to have been at his wife's hideaway while she was building the extension and bringing in furniture, and in so small a house a decorative item as big as the show-show was not likely to have escaped his notice. Had he helped her plant it next to Lattner's corpse? In that case, his performance as the self-pitying innkeeper suggested hidden depths of cunning.

In the long, frowning pause Searle's momentary aggressiveness faded. He said nervously, "I have no idea how the machete got into Lattner's cottage. Neither does Margaret."

Xavier nodded, as if he accepted the denial. "Then let's take up another point. I'd like a little information about your own background. I mean in the States, before you took up residence in St. Caro. I could get it, of course, by asking the FBI to make inquiries, but I think you would prefer to tell me yourself."

"What do you want to know? I've got nothing to conceal."

"Did you ever serve in the Army?"

"That's a peculiar thing for you to ask. If it's any concern of yours, the answer is yes. In the Korean War. I was too young for World War II, but I'd had ROTC training at college, and they gave me a commission in the Quartermaster Corps. I was in Seoul for a while and in Japan for over a year. Why?"

"Did you study unarmed combat?"

The mystification in Searle's face was almost too convincing. "Yes, sure. Practically every American officer in Japan got some. of that. It was the thing to do. Judo, karate, and all that. I wasn't very good at it but I went through the basic course. Why?"

Xavier ignored the question. "And Mrs. Searle. Did she ever study unarmed combat, the way a lot of women do nowadays?"

"No, I don't think so. What put that into your head?"

"Can you tell me something about her background?"

Searle hunched his shoulders. "What is there to tell? She led a very conventional life. Right after she graduated from college she got married, not to me, to somebody else. Lived in a mainline suburb of Philadelphia. After her divorce, she came down here, where we met. What are you getting at?"

"Just filling in some details. The only other thing I need to know is whether you have such a thing as a master key to the inn's fleet of cars. The ones I've seen are all MG's."

Searle's eyebrows rose halfway up his forehead and some of his normal tone of complaint returned to his voice. "I hope you know what you're doing, Brooke, because I'm damned if I do. Yes, I have a master key. Couldn't get along without it, the way the guests keep losing theirs or carrying them away."

"Does the same key open the trunks of the cars?"

"Why, yes."

"I'd like to borrow it."

"I don't understand."

"You don't have to. If you will let me have the key for a few hours, it will make it unnecessary for me to ask for a court order. I'm pressed for time."

"I'm not resisting you. Certainly you can borrow the key if you want to." Searle reached into a desk drawer, took out a car key bearing an identifying tag, and passed it to Xavier. "It's just that your methods don't seem to make any sense."

"We'll be able to judge that better in a few hours." Xavier rose and looked out of a window. "I believe your own cottage is that big one nearest this building? That's your car outside it, the red one? You won't mind if I examine it, I hope."

"Go ahead. What are you looking for?"

"Evidence. I will also want to inspect the car Mr. Lattner used. Where is it now?"

"In the garage. A yellow car. I haven't yet assigned it to anyone. The way the guests are leaving," he added bitterly, "I won't have to."

"Just one more question. Have you any idea where I can find Mrs. Keys?"

"I believe she drove into Gracedieu. She's leaving tomorrow morning. Do you have to bother her? She complained you came to her cottage the other night and were very rude."

"Murder is a rude business."

"You're just driving our guests away."

"It will be over soon. Thank you for your cooperation. If you don't mind, I'll stop at the bar a little later and have a drink and a sandwich. I'll pay the check this time."

"You don't have to do that. Just tell the boy—"

"Thank you, but I'll pay."

"Does that mean you won't accept my hospitality because you suspect me?"

"Let's just say I don't want to be a freeloader."

On leaving the office, Xavier walked directly to Searle's little red MG, where he first scrutinized the leather upholstery of the divided front seat and then opened the trunk. Searle, he noticed, was standing in the doorway of the inn, watching him. There was nothing in the trunk except a spare tire and a tool kit, but he spent some minutes inspecting the rubber mat, scraping at a spot or two. While he was bent over, he heard footsteps and raised his head to see Margaret Searle entering the cottage, dressed in a sport shirt and white slacks that emphasized her athletic carriage and trim hips. She did not glance at him or speak. When he closed the lid of the trunk, Searle had gone back into his office.

23

THE drinking room of the Mango Beach Inn was a spectacular achievement in tropical decor, featuring a huge circular bar made of light native woods, huge bamboo armchairs, and large, low wooden tables exotically inlaid. The place was almost empty at that hour, and only one barman was in attendance, a well-spoken youngster from Gracedieu. He greeted Xavier with respect and opened a bottle of St. Caro beer, which was inferior to Mexican beer but potable.

"Ray," said Xavier, "I want to talk to Percy. The page. Do you know where he is?"

"Ought to be helping set the tables in the luncheon room about now. Or maybe trying to lay one of the maids. You never know with that kid. A young devil. Want me to send for him?"

"Please. Tell someone in the kitchen to find him and have him bring me a sandwich. Make it beef."

He drank his beer slowly until Percy arrived, carrying a tray, his eyes wide with excitement. "Everybody say you shot Maubee dead, Chief," he said with a broad grin.

"Everybody is wrong, Percy."

"He dead, they say you did it cause he kill Lattner."

"I didn't shoot him. He jumped in the sea and it looks like the sharks got him."

"Sharks! That a bad way to go." In this epitaph Percy conveyed the fading of his interest in Maubee. No dead hero is as interesting to youth as the man who conquered him.

"Put the tray down there." Xavier motioned to a distant table and, as they crossed the room, said, "Would you like to be a policeman someday, Percy?"

"Yes, sir!"

"One of the first things a policeman has to learn is to keep his mouth shut. Never show off how much he knows. Think you can keep a secret? Not go blabbing it to the maids?"

"Yes, sir. Me can do that."

"Good. Then I'll let you in on something. Maubee didn't kill Lattner."

The boy looked incredulous. "But me saw his fingerprint on the show-show."

"He handled it some time before the murder, but somebody else did the killing."

"Who?"

"I'm not sure yet. Mr. Searle make any trouble for you after you talked to me, Percy?"

"No, sir. Not much. He wan' know what we talk about. Me tell him, you ask about Lattner but me jus' keep sayin' don' know, don' know. He say he don' wan' me talkin' 'bout the guests, and me say, yes sir, won' never do that. Who we talk about now, Chief?"

"Mrs. Dillon."

"Yes, sir!" Percy's face lighted up at the prospect.

"When she was here last year, did she have a man?"

"Yes, sir! Everybody know that. Dr. Richardson her man las' year an' year before that. They say he her man back in California."

"Who says that?"

"Maid who had his cottage last year, she read a letter. She say he got wife in California an' she make trouble, so this where the doc and Mrs. Dillon team up. He in her bed all the time las' year. The maids say when he come this year he think she his woman, but Lattner got to her first. The maids, they laugh their head off. All the time she layin' Lattner, she don' give nothin' to the doc. They say he had a big picture of her in his cottage and he tore it up. They found the pieces in his trash basket. But he don' go way. He stay. He mus' be glad Lattner dead, because now he gettin' it again from Mrs. Dillon, an' he got a new picture of her in his bedroom. You think he kill Lattner?"

"I'm trying to find out. You can help me. Would you like that?"

"Yes, sir!"

"You remember the morning Lattner was found dead, Mr. Searle sent you to the golf course to fetch Dr. Richardson. Do you happen to know what his score was that morning, good or bad?"

"Me don't know that, but I bet Sam Greer do."

"Who is Sam Greer?"

"He caddy for the doc, regular."

"You and Sam friends?"

"Pretty good friends. Me and him shoot craps sometimes."

"Do you know how he feels about Dr. Richardson?"

"Okay, I guess. He say the doc tip mean when he play bad but tip good when his score is low."

"I want you to walk to the golf course with me, Percy. Something I want you to do. I'll tell you when we get there."

The clubhouse of the golf course was a five-minute walk from the inn. Percy strained to keep up with Xavier's long legs, looking up at him with manifest pride.

"Is that the doctor's car? Good. Now Percy, see if you can find Sam Greer. If he's in the clubhouse, bring him to me."

The undulating sweep of the well-kept green course against the distant sea had the excessively pretty, slightly unreal quality that Xavier associated with everything at Mango Beach. Here and there correctly dressed players dotted the fairways, followed by small black caddies carrying big golf bags. In the distance someone called "Fore," and there was the smack of a club hitting a ball.

Xavier opened the trunk of the little white car and was peering into it, when Percy returned to report that Sam was out on the course, caddying. "Me think that him way over there, about the sixth hole."

"All right. Now I want you to help me in a little detective work."

"Yes, sir!"

"I haven't time to wait until Sam comes back. Go out there and talk to him. Ask him about the other morning, whether he remembers the doctor's score. Tell him you are asking for me. Tell him I'm up here looking into the trunk of the doctor's car."

Astonishment competed with eagerness in Percy's face. "You want him know that? He tell the doc, for sure."

"That's what I want him to do. Now move."

He watched the boy run across the links, keeping off the fairways, until in the distance he came together with another tiny figure. Percy pointed at the clubhouse, and they stood talking until Sam broke off to watch where a drive landed. As he began to run toward the ball, he seemed to call something back over his shoulder. Whatever it was satisfied Percy, who turned and trotted steadily back to Xavier. As he came close, he panted, "He play real bad that morning. Eleven holes, had a fifty-six. He only tip Sam a dollar. Sam, he pretty sore about that."

"You told him what I was doing?"

"Yes, sir. Like me was doin' him a favor. Tol' him he could get an extra buck from Doc Richardson if he tells him you lookin' at the car."

"After the season is over, Percy, come to see me, and we will talk about the things you will have to learn in order to get on the police force when you grow up."

"Yes, sir!"

24

AS Dr. Richardson's car swung off the inn's driveway toward his cottage, Xavier and George Michelle stepped forward from the terrace where they had been waiting. The impression that they had been inside the cottage brought a flush to the doctor's face and a blaze to his eyes as he stepped out of the car. "God damn it, have you been in there?" He tried the door of the cottage and found it locked.

"No, doctor, we have been waiting for Mr. Motley."

"I think you're lying. Did Searle give you a key?"

"No, doctor," Xavier said quietly, "I tell you again, I have not been inside your cottage. Something seems to have upset you."

"You're damned right something has upset me. You've been snooping around my car, and don't try to lie your way out of that."

"Just a minute, doctor. You'll have your chance. I want to hear what Mr. Motley has to say. Ted, did you find anything?"

The doctor held his fire impatiently while Ted replied. "Negative. Not a sign. I went over the trunk inch by inch. No incision of any kind that could have been made by a sapper."

Xavier nodded. "All right. Then at least we know where the manchineel didn't come from."

Unable to contain himself any longer, Richardson broke in. "Damn it, Brooke, I want an explanation and I want it now."

"I'll be glad to explain, doctor, but first I want to give some instructions to Deputy Michelle. Got those envelopes safe?" George patted a pocket. "Rush them to Dr. Evans. Tell him

190

I'm asking him to drop everything else. As soon as you have his report bring it to me at Governor Chalk's office." With a formal salute, George turned in military style and marched off to his motorcycle. "Now, doctor, what's on your mind?"

"The hell with you," Richardson said. "It's a waste of time to discuss anything with you. I should have known better than to cooperate with a—" He left the word dangling. "I'll have a word to say to Governor Chalk about this."

George's motorcycle roared into motion, and Xavier smiled. "A number of people are planning to complain to the governor about me, doctor. There will be a meeting at his office at five o'clock. I'm going to Mr. Searle's office right now to phone him, so he will know where we stand and who will be there. Why not wait with what you have to say until then?"

"I may just do that, Brooke. You'll be sorry you ever tangled with me." The doctor unlocked the cottage door, went in, and slammed it behind him.

"Come along, Ted, while I phone the governor."

"Putting your head in the lion's mouth, aren't you?"

"I figure if I confuse the lion he may not bite."

Searle looked up from his desk with an unwelcoming expression. "Now what?" But he raised no objection to the use of his phone and even rose from his chair as if to step out of the office.

Xavier stopped him. "Don't disturb yourself. Nothing secret about this call, and I think you will want to know what the governor says." The usual difficulties with the exchange out of the way, he said into the telephone, "Governor, I'm calling from Mr. Searle's office with his permission. He is here with me and so is Ted Motley—"

"I've been meaning to talk to you about that. What's the idea of deputizing Motley?"

Xavier preserved a smiling voice. "Yes, he has been very helpful. I have just sent Deputy Michelle into Gracedieu with two pieces of evidence which he will bring to Dr. Evans for testing. Some scrapings that may be blood and a human hair. Both came out of one of the cars here at the inn and I think will prove decisive."

"That's your business. I've told you before, I'm interested in results, not details."

"Yes, I agree we ought not to reveal which car until we receive Dr. Evans's confirmation. But if the scrapings test out positive and the hair is Carolla Peters', that will be all we need. I expect to have Dr. Evans' report in time for our meeting later this afternoon."

"I don't follow you, Brooke."

"Right, Governor. I think we will have the solution of the case in our hands, with all the evidence needed for a conviction of murder. Just one thing I'd like you to do if you will. It would be helpful if all the people concerned joined us at your office. That way we can put the evidence together quickly."

"I can't see the point of it."

"As you say, considering how it would look if they refuse to come, I think they'll put everything else aside in order to be there. The persons I have in mind are Mr. and Mrs. Searle, Mrs. Dillon, Mrs. Keys, and Dr. Richardson."

"I hope you know what you're doing, Brooke, messing with people of their standing. Let me tell you, you could get into even worse trouble than you're in already."

"I understand, Governor." Xavier cradled the phone and said to Searle, "The meeting will be at five o'clock. I hope you and Mrs. Searle will accept the governor's invitation to be present."

Searle's eyebrows rose while his lips protruded, combining an effect of mingled curiosity and exasperation. "Well, I don't know. I've got a lot to do here, and we've asked some people in for drinks."

"You may find that the meeting is important to the inn. Thank you for letting me use your phone."

On the way out, Ted Motley muttered, "Think they'll all come?"

"I'd be surprised if they didn't. The murderer won't be able to resist finding out what we have got on him. The innocent will be worried about what I might say about them if they're not there. They'll come."

"You mean you know who the murderer is? Who?"

"We'll all know before the meeting is over, I hope."

"Gambling a little, aren't you?"

"Maybe, but what have I got to lose? Ted, I see Barbara Keys' car outside her cottage. I want to talk to her. While I do that, I wish you would knock at Mrs. Dillon's door and extend Chalk's invitation. If she says she isn't feeling well or something like that, tell her we hope to clear up the Lattner case at the meeting and that the other people from the inn will be there. Say you feel sure the governor would appreciate her coming."

"In other words, don't take no for an answer. I'm on my way."

When Barbara Keys opened her door to Xavier's knock, he saw a disarray of opened suitcases behind her. "I've no time to talk to you now." She was immaculate in an ice-blue linen dress that matched her tone.

"When do you intend to leave?"

"Tomorrow morning."

He held up a hand to prevent her from closing the door. "I'm afraid you will have to postpone your departure until you have answered a few questions."

The rasp of his voice surprised her, and she hesitated before saying, "Don't be ridiculous. I'll leave when I choose."

"If you take that attitude, I shall get an order from the court that will keep you here."

Behind the ivory-framed spectacles her gray eyes flashed warning signals. He thought she was going to slam the door, but after a difficult moment she said, "Talk here, then. You're not coming in. What do you want to know?"

"The night of Lattner's death, when you went to his cottage. Did you see anyone nearby?"

"I told you I didn't go to the cottage."

"You started to. I think you saw someone. Who?"

"No one."

"Then why didn't you knock at Lattner's door, as you intended?"

"I told you. I changed my mind. I was tired and decided to go to bed."

"Mrs. Keys, I can understand your desire to avoid being

involved in a murder trial. But if you withhold vital information you will be stopped at the airport if you try to leave the
island."

The hauteur and confidence in her face he thought were
assumed, but she said, "Who do you think you are? If you
interfere with me, I'll appeal to Governor Chalk. I've dis-
cussed my leaving with Mr. Searle, and he told me where
you stand with the governor."

He acknowledged the thrust with a grim smile. "Even
governors have been known to put the law above their wish
to oblige a lady. Whether you like it or not, you are involved.
I advise you to cooperate with the police—unless, of course,
you murdered Lattner yourself."

She drew in her breath sharply. "Are you accusing me?"

"The facts don't exonerate you. We know now that Dr.
Lattner was poisoned by manchineel. You had access to
manchineel. I'm informed on good authority that you and he
had a relationship that could conceivably have threatened
your marriage." He ignored the anger in her face. "If he was
putting pressure on you, that might have given you a motive.
Someone visited his cottage late that night and tried to
conceal the poisoning by cutting his neck with a machete.
You were nearby around that time. I am not accusing you.
But we have good reason to hold you as a material witness. I
am only asking you for information that you should be
perfectly willing to give, both as a friend of Lattner's and as a
citizen."

She had collected herself, and his hope of shaking her was
dashed by her ironic smile. "You know perfectly well I didn't
kill Lattner and I don't believe you can stop me from
leaving."

He inclined his head a fraction of an inch. "We'll see. I am
instructed to tell you that there will be a meeting in the
governor's office at five o'clock this afternoon to discuss the
case. I have his authority to request you to attend. If you
expect to leave tomorrow, that will be your best chance
to get him to intervene on your behalf. Others from the inn
will be there, and we expect to clear up the case at that
time."

She looked surprised, but all she said was, "I'll think about it."

As she closed the door sharply, he glanced at his watch for the tenth time that afternoon. What he wanted now was time to think.

25

"I haven't come here," said Barbara Keys, "because I have anything to contribute to your investigation, Governor. I came because I want to make a complaint." She gave Xavier a disdainful glance that warned him she had pulled the pin of a verbal grenade. "The attitude of your chief of police, Mr. Brooke here, has been highly distasteful to me and I think to other guests at the inn. More than distasteful." The governor glanced at Xavier suspiciously. "Twice," she went on, "he has chosen the most inconvenient times, invaded my privacy, to ask me a great many irrelevant questions in a manner I can only describe as insolent. When I told him I plan to leave St. Caro tomorrow morning, he threatened to have me stopped at the airport."

From the moment she had sat down it was plain that her highbred style and cultivated voice attracted Chalk. It was an effort for him to keep his eyes from the smooth gleaming display of bare, tanned, classically shaped leg below and above her crossed knees. Perhaps the sailor in him was also stirred. She had changed into a blue tropical suit with white trimming and gold buttons. "Welcome aboard, Mrs. Keys," he had said to her warmly when she entered the office with the Searles. The three of them were sitting directly in front of the big gubernatorial desk. To Chalk's left were Andrea Dillon and Dr. Richardson, he with his usual stern expression, she smiling faintly, as at some private joke. The wild and swirling colors of her miniskirted Pucci print demanded attention, and she was getting it from Marco Ferrer, who was sitting next to Xavier and Ted on Chalk's right. When Marco was introduced to her he said, "You are Andrea Morse? The famous actress?" Her reply, "And you must be the Moshe Dayan," made everyone laugh. Marco was wearing a black patch over one eye that might have given him a dashing air if he had not seemed strangely subdued. The corners of his mouth were turned down, and several times he nervously patted the top of his head, although his glossy black hair did not need smoothing.

The fact that Chalk had brought Marco into the group added to Xavier's feeling that he was under siege. He saw unconcealed hostility in Marco's good eye when it turned toward him. Replying to Barbara Keys, he said, "Governor, I don't know what Mrs. Keys considers insolent, but whatever it is, surely it can wait. We have come here to identify a murderer. Once that is done, I'll be glad to hear anything she has to say."

Barbara Keys and Dr. Richardson both began to speak at once. He deferred to her with an outflung palm, but she said, "No, go ahead, doctor." He had an empty pipe in his hand and he pointed the stem at Xavier, but addressed Chalk.

"I've had enough experience in my life, Governor, to know that the first essential in a murder case is competent police work. That's what I'm questioning here. Mrs. Keys doesn't like Brooke's attitude, and she is quite right. But it's not his attitude that bothers me so much as his methods. I've watched him. This was a clear-cut case from the start, no problems at all, and somehow he has managed to make a mystery out of it. I don't know his reasons, but I've heard he is an old friend of that rascal Maubee, and I can't help asking myself if that isn't why he keeps looking elsewhere for Lattner's murderer. I'm familiar with problems of medical jurisprudence, Governor, and I can smell a cooked-up police theory a mile away."

Xavier said softly, "That's a broad statement, doctor. Suppose you tell us specifically why you are so worried?"

"There you are!" Richardson exploded. "Worried, he says. That's precisely the kind of thing I mean, Governor. He keeps hinting that he suspects one of *us*—but does he produce evidence of any kind? No. He is simply trying to muddy the waters. My question is, who is he protecting?"

In a voice that was colorless but scalding, like hot water, Margaret Searle said, "Dr. Richardson is absolutely right. I couldn't agree more." She did not look at Xavier. "Brooke is protecting Maubee, of course. I believe he would say anything, invent anything, so as not to have to arrest him." Xavier resisted a temptation to smile. She was setting up her defense against any possible revelation that he might make. In a close-fitting blue and white seersucker dress and dark glasses, she gave her customary impression of having just stepped out of the advertising pages of a travel magazine. Who would ever believe that a woman like that a few hours earlier could have stood naked in front of a black stranger and offered herself to him?

Chalk said, "I guess you people haven't heard. Maubee is dead. Sharks got him while he was trying to escape by swimming across the harbor at Port Cambo last night." He stopped short and a frown creased his forehead. "At least, that's Brooke's report."

"And you believe it?" Mrs. Searle asked.

"Well," said Chalk dubiously, "I understand there was another witness. Ted Motley."

Searle stirred restlessly in his chair and said, "That's another thing. We all know Motley is a pal of Brooke's."

Their stares at Ted practically accused him of being a traitor to his race. He was in fact present only over Chalk's objection. "Damn it all," the governor had said, "there's no reason to have a newspaperman in on this." Xavier's reply, "At this moment he is a special deputy, and far more necessary to our discussion than Marco," had caused Chalk to subside, but he had not forgiven. He said to Searle, "That's true. I don't know how far Motley would go to back Brooke up."

Ted grinned. "Pretty far, Governor, but I'm stating the plain truth when I say I saw Maubee go under yelling 'Shark!' "

Xavier glanced around him. The only friendly eyes in the room were Andrea Dillon's, and they were slightly glassy, as if she had come to the meeting well fortified with her favorite daiquiris. With a slight slurring of her speech, she said, "Why are you all picking on poor Mr. Brooke? I think he and Mr. Motley have both been perfectly charming." At a reproving shake of Richardson's head she smiled at him innocently.

The moment struck Xavier as too decisive to let pass. "Governor," he said, "if the personal criticisms are now out of the way, can we get down to business? In a few minutes I expect Deputy Michelle to arrive with a report from Dr. Evans. I believe it will tell us what we want to know. Until he gets here, with your permission I will review the main points of the case, so there will be no doubt where we stand."

Before Chalk could reply, Richardson rose and said, "I only came here as a courtesy to you, Governor, to let you know how I feel about the way this case has been handled. I don't think I'm under any obligation to listen to any more of Brooke's theories, and anyway I've promised to meet some friends who are leaving for the States"—he looked at his watch—"and I'm a little late already. You can always reach me at the inn if you want to talk to me." Turning to Mrs. Dillon, he said, "I'm sure Walter and Margaret will be glad to give you a lift back to the inn, Andrea. I'll see you there for dinner. Will you be ready by eight?" He looked hard into her eyes. She evidently caught the unspoken question, whether she would still be sober enough by then to have dinner, because she wrinkled her nose at him. He shook hands with the governor, nodded to Barbara Keys and the Searles, and left the room.

"I feel very much as Dr. Richardson does," Barbara Keys said. "Totally disgusted at having been drawn into this unpleasant business." The phrase brought a giggle from Mrs. Dillon, but the other woman appeared not to notice. "As a friend of Carl Lattner's," she continued, "naturally I take an interest in the solution of his murder, but I may tell you that I have no confidence whatever that this discussion is going to get anywhere."

"It certainly won't if we keep interrupting poor Mr. Brooke," said Andrea Dillon.

Marco leaned forward to mutter something to Chalk, who nodded and said, "Good point. You told me over the phone,

Brooke, that you were sending Evans some blood samples and a hair for testing. What do you expect them to prove?"

"As soon as Michelle arrives, I hope to be able to tell you who killed Carolla Peters, and who put manchineel juice in Carl Lattner's refrigerator so he would mistake it for green coconut water."

"You mean you don't yet know who did it? You asked me to call this meeting just on a fishing expedition?"

"The fish is hooked, Governor. We're close to the end of the case, now. I'm in a position to reconstruct most of what happened." His voice took on a depth that made interruption difficult. "On the night of the murder, about nine o'clock, Carolla Peters went to Lattner's cottage, carrying a bottle. In it was juice made mainly from manchineel apples, and extremely poisonous. She had obtained the apples when Mrs. Keys threw out a manchineel branch she had used as a subject for a botanical painting. The poison was brewed from the apples in Carolla's house." He was determined to say nothing about Francie Peters if he could help it. "She obtained the empty bottle at the inn. There is reason to believe it was a pint club soda bottle made of clear glass—the same kind of bottle the bartenders used for the green coconut water they sent to Lattner's cottage every day." He forestalled an impatient remark from Chalk by adding, "As you will see, that's a point of some importance. Carolla carried this bottle because she intended to sprinkle the juice around Lattner's cottage as part of an obeah ritual."

The governor exploded. "Obeah again! Why do you have to complicate a plain murder case with black magic?"

"The girl had been victimized by Lattner, Governor. She was taking revenge in the traditional way. The point is, the manchineel that poisoned Lattner came from that bottle. I want to make that perfectly clear. The tree from which the apples came is one of the few left on the island and certainly the only one near Mango Beach. Mr. Motley has inspected it. No one has drawn sap from the trunk. Only one small branch was taken from it—the one that Professor Keys cut down for Mrs. Keys to paint. I think we can dismiss the possibility that Mrs. Keys or any other guest of the inn boiled up manchineel apples to extract the juice. That could not be done in one of the cottages without a maid or someone else noticing. We must conclude that Carolla's bottle contained the poison that did the killing."

Now he had their undivided attention. Even Chalk did not interrupt. "At first, as you know, Governor, I thought Carolla had committed the murder and that Maubee had covered for her with the machete. Later I saw some serious flaws in that theory but couldn't think of a better one. Then came the news that Carolla's body had been found. Why was she killed? The best answer I could find was that while she was alive she was a threat to someone, and who would that be if not Lattner's real murderer? Of course, if Carolla had not committed the murder, I had to find a new explanation for the machete and the robbery. Maubee might have tried to cover up for Carolla, who was the mother of one of his children, but I could not see him incriminating himself to help anyone else."

Chalk compressed his lips. "I wish you would get to the point."

"I want you to see the whole picture, Governor." Xavier wondered whether he would be able to keep them quiet until Michelle arrived. "Another thing that stopped me. Even assuming Carolla knew who the murderer was, why was it necessary to kill her? Wouldn't it have been easier and safer merely to let the police investigate? No matter what Carolla might claim to have seen, she was the one who would have been thought guilty. She had the motive, the poison, and the opportunity to put the bottle in Lattner's refrigerator. All the murderer would have had to do was deny anything Carolla said, and the girl would have gone to jail. The more I thought about it, the more I became convinced that Carolla must know something more than the identity of the poisoner to make her such a menace that she had to be killed.

"It was something Ted Motley said that put me on the right track. If the obeah ritual had been interrupted by the real poisoner, what would Carolla have done? She would have gone back home. But would she have stayed there? I doubted it. Until the ritual had been completed, she would have feared the obeah would fail. In that case, she might well have gone back to Lattner's cottage again, hours later when no one would be likely to see her. I checked with Carolla's grandmother and found that was what had happened. Carolla made another visit to the inn, probably around three in the morning, and after that never returned home. It began to look as if whatever she saw at Lattner's cottage on that second visit led to her murder."

"Well, what did she see?" Chalk pressed him. "I've told you again and again all those details about what you thought or didn't think don't interest me. Who killed Lattner?"

"I'm almost there, Governor. Now we come to another essential point, which so far only you and the police know." Xavier looked around at the others. Tension, rather than hostility, now pervaded the room. He could guess at their inner anxieties—Barbara Keys' for her reputation, the Searles' for the future of their inn, Chalk's for his hoped-for appointment as governor, Marco Ferrer's for his chance of becoming chief of police. Almost imperceptibly they craned toward him as he said, "The blood on Lattner's clothing was not his own blood. It was not human blood. It was dog's blood. I'm sorry to say, Mrs. Dillon, that is what happened to Pepe. Dr. Richardson killed him in order to get the blood he needed to cover up the poisoning."

Her pretty face was frowning slightly as if she had not quite understood him. Suddenly she turned very pale. "I don't believe you," she said finally.

The room was suddenly very still, as if everyone had stopped breathing. Xavier said gently, "He did not want to tell you the truth. He knew how much you loved Pepe. But he must have told you something to explain how he obtained the blood he needed. Did he say he cut himself?"

She stared at him in astonishment. "Then you know. But I saw the bandage on his leg." She touched her thigh. The implication of her words escaped her. She was completely absorbed in the manner of the dog's death.

In the same low, conversational voice, Xavier said, "Yes, he wanted to be sure you would not connect him with Pepe's disappearance. Sooner or later it would occur to you that there would have to be blood to make it look ·as if the machete were the murder weapon, and you would wonder where it came from. To forestall that possibility he would show you the bandage. Probably you praised him for his courage." He did not wait for her reply. "I would not be surprised if he even went so far as to make a little cut under the bandage for the sake of realism. He is a careful man. But he had to have much more blood than would come from a small cut, so he went to your cottage while you slept and took Pepe away."

"Jimmy wouldn't do that. Not to Pepe." She buried her face in her hands and began to cry. "Oh, poor Pepe. Poor Jimmy."

The others in the room looked uncertainly from one to the other, like spectators at a tennis match. Walter Searle said finally, "I don't understand. Are you saying that Dr. Richardson killed Lattner?"

"No, Mr. Searle. He killed Carolla."

"Then who murdered Lattner?"

The glance that Xavier gave Mrs. Dillon was more that of a friend than of a policeman. "It must all come out now. I've been wondering," he said to her, "whether you did not intend merely to make Lattner a little sick."

She took her hands from her tearful face and looked at him gratefully. "Oh," she said, "you do understand, don't you? I didn't think he would drink enough to kill him. I only thought it would serve him right to suffer a little. He made me suffer so much."

Governor Chalk's eyebrows fluttered, as if unable to decide whether to rise or scowl. "You mean to say—" He interrupted himself. "Now see here, Brooke. None of this makes any sense to me. I want a plain explanation and I want it now."

Xavier said amiably, "Certainly, Governor. There are still many details to be filled in, but in broad outline, this is what must have happened. On the evening of the murder, Mrs. Dillon went to Mr. Lattner's cottage. I don't think she would

have done that unless Lattner had suggested it. Isn't that
right, Mrs. Dillon?"

She dabbed at her face with a little handkerchief. "When I
saw him on the beach that morning he—" She stopped,
looking at Barbara Keys, who averted her head indignantly.

"He told you he would meet you at his cottage, is that it?
Yes, he would have enjoyed that. No doubt the door was
unlocked, you went in, you switched on a lamp, you waited.
He didn't come. You became bored. You poured yourself a
drink out of his bottle of rum, perhaps two or three. You
poked around, opened the refrigerator, saw the usual bottle
of green coconut water there. You turned down the bed."

"How ever did you know?" Her eyes showed admiration, not
fear, as if the peril of her situation had not yet come home
to her. She might have been applauding a theatrical turn.

"When he still didn't show up, you became angry. Finally
you went out again. That was when you saw Carolla sprinkling something on the ground around the cottage. You
guessed at once what it was, didn't you? You remembered
the obeah ritual from the time years ago when you made
your voodoo picture in St. Caro."

"Oh," she exclaimed, "you *are* a clever man! I told Jimmy
so, but he wouldn't believe me."

He acknowledged the tribute with a smile. "I've been
wondering how you persuaded Carolla to give you the bottle.
Did you pay her for it?"

She murmured, "Ten dollars. She was very pleased."

"Did she try to leave the deadies? You know what they
are?"

"Those revolting little corpses and things? Oh, yes, but I
made her take them away. I said it would spoil everything if
Carl saw them. I told her I would help make the obeah
work."

They might have been alone in the room. "Did she tell you
why the big fix was on Lattner, because he had got her
fired?"

"Yes, she said she was going away in the morning to look
for work."

"Did she say where?"

"To Bamboula. We always were friendly, Carolla and I, even though I knew about Carl's thing with her last year."

"And when she left, there you were outside the cottage, holding the bottle. In the dark you would not have been able to tell much about the contents so you went back into the cottage. That must have been when you noticed that the obeah juice resembled the green coconut water you had seen in Lattner's refrigerator. Until then you were not sure what you would do, were you?"

"Oh, that's so true," she said. "First I thought of just putting a little into his rum bottle. Then when I noticed the color, I decided it would be much more fun to switch bottles and let him hocus his own drink. I really didn't have any idea he would drink enough to kill him. Really."

Barbara Keys stood up abruptly. "All this has nothing to do with me, Governor Chalk, and I'm not interested in knowing the obscene little details. So if you'll excuse me—"

Mrs. Dillon's eyes grew wide and bright, and her voice took on sudden resonance. "Considering, Barbara, that you were one of the obscene little details yourself, you really shouldn't be so hoity-toity. You were quite enterprising with Carl, remember? There was one night when I couldn't sleep and went out for a walk and happened to pass your cottage, and one of the jalousies wasn't quite drawn—" She stopped and put a hand to her mouth in an actress's gesture of contrition. "But I mustn't blurt out things like that, must I?"

Barbara Keys flushed deeply and the purse in her hand trembled as if she were about to throw it. Rising swiftly, Xavier stood in front of her and met the blast of fury in her gray eyes. "You had better sit down," he said. "We will want your evidence. You should have told me the truth when I asked you who you met near Lattner's cottage that night. It was Dr. Richardson, of course. What did he say to you—that he had just been at the cottage and Lattner was not there? Is that why you turned back?"

"You've no right to speak to me like that!" She looked to Governor Chalk for support, but he avoided her eyes.

Xavier said, "Your only hope now of escaping publicity is to tell the truth. Was it Richardson you saw?"

She sat down slowly and, as if the word was being wrenched out of her, said, "Yes."

"Now just a minute, Brooke." Chalk was unhappy. He broke off to listen to Marco Ferrer mutter something in his ear, and it seemed to encourage him. "So far, so good. I can see Mrs. Dillon's part in this thing. Unfortunate, but she evidently thought of it only as a sort of practical joke that went wrong. But what about Richardson? You flatly accused him of murdering Carolla Peters and you haven't connected him with her in any way. That's a serious thing, accusing a man of his prominence when you haven't any real evidence."

"Perhaps he will tell you about it himself, Governor, because I think I hear his voice." Xavier hoped that his relief and elation did not show, as sounds of anger and heavy footsteps came from the adjoining room. Chalk's frightened secretary poked her head in the door to say, "Governor, is it all right if—"

Richardson's bulk filled the doorway and his voice boomed, "Chalk, do you realize that this moron has actually arrested me? Have you gone mad?" Close behind him stood George Michelle, a firm grip on one of the doctor's wrists. They came into the governor's office almost together.

"You can let go of his arm now, George," Xavier said. "Where did you find him?"

"Just like you said, Chief. At the airline office. He don't see me. I hear him ask for a ticket on the evening plane to New York. It leave in an hour. I wait until he buy the ticket and has it in his pocket before I arrest him."

"God damn it, I've a right to buy a ticket on any plane I choose!" His eyes flamed at Xavier as if trying to incinerate him.

"But you don't seem to have any luggage, doctor," said Xavier courteously. "You must have made up your mind to go rather suddenly."

"What of it? I just talked on the phone with Los Angeles. A patient of mine has taken a serious turn for the worse.

Naturally I didn't go back to the inn to pack. I must catch that plane. Governor, tell these fools to get out of my way."

Xavier smiled. "A very good try, doctor. If you actually held such a conversation to give yourself an excuse for catching the next plane, it would have been a brilliant stroke on your part. But I don't think you did. You would not have felt it necessary, dealing as you are with stupid island policemen. You would not have taken the time for the call. But that can be checked. Where is the phone you spoke from? Where are the friends you said you were going to meet? Shall I ring the long-distance operator now to verify your statement?" His voice hardened. "Don't try to evade it now, doctor. You knew you were in danger when you heard about the blood traces in the trunk of the car. You knew they would be dog's blood, because that was where you had put little Pepe's body, wrapped in a towel, I suppose. As well as all the equipment you took from Lattner's cottage."

Andrea Dillon said, "Did you do that to Pepe, Jimmy? Did you?"

Xavier gave him no chance to reply. "And as soon as you heard of the hair I found in the front seat of your car, you knew it would be Carolla Peters' hair and would tie you up with her murder." He turned to Searle. "Am I right in saying he came to your office after I finished talking on the phone with the governor to find out what I'd sent to Dr. Evans for testing?"

"Why, yes." Searle was startled. "He said he was going to complain to the governor about you. I told him what you'd said about blood spots and the hair. I didn't see any reason not to."

"Of course. And it was then, doctor, you realized you would have to get out fast if you were to escape arrest."

"Damn it, do I have to stand here and listen to this stupid ass? Governor, I warn you, if I miss that plane I'll raise a stink in Washington you'll never hear the end of."

The governor's incredulity was thawing fast. "Well, now," he said restively, "I don't think you've any call to take that attitude. We're only trying to clear this thing up."

As if he had not been interrupted, Xavier went on, "Another worry that must have made you anxious to get away, doctor, was that you could not be sure what Mrs. Dillon might say when she learned about Pepe."

"You're out of your mind!" The doctor looked at Andrea Dillon as if he were trying to hypnotize her. "Don't say a word, Andrea. They'll twist anything you say. Not a word!"

The thought flickered through Xavier's mind as his eyes locked again with Richardson's that they had been looking at each other like that for centuries. "It's too late, doctor. Mrs. Dillon has already told us that she put the manchineel juice in Carl Lattner's refrigerator. We know from Mrs. Keys that she met you coming from Lattner's cottage. You obviously knew where to find the machete with Maubee's fingerprints on it." He carefully avoided looking at the Searles. "And it was, of course, when you went for the machete that you came across Maubee's little black book."

Richardson's face took on a greenish tinge under its tan and he sat down heavily. After a moment he closed his eyes tight as if trying to blot out the world. With a last effort at self-assertion, Chalk said to Xavier, "You mean to say you knew he was guilty all the time and you let him walk out of here? That was damn foolish. He might have gone directly to the airport and boarded a plane."

"He couldn't do that, Governor. I alerted the airport constables and the airline personnel before I came up here."

Chalk threw Marco a glance of frustration, and the alarm that each read in the other's eyes prompted him to try again. "What about that report from Dr. Evans? Didn't you say Michelle was bringing it? Where is it?"

"Not ready yet, Governor," said George, looking at Xavier.

"We won't need it now," Xavier added. He did not quite give George the St. Caro wink, but he came close to it.

26

TOINETTE was radiant. When Xavier and Ted entered the house, she embraced them both with bubbling enthusiasm. Xavier thought for a moment she had somehow heard that the case had been solved, but it turned out that her happiness had a different cause. "Wait till I tell you! That Marco! He never bother this house no more, you bet on that." Her grammar was vanishing fast in her excitement. It was late—the formalities of arrest and arraignment had taken hours—and the children were in bed, so she could talk freely.

"What happened?"

Xavier's apprehensive tone added to her pleasure in the telling. "He come here early this afternoon, same like last time, drove up and parked his motorcycle right in front. Soon as I see him, I know something bad is going to happen. I run out the kitchen to the back yard and call Celia Jennings from next door. After he was here before, I ask Celia if he come again would she help me and she say she would sure. She come back into the kitchen with me an' wait while I answer the front door an' let Marco in. Oh, he jus' like honey. He take off his helmet, he smile an' say he come because there is something he must tell me. He say he want me to know he always think I the best-looking girl in Gracedieu. I the kind of wife any man would be proud to have."

"That is true," said Ted.

"The way he say it, he don' mean it, he lookin' for something. He begin to talk real fast. Sweet butter an' honey, they jus' pour out of him. He say he can't sleep because he keep thinking about me. I stand there smilin' like he is gettin' to me. He take my hand and kiss it. He stroke my arm. He so sure of himself, I want to kill him. He begin to whisper, he love me, he need me. Then he reach out for me an' try to kiss me on the mouth. He very strong and I have a hard time holding him off. I whisper too. I say, 'Marco, let go just one minute, I be right back.' I guess he think I mean get ready for a big time with him, because he let me go. He got a look on his face like a cat lickin' cream. I go to the kitchen an' tell Celia, 'Come on.' We each pick up a pan an' go to the front room. When he saw us he look like he don' believe it. I say to him, 'Marco, you a coward. You no brave enough fight Xavier, so you try steal his wife.' "

She was acting it out with gestures, imitating Marco's voice and expression. "He put on a grin but he mad clear through. 'All right,' he say, 'I go. I didn't know when I come here there going to be two nigger whores in the house. I only want one.' He open the door to go out, and that is when Celia conk him on the head with the pan. Oh, she conk him good, that a real heavy pan. He almos' fall down. She don' like bein' call' a whore. I would conk him too, but she in the way an' I can't get at him. People in the street stop to watch. He look like he goin' to hit us, but then he put his hand on his head an' go out the door. I remember his helmet so I get it an' skim it at him, jus' as he turn to say somethin' else. It hit his face and he swear an' put his hand to his eye."

"He's wearing a black patch on that eye," Xavier said.

"Good! Maybe it will help him remember not to fool around with married women. When he get on his motorcycle, Celia yell, 'If you come back, we break your head again.' An' she say to the people, 'He come bustin' in here, he talk dirty, he call us niggers.' Marco heard her and he drive away real fast. He never dare come back this street no more. By tomorrow, everybody in Gracedieu know we conked him. Wait till the Councillors hear 'bout *that*!"

As she talked Xavier's initial anger changed to something like awe at the simplicity, competence, and thoroughness of female revenge, compared with his own futile effort to deal with Marco. He even felt sorry for the man. To have been conquered by two women would disgrace him in the Puerto Rican community, while making him a laughingstock among the blacks.

"Now let him try be chief of police!" Toinette burst into laughter as she flung her arms around Xavier and kissed him again.

He could feel the triumphant tingling of her body under her thin dress. "You are a wonderful woman," he said, caressing her. "After all these years you can still surprise me."

Ted Motley said, "Don't mind me, but if you are going to make love in my presence, at least bring out the booze." Toinette made a face at him, detached herself, and bent down to the liquor cupboard. She said, "Rum all right? It's all we got."

"The right drink for tonight," said Ted, examining the bottle. "I will drink to you, Toinette, because you are a wife right out of an old Greek play, the kind who killed her husband's enemies."

"Greek?" she said doubtfully, as she handed them jiggers filled with rum.

"It's a high compliment," he assured her. "When I write my story, Xave, I am going to put in a photograph of Toinette standing victorious with a frying pan in her hand. Caption: Police Chief's Wife Clouts Ardent Wooer While Husband Solves Murder Case."

She lighted up all over again. "You solved the case? You know who kill that man at the inn? I want to hear. Come into the kitchen and talk while I get dinner on the stove. I got a lovely snapper."

When they were seated at the kitchen table with the bottle of rum before them and their mouths salivating at the unique and irresistible odor of fish cooked in the Carovian manner, sautéed in butter and the juice of fresh limes, Ted said, "First off, Xave, there's one thing I've got to know. Did you really find blood spots and one of Carolla's hairs in Richardson's car, or was that a put-on?"

Xavier chuckled. "I scraped something out of the trunk of the car. It could have been dried blood. Or it could have been dried grease. There was a hair in the front seat of the car. It wasn't Carolla's—it was short and white, Richardson's—but it was a hair. I like to be truthful when possible."

"You staged all that just to make Richardson think you had found something in his car?"

"That's it. I knew if he was guilty he would not be able to rest until he knew what I had found. He heard me say I was going to call Chalk from Searle's office. That's why I made sure Searle heard me tell the governor about blood scrapings and a hair. I expected Richardson to get that information from him as soon as I was out of sight."

Ted whistled. "If it hadn't worked out that way you would have been in big trouble."

"No bigger than the trouble I was in already. My only hope was to push Richardson into making a false move."

"My God," said Ted, "underneath that easygoing manner you are a Machiavellian character, my black friend."

"Got to be, to deal with you white folks."

Toinette brought a platter of tawny, aromatic red snapper to the table, garnished with greens and potatoes, and said, "Now lay off that rum and eat your dinner. I don't understand a word you been saying. Who killed who? No, don't tell me now. Eat first."

"Marco was right," said Ted, after swallowing his first mouthful. "A woman who looks like that and can cook like this would make any man happy. What did you do to earn your good luck, Xave?"

"Well, one thing, I burned my little black book."

"I made you do it," Toinette reminded him. "It almost broke your heart. Don't drink all the rum. Save some for later. We have mango pudding for dessert." When they were well into the fish, she said, "Last time we talk—I mean, talked—just the other night, you said Dave Maubee and that girl did it. What happened? Did you find Dave?"

"The last time Ted and I saw Maubee, he was swimming across the harbor at Port Cambo, trying to escape," Xavier told her. "All of a sudden he yelled, 'Sharks!' After that we didn't see him any more."

"Oh." Toinette's eyes filled with tears. "That must make you feel awful, Xave."

Ted cleared his throat and said, "Something I've got to tell you about that, Xave. I don't think the sharks got Maubee."

"You don't?" Xavier's face was enigmatic. "Why?"

"When we stood there after you climbed back on the dock, I happened to look at one of the small boats out on the water, and I saw it give a sudden lurch. As if somebody had grabbed hold of the side and climbed in. Maubee could have swum that far under water from where we saw him last without any trouble. I thought I'd better not say anything at the time because you might have felt obliged to go after him and somebody could have got hurt. On the way back to the hospital I started to tell you but you cut me off. Early this morning I went down to the dock and the boat I saw move was gone. So was the *Corinto.*" He examined Xavier's face and added, "You don't seem surprised."

Xavier said, "You're not the only one with good eyesight, Ted."

After a startled moment, Ted gave a mighty laugh. "You sonofagun! I wondered why you seemed so indifferent. I thought you were just being the stoical policeman."

"No, it came to me at the time that there hadn't been any real pain or horror in Dave's voice when he yelled. He didn't scream the way a man would if a shark had him. When I saw the boat tilt, I was pretty sure. Reason I didn't say anything, I thought it would be best for everybody to think he was dead—especially Chalk."

"Why he do it?" Toinette asked. "So you wouldn't go after him?"

"Maybe that, but I think mainly he was trying to help me. He knew I'd been told to bring him in dead or alive, and he figured I'd be in trouble with Chalk if he escaped, so he gave me an easy out. Chalk couldn't object too much if he was food for the fish."

"That a horrible thing to say when we are eating fish!"

"This is not fish. It is ambrosia," said Ted. While she wrinkled her forehead at the word, he went on, "St. Caro won't be quite the same without Maubee."

"Maybe the Dominican Republic won't be quite the same, either."

Toinette burst out, "You are both crazy. I don't know what you are talking about. First Dave Maubee is killed by sharks, now he isn't. You say you solve the murder, but you don't arrest Dave. I still don't know who killed that man. What is am-ambro-what you said?"

"Ambrosia is food for the gods, which is what we are right now," said Ted, plunging a spoon into his creamy mango pudding. "And you are absolutely right, Toinette. What we want from you, Xave, is a coherent story. This morning you were as confused as I was. What happened to put you on the right track?"

"I guess it was right after my talk with Francie Peters. That convinced me Corolla had not planted the manchineel in the refrigerator. So I asked myself the obvious question. Who else had a strong motive for killing Lattner? You suspected the Searles, and a lot of what you said made sense, but the motive was pretty farfetched. If not the Searles, then who? Mrs. Keys had no motive that I could see. But Andrea Dillon did."

"Yes, but wait. If it comes to that, Richardson had a motive too." Ted pointed out. "Jealousy."

"That's right, but I could not see a trained physician using such an uncertain way to kill as to put manchineel in a man's refrigerator in the hope that he would drink it. That sounded to me more like an impulsive woman—a woman who is a little—I can't think of the word."

"Neurotic? Fey?"

"Fey, that's it. She would have thought it amusing to switch the bottles. So I followed that line of thought to see where it led. Where would she get the manchineel juice? That stopped me for a while. I couldn't believe she would make the effort to tap a tree or would know how. All at once I got a picture in my mind."

"You and your pictures," said Toinette. "I thought detectives went by clues. Here's your coffee. I'm going to do the dishes. You keep talking—I want to hear."

Xavier patted her rear as she left them, and she smiled at him. He said, "I wondered whether Andrea saw Carolla at

Lattner's cottage with the obeah juice and got the poison from her. But why would Andrea be there? Perhaps in the hope of starting up her affair with him again? I liked that idea. There was what the books call a corroborative detail, too. The turned-down bed. I couldn't see why anyone else would have turned it down. But Andrea, sitting in his cottage with nothing else to do—it would be just the kind of thing she would do."

Ted nodded appreciatively. "I see what you mean. A symbolic gesture. A subtle invitation to him if he came in while she was there."

"It began to look like Andrea could have had motive, means, and opportunity. So I simply applied the same reasoning I used when I thought Carolla was guilty and Maubee covered for her. Only now I saw Andrea poisoning Lattner and her friend Richardson trying to help her. And not only her friend—her lover, as Percy told me."

"She sound to me like a big sleep-around," Toinette remarked from the sink, over her shoulder. "What she look like?"

"Not bad," said Xavier. "But she had her face lifted."

"You mean an old woman, carrying on that way?" Toinette said with the callousness of the young.

"The doctor is even older. Anyway, he loved her. If she asked him for help, he would want to give it. What would he do? He would volunteer to go to Lattner's cottage and wipe off the bottles and the glass. He would tell her not to worry, take a sleeping pill and go to bed, leave it all to him. She would tell him he was wonderful, and do like he said. That was the picture I had."

"He was taking a big chance," said Ted. "Suppose Lattner was home and alive?"

"Richardson could have made up a story for Lattner. For instance, he could say he had seen a black girl sneaking into the cottage earlier that night carrying a bottle. They could look for the bottle and he could pick it up and take it away to be tested. Something like that. But Lattner was dead."

"In that case," Ted objected, "why did the doctor have to

cover up the poisoning? As soon as he took care of the fingerprints he could walk out and Andrea would be safe."

"Yes, and that meant it was something that happened after Richardson left the cottage that made the situation dangerous for them. So now the big question was, what did he see? Soon as I asked myself that I knew the answer. Barbara Keys. By her own statement, she was on the way to Lattner's cottage. That must have given him a shock. He had to stop her. He could not risk telling her Lattner was dead. Everyone knew he and Lattner were rivals, not friends, and she would have wanted to know, what was he doing at the cottage? His best bet was to say he had just looked in and Lattner was not there."

Ted scratched his long nose thoughtfully. "But he would have to give a reason for looking in."

"Richardson had a quick mind. We will find out from her what he actually said, but I have thought of one or two stories he might have used. For example, he could say Andrea Dillon was not at her cottage, either, and put on a show of jealousy. He could wonder whether she and Lattner were not down on the beach—did Barbara want to come along with him and look for them? She is too proud to do a thing like that. She would say, no, certainly not, and march back to her own cottage."

"I buy that. It's just what he would say and just what she would do."

"But now look at Richardson's position. He is still in a trap. Lattner's corpse will be discovered in the morning. If Barbara Keys says she saw him coming from the cottage, and if Carolla tells her story, he and Andrea will both be under suspicion. They might be arrested. The story might be picked up by the mainland press. Even if he was not convicted, his reputation could be badly damaged. You can see him standing there in the night, watching Barbara Keys walk away, groping desperately for a way out."

"I begin to feel sorry for him," said Ted. "He starts out to help the woman he loves and he finds himself getting sucked in deeper and deeper."

"He was a victim, all right. And he is not used to being a victim. What would a man like that do? There was one way out. If he could make it seem that Lattner was killed after he met Barbara—not by poison but in some way that nobody would associate with Andrea or himself—if he could do that, Barbara would have no reason to suspect him and Carolla would not suspect Andrea. In other words, he needed a new murder weapon that would convince the police. That was when he had his inspiration. The machete."

Ted poured himself another tot of rum from the shrinking contents of the bottle and said, "How could he know where to find the machete?"

"It took me a long time to figure that out. Then I remembered something Percy said about Andrea Dillon. 'She a great big snoop.' She enjoyed spying on people. She told me herself that last year she used to spy on Lattner. It was a form of entertainment for her. If she saw Margaret Searle driving out of the inn after everybody should have been asleep, it would have been natural for her to get in her car and follow.

"Once she discovers the hideaway, would she keep a juicy piece of gossip like that to herself? You can bet the first chance she got she would tell Richardson. I could see her proposing that they both go to watch what went on up there. My guess was that one night after Margaret drove out they followed her and climbed the hill to the hideaway. Then I asked myself, suppose that was one of the nights Dave Maubee was there? Suppose they saw him in the moonlight, doing his trick with the machete, splitting green coconuts."

"Green coconuts!" Toinette commented as she wiped a dish. "Never be able to look at one again without thinking of murder."

"You'll have to learn to drink your rum straight, like me," said Ted. "But I get the picture, Xave. There's the doctor outside Lattner's cottage groping for some way to cover up the poisoning and the answer flashes into his mind. The machete. Probably Maubee's fingerprints on it. He can slice Lattner at some vital spot, spill some blood around, stage a robbery, and who would think of looking for poison? Especially when he will be there to certify the cause of death."

"That's it." Xavier raised a hand toward the rum, noted the depleted condition of the bottle, and changed his mind. "Everyone would agree the murder was committed by a native. For Richardson, that was the way out. He wouldn't have wasted a moment before driving to the hideaway."

"Suppose Margaret Searle had been there?"

"Then he would have had to try something else. But he was lucky—or unlucky. No one was around. A place like that is easy to get into. He goes in, checks the rooms, sees the machete, and wraps it up in something so as not to damage the fingerprints. While looking around he sees the little black book that Margaret Searle took from Maubee's jeans. We don't yet know why she kept it."

"No mystery about that," said Toinette. "She hoped Dave Maubee would come back for it."

"You are a bright girl. That's it. Richardson picks up the book and sees Maubee's name inside. That could have been the first time he realized who Margaret's black lover was. Now he is riding high. The little black book will definitely pin the murder on Maubee and nobody will question it. Back he goes to Lattner's cottage. He plants the book near the corpse where he can call it to Searle's attention the next day if nobody else sees it first."

"Wait a second," Ted objected. "Would he do that when Margaret Searle could give the show away? As soon as she saw the book and the machete she would suspect a frame-up."

"Yes, but she couldn't say so without revealing that Maubee was her lover. Richardson could be pretty sure she wouldn't do that. And even if she did, everyone would assume she was trying to protect Maubee by lying for him. Richardson did not have to worry much about her or Searle. I see him picking up the machete carefully with a handkerchief and making that nice surgical cut at the back of Lattner's neck—not too deep, just enough to make death certain and instantaneous if Lattner had been alive. He needed a lot of blood, but he knew where he could get it. Andrea Dillon's dog. When he went to her cottage and found her sound asleep he must have felt that his ordeal was nearly over. The dog knew him—it would not raise a fuss when he picked it up. I see him taking it back to Lattner's cottage, wrapping it in a towel, and cutting its throat."

Toinette was wiping the last pan. "That poor little dog."

"There is nothing sentimental about the doctor. And he has great confidence in himself. He takes it for granted that people will bow down to him. That is why he did not worry more about an autopsy. He would feel sure that if he signed the death certificate, no one in a place like St. Caro would fool with an autopsy. So there he is, holding the dead dog. It is very late, very dark—he does not expect anyone to be around. First he puts the dog's corpse in the obvious place, the trunk of his car. Now he is almost through. He goes back inside, removes the wristwatch, searches Lattner's pockets, finds the wallet, travelers' checks, and the key to the locked closet. He picks out the camera and other things he imagines Maubee might take if he had robbed the cottage and goes out again to put everything in the trunk. I think he must have made a third trip for the poison bottle and the glass Lattner had drunk out of.

"That is where everything went wrong. It was bad enough when he met Barbara Keys. Now it is Carolla Peters, coming back to leave the deadies on her grandmother's orders. You can guess her feelings when she saw this big man coming out of the cottage."

"That poor child," said Toinette, joining them at the table. "The big fix bounce back on her."

"That's the way she must have felt. And what about Richardson? He could not afford to let her get away. If she talked, he would have to face a charge of murder. I don't think he hesitated. The mark on her chin indicates he knocked her out with a blow before killing her. To remove any suspicion that she might have been killed at the inn, he drove toward Bamboula. Probably Andrea had told him

Carolla was planning to go there. He dumped the body in a cane field and hid the stuff in the trunk somewhere else, we don't know where yet. Then he went back to his cottage. He couldn't have got much sleep, but he was ready when Mrs. Searle found the body and Searle called him. No one doubted that Maubee committed the murder."

"Except you," said Toinette proudly.

"Yes, but I got off on the wrong track. Richardson had good reason to feel secure. If he hadn't, he and Mrs. Dillon would be safely in the States by now."

Ted was squinting at the empty rum bottle in a marked way, but seeing no encouragement in Xavier's face, he sighed and said, "What I don't get is why you bothered to check up on his golf score. Okay, suppose he lied about it. Lying golfers are as common as weeds. What did you expect to prove?"

"Come on, Ted. Here's a man who commits one murder, covers up another, kills the pet of the woman he loves, and is up most of the night under great strain and anxiety. Is he going to go out the next morning and play his best game?"

"But why would he lie about the score in the first place?"

"Probably he wanted to make us feel we were imposing on him. Since he was going to all that trouble, the least I could do was take his word for the cause of death. It never occurred to him that I might check up on the score. That and my mention of blood spots and a hair made him feel I was breathing down his neck."

Toinette said disparagingly, "So that's what it takes to be a detective. Why, it's just a lot of remembering and supposing and probably."

"You've got something there, Toinette," said Ted. "Great detectives are supposed to be masters of logic, but Xavier is a master of guesswork. How am I going to write up this case so the American public will believe it?"

"You're just trying to get out of all that work," Xavier told him.

"An unkind remark, even if true. Still, I may surprise you. You may wake up one morning and find your fame spread all over the States."

"With a picture of me. You promised," said Toinette.

Ted sighed and got up. "I see I'm going to have to sit many an hour at my desk that would be better spent at a bar. Well, let's see what happens. You are my favorite woman, Toinette." As she kissed him good-bye, he looked at Xavier wickedly. "She is even prettier than Isabel Cannon."

She stood apart from them, her hands on her hips. "You mean that singer at Port Cambo people are talking about? What you doing in a night spot when you supposed to be chasing criminals?"

Ted bowed to Xavier. "A good question. On that note, I leave. A beautiful dinner, Toinette, and a fine, if singular, bottle of rum, Xave."

When he had gone, Toinette looked hard at Xavier and said, "Tell me then, man, you get mixed up with this Isabel?"

Xavier laughed. "Ted just said that because I did not bring out another bottle of rum. I like him too much to get him drunk."

"You're not answering me straight. What about Isabel?"

What would she say, he wondered, if he told her about Margaret Searle? But to mention that he would have to be far gone in insanity. "Isabel is Dave Maubee's best girl. I found her name in his little black book. We went looking for him at the bar where she sings. That's all."

She accepted that. "What she like?"

"Not pretty, exactly, but she got something. A good singer."

"Good as me?"

He said promptly, "When you were singing nobody was as good as you."

"You think I don't sing so good any more?"

He recognized her tricksy mood and enjoyed it. "Honey, last time I heard you sing, that was the best."

"When was that?"

"The other morning."

She frowned, trying to remember, and then laughed. "You mean Little Black Book?"

He nodded. "If I had one you would be on every page."

She gave him a sidelong look under her long lashes and

crooned a verse he had not heard before. "If you like the way
I wiggle—if you like the way I look—just mark my name A-1
in your little black book."

"That sounds to me like an invitation," he said. "I accept."